Praise for *The Scent of Oranges*

"The elegance of Joan Zawatzky's writing is a big part of what makes this story so memorable and delightful. Her words flowed right through me and led me into a story so full of life, nature and relationships. I never wanted it to end."

Ashley Merril, Front Street Review

"The Scent of Oranges by Joan Zawatzky is the first book I've read by this author but hope to read more. Right away I was transported to South Africa. I could picture everything that Linda saw as if I was her. Joan captures the essence of South Africa with the mystery and intrigue of murder."

Cheryl's Book Nook

"I think this novel will really appeal to people who like to sit and savour the writing and ...a mystery unfolding."

Peeking Between the Pages

Praise for *The Elephant's Footprint*

"Joan Zawatzky has a very smooth writing style. I enjoy reading her books as they take you through the story with just the right amount of detail. The romance is an added bonus for the romantics out there. This was a very enjoyable read."

Ashley Denis, Front Street Review

Other books by the author

The Third Generation

Dawn in Catland

Bella: An ordinary cat with an extraordinary gift

Stories of Love, Hope and Healing for All Ages

STOP Family Anxiety: A guide for anxiety disorders in parents, grandparents, teenagers and children of all ages

Depression: Light at the End of the Tunnel

The Elephant's Footprint

The Scent of Oranges

THE
WIND'S SONG

Joan Zawatzky

First published in Australia in 2022 by:
Veritax. Victoria, Australia

Website: www.placeofbooks.com

Front cover image by stock unlimited
Typeset by BookPOD

ISBN: 978-0-6455062-0-4 (pbk)
ISBN: 978-0-6455062-1-1 ebook)

For my husband, Hymie.

Prologue

Josef stared out of the window at the bleak morning sky and the endless white landscape. His grandfather was up early and sat in front of the fire rubbing his hands.

"It's been snowing all night. A miserable day for a trip to the harbour to visit your friend, the mermaid. What a crazy idea!"

"I didn't pick the day. We're leaving Copenhagen in three days, *Farfar*, and you promised to take me to say goodbye to her," Josef, said using an affectionate Danish term for his grandfather.

The old man nodded. "I know, I promised. We'd better eat and dress quickly, or I'll change my mind."

"I'm glad I don't have to come," Lars, Josef's younger brother said with a smirk.

Josef ignored his brother and gulped down a breakfast of oats and hot milk. Lars watched Josef dress in long, woollen underwear, boots, his warmest, handknitted jumper and his lined coat.

"Don't forget your gloves, scarf and hat, my boy, or you'll freeze," the old man said as he opened the front door. A gust of icy wind almost drowned his words, "Come on! If we don't hurry, it might snow again."

Josef, usually independent, clutched his grandfather's gloved hand as they trudged through the snow to the bus stop. At nine, he was small for his age and took uncertain steps as he battled to keep up with his grandfather's strides. Though Josef would have preferred a slower pace, he knew that his grandfather did not appreciate signs of weakness. As they waited for the bus, Josef turned to look back at their house on the hill and the road curving downwards to the white, carpeted forest. He felt a twinge of guilt about dragging his grandfather out on a freezing Copenhagen morning to satisfy his need to say goodbye to his special friend, the mermaid. It was his last opportunity to see her before they left for Australia as his mother couldn't tolerate the cold. He was accustomed to being alone. His mother was ill in bed most of the time. His father arrived home late from work, ate his meal before the fire, drank heavily and then went to bed. Though his grandfather was kind, he wasn't one to discuss anything that mattered to Josef. It was the mermaid's unchanging, sad expression as she sat on the rocks in all weathers, that led Josef to believe that she understood his loneliness. Only *she* understood how different he felt to his brother and schoolmates.

Josef jumped about to keep warm until the bus arrived. After the heated bus ride, they were thrust into the cold again. The wind was bitter and slits of sunlight were obscured by clouds. They walked briskly past the cruise liners berthed at the Langelinie Pier. Lines of tourists bundled in warm clothing poured out of the ships to view the famous Copenhagen sculpture.

"How small!", "how insignificant, disappointing," or "how lovely," he heard some of the tourists say as they returned to their busses.

Vapour gushed from his grandfather's mouth as he talked, "let's get on with it, move out of the cold. Then we can have something warm to eat and drink."

Joseph nodded, pulled down his woollen cap and tugged at his matching scarf.

The old man sighed. "We can only hope the weather will be better in Australia. I don't know much about Australia, but your mother can't take the cold in Denmark, so we are going there for her health. Doctor's orders."

Josef ignored his grandfather's chatter. Instead, he listened to the pounding surf and sniffed the salty air as they neared the water's edge and the bronze statue. He felt a surge of excitement. As they moved closer, he was frustrated that only her head and shoulders were visible in the swirling waves that day. Her body was seated on a pile of rocks and her fishy tail lay beneath the water. Other than his mother, the mermaid was the only female he admitted he loved. The first time he saw her, he was four-years-old and she enchanted him. It wasn't her nakedness. He had seen his mother naked in the shower and watched her breastfeed his younger brother Lars. The satin lustre of the mermaid's skin made him want to touch her, even on such an icy day.

"There are too many people around her now, let's wait until this lot leave," his grandfather suggested.

"She looks so sad and cold," Josef said with a shiver.

"Mermaids don't feel the cold," his grandfather replied with his first smile that morning. She's half a fish anyway and she's tough."

"Oh?"

"She's been sitting on her rock every day for as long as I can remember and survived many attacks by vandals."

Josef looked concerned. "Poor mermaid!"

"She was even here during the Second World War. I expect she was too small for the Germans to notice her,"

"That is a long time," Josef said looking up at his grandfather.

"I've told you a little about the war. You're old enough now to know more about it."

Josef looked at his grandfather uncertainly. "The war when the Germans came to Denmark?"

"Yes, they invaded Denmark and occupied our country."

Josef stared at his grandfather, not fully understanding.

"I remember it clearly. Before dawn on April 9, 1940, three German ships arrived here at the docks in Copenhagen and soldiers poured out of the ships," he said pointing to the water's edge. "At the same time, German planes dropped leaflets telling us to accept occupation. What a terrible day it was for Denmark." His grandfather lifted his head in the direction of the rough sea. "I was a member of King Christian's small regiment then. We were a small army, but we held our own against the enemy for hours until we were overwhelmed."

"Scary!" Josef said with a shudder.

"I'll tell you more about the Occupation and the Danish Resistance when you're older."

Josef nodded. The war did not interest him. He was more interested in the mermaid, a mysterious part-fish and part-human creature. The mermaids that swam among the fish and corals in his picture books had appeared in his dreams. The previous night, he dreamed that he swam with a mermaid across the sea to a new land. He smiled remembering. As the swell rose, icy spray slapped Josef's face and his attention returned to the harbour.

He's not who you think he is, the winds called. Josef was aware of the message but he did not grasp its meaning – not then.

He ignored his grandfather's droning voice and tugged at the old man's sleeve.

"I'll wait here while you say goodbye to your mermaid friend," *Farfar* said, battling to speak above the blasting wind.

Josef took a few steps towards the mermaid, stared at her and then closed his eyes as he tried to commit her image to memory. He knew he might not see her again for many years.

"Goodbye, sad mermaid," he whispered and waved. Then he took his grandfather's hand. "Okay, *Farfar*, let's go."

They walked along the cobbled streets of the harbourfront lined by ancient wooden ships, brightly coloured 17th and early 18th century apartments, taverns and cafés. After a long walk, Josef was relieved when music and loud voices drew them into the warmth of a café. They removed their warm outer clothing and concentrated on the menu. With music in the background, they enjoyed a hot meal with cream doughnuts and coffee to follow.

"Skol...here's to our new life in Australia," *Farfar* said attempting a smile as they clinked their coffee cups.

"Skol," Josef replied uncertainly.

Chapter 1

Josef sank into the couch, tugged the metal ring of his beer can and licked the surge of froth. After a few sips, he sighed. He was lonely and missed his grandfather. It was three months since his grandfather's death but each day he felt the loss more acutely. Nothing seemed to matter - his surroundings, food or sleep were no longer important. Work hovered in the distance. He was lost, caught in a web of memories. A week after the funeral, he returned to the office, to the comfort of his colleagues, but as the days passed emptiness gnawed at him. Trying to push himself to go to work did not help. Tim, the senior partner of the architectural firm phoned offering help, but Joseph brushed aside his kind words as well as his suggestions of a slow return. He knew that he couldn't face work.

He ached to see his grandfather's face again and stretched for the family photo album that had sat on the shelf unopened since he moved into his house. His mother, a keen photographer had taken the pictures and arranged them. On he first pages of the album there were photographs of himself and his family. As he flicked through the pages, he noticed a picture of himself on a beach near Copenhagen. He was with his parents, brother, Lars, and his grandfather celebrating Midsummer Eve or *Sankhansaften*, as it was called in Denmark. It was the last time they spent together before they left for Australia. The long days and short nights of Midsummer on the crowded beach were among his most precious memories – picnics, the treat of ice cream and the fantasy of 'forever time'. The beach was packed with families. At around 10 p.m. bonfires were lit. Black effigies of witches were thrown into the flames to represent the burning of evil spirits. He was young enough then to believe the legend that burnt witches once set free flew away to the mountains on their broomsticks. Part of the fun of Midsummer Eve was joining the raucous singing of popular Danish songs. In one photograph, he was singing and in another jumping excitedly as he tossed sticks into a raging bonfire. He recalled the smokiness in the air and the red and blue shooting sparks. The camera's flash had captured his grandfather's broad grin. Farfar was in his sixties then, his body lithe and his silvery hair shimmering in the firelight.

He continued turning the pages. A photo of his mother smiled at him. Six years had passed since she died and this was how he liked to remember her – healthy, tanned and willowy, her blonde hair touching her shoulders and her blue eyes smiling just at him. His parents' wedding photograph was on the next page. His mother made a lovely bride and his father was grinning. His father was alive, but Josef preferred to have little to do with him. Childhood memories of an uncaring, harsh man still lingered.

His mother's hobby was photography and faces fascinated her. Josef examined her portraits of his grandfather at different stages of his life. When they arrived in Australia, *Farfar* was seventy and still a handsome man with many admirers. Increasing age revealed less of his silvery hair, a few facial lines and a constant smile. Towards the back of the album, there were more recent photographs of his grandfather. Josef noticed that the smile had gone and his blue eyes looked pensive and distant. Josef recognised his grandfather's cold indifference. In the two years before *Farfar's* death, Josef recalled talking to him about his work. The old man appeared to listen and show interest, but within minutes, his expression changed, and he was focussed elsewhere.

Josef glanced at photographs of his grandparents in affectionate poses. His mother had taken a few portraits of his grandmother, a beautiful young, blonde woman with delicate features who Josef had not known. She died of cancer at thirty-eight.

Josef's thoughts shifted to how *Farfar* had cared for him when they first arrived in Australia. His mother's health had improved in the warmer climate and she returned to her work as a medical technician. Fortunately, her certificates and references from Copenhagen ensured her a job in a laboratory in Melbourne. As she worked full-time, his grandfather fetched him from school, made him lunch or put a band-aid on a cut. They talked about Josef's day at school and his plans for the week, but his grandfather avoided discussing himself and any questions about his past. Talk about feelings was discouraged. Despite spending long periods with the old man he knew little about him.

He disliked the photos of himself as a child shyly looking away from the camera. Despite his adult mask, he realised that he hadn't changed much. Bored with the photographs, he returned the album to the shelf and turned on the television. The daily news drifted past him in a blur and he fell asleep.

The crunch of his neighbour's car on their gravel driveway woke him. It was morning and the room was bright and cool. He shivered and drew up the blanket that had slipped onto the floor. Only three months ago he was leaving for work to battle the traffic on the freeway. He stretched and then strolled into the kitchen to make coffee. He was about to pour his first cup for the day when the piercing sound of the doorbell was an unwelcome intrusion. No one had visited or phoned him that week and he preferred his isolation. His brother Lars stood on the doorstep carrying food and drink.

Lars deposited his parcels on the kitchen bench. "I needn't ask how you're doing. You haven't showered or changed your clothes in days."

"Stop being a pain, bro, I'm fine," Joseph replied, peeved. The last thing he needed was comments from his brother.

"I bet you haven't eaten."

Josef shrugged. "I'm not hungry."

"You're a mess, bro. You need to see a doctor."

Josef looked down and grimaced.

"Head office is insisting on a medical certificate."

"I guess I could come with you."

"No way! I'm not a child." Lars was becoming more annoying by the minute.

"Maybe a doctor can help. Make an appointment, Lars said with a shrug."

"Okay, okay! I'll phone, but stop hassling me. None of those happy pills. I'm feeling down – grieving, that's all. There's nothing wrong with me. Just let him write a certificate for work."

Lars stood and tapped his brother on the back.

"I'll check to find out what the doc said," he called halfway through the door.

That week and the next, Josef forgot about his promise to make a doctor's appointment. When Lars phoned, Josef made the same promise again. Admin at work was insisting on a doctor's certificate.

Each day he drifted listlessly. He thought of vacuuming the carpet, washing his clothes or cleaning the dirty plates, but somehow it all seemed too hard and another day passed without doing anything. A call from his bank warning him that his account was almost overdrawn, finally urged him to search the Internet for a doctor in his area. He needed a certificate or his work payments would dry up.

After a long wait in the doctor's consulting room, a skinny man with balding hair called his name. He followed the man down the passage into a small room.

"Geoff Parker," the doctor said extending his hand. "How can I help you?"

When Josef explained his need for a medical certificate for work, the doctor looked at him with concern. Numerous questions followed and Josef answered tersely.

"I don't have a problem providing you with a medical certificate as you're obviously in poor shape. I bet you haven't eaten much and you're hardly sleeping. From what you're telling me you don't even want to see your friends or family."

Josef looked away and waited for the doctor's next comment.

"A certificate isn't all you need. You appear to be depressed."

"I'm not taking happy pills,' Josef replied.

"That's your choice, but your depression won't lift by itself."

"Depression? I'm grieving for my grandfather. Feeling down is normal when one loses someone close." His eyes filled with tears.

The doctor's expression was stern.

"A grieving person usually wants people around and to stay connected. There are occasional experiences of pleasure and he or she continues to function as before while slowly rebuilding their life."

"So, you're telling me that my grief has morphed into depression," Josef said.

"I guess so, but medication isn't always the answer for depression. What about seeing a counsellor?"

"A shrink?"

The doctor ignored Josef's comment and consulted his computer. "I know someone who can help."

Josef looked through the window at the ugly cement path.

"Think about it and come to see me early next week. We'll talk about the counsellor again. Meanwhile, I'll give you your certificate...and try to eat a little."

Before Josef could reply, the doctor stood and was herding him out of the room.

When Josef reached home, he was exhausted. He threw his coat on an armchair and flopped onto the couch. He thought about the doctor and that he felt lighter and less alone after talking to him.

He seems to know his stuff but I'm not happy about seeing a shrink.

It was dark when his phone rang. Lars was arriving with dinner in about twenty minutes. Josef muttered to himself about not being able to rest in peace. Quickly, he tidied away papers, closed the blinds and switched on the lights. Dirty glasses, cups and plates lay on the kitchen benchtop. The least he could do was to put a few plates and glasses in the dishwasher.

Lars arrived with enough Chinese takeout for three. Josef looked at the amount of food and shook his head.

"Before you ask, I went to a doctor, Dr Parker. He wants to see me again. He's checking up on me." Josef kept the doctor's suggestion about seeing a counsellor to himself.

"You'll get over this dark mood, bro."

Lars told jokes and stories about his work colleagues to cheer his brother up. Though Josef tried to appear interested, he found his concentration lapsing.

"I've been thinking about work. I don't know if I want to go back to my old job," Josef said.

"But you enjoyed your work and stayed back for hours finishing a project," Lars said looking puzzled.

"I've changed. Maybe I should try something different."

"Get real, bro. You're not trained for anything else. You'd be doing unskilled work."

"I don't care. Maybe I'll leave Melbourne and move somewhere else...even go back to Denmark for a while."

"Back to Copenhagen?"

"We still have a huge family there and I miss them," Josef said. "It would be great to be part of the easy-going life there again - the bikes, great bars, canals and old architecture."

"Are you crazy, Bro? Have you forgotten the freezing cold, wet and long and dark winters?"

"Maybe a change would do me good and shift this mood,"

Lars looked intensely at his brother and shook his head.

"You've got a fairy tale in your head. If you go back to Copenhagen you'd have to find a job and maybe stay with family for a while. You haven't been back for at least six years. Life in Denmark has changed and not as easy going as you think. Since the arrival of refugees, things are different there. I was in Copenhagen on holiday five months ago. Some Danes welcomed the new migrants, but there has been a great deal of hostility towards them. Extremist groups have sprung up too. I don't know if I would want to live there now. Of course, there are problems everywhere but the weather in Australia and the lifestyle here is amazing. It's safe and people are friendly. What more do you want?"

Lars was probably right. Why go back to Copenhagen when life is so good in Australia. He would tell Dr Parker that he agreed to see the shrink. If it didn't work out, he could walk away.

A week later, Josef went back to Dr Parker. The long wait in his stuffy reception area among other patients irritated him. At last, the doctor called his name.

"How are you, Josef? Any improvement in your mood"? the doctor asked.

"Nothing has changed."

Dr Parker nodded. "Have you thought about medication or seeing a psychologist?"

"No tablets but I could try the shrink – see if she can help."

While Dr Parker was typing on his computer, Josef glanced around the room. Two ships on the shelf opposite caught his attention. They were both clippers beautifully crafted with masts and sails.

"Those clippers are magnificent. Did you make them?" Josef asked.

'Yes, models are a hobby that keeps me sane with all the stress of a busy practice."

"You've done a good job with them," Josef said.

"This is a referral an for excellent counsellor who has helped many of my clients - Carla Rosen. I think you'll like her and I hope she'll help you," he said passing an envelope to Josef. "I'll phone her for an urgent appointment. My receptionist will call you with the appointment time."

Dr Parker stood and smiled at Josef.

"If you need further help come back any time."

Chapter 2

Carla tore open the letter. Her eyes snapped shut in shock. The letter was from a solicitor representing her landlord, the owner of the house where she held her practice. He was selling the house and giving her three month's notice. Thirteen years ago, she rented a room in the red-roofed, old-fashioned house and since then she had not considered moving. The high-ceilinged room was filled with her parents' furniture and ornaments. Her father's paintings decorated the walls. The room had an ambience that her clients found relaxing and comfortable.

The letter came when she was thinking of reducing her work hours but hadn't made any firm plans. Exhausted, worn out, flattened, bombed, done in and dog tired were the words she used to describe her feelings after a day's work. Though she tried almost everything to boost her flagging energy, from vitamin B shots to taking a short nap during the day, none of it helped. She had a vibrant practice but no idea of how to cut it back. Though she was good at telling others to say "no", she had not mastered the knack herself. Over the years, immigrants, refugees and elderly Holocaust survivors and others had gravitated to her. Working with them was a privilege. If she could bring hope and peace to even a few, she considered her efforts worthwhile.

That morning, she started early, hoping to catch up on a pile of outstanding reports before her first client arrived, but her thoughts darted to the letter. Where would she go? Would she find another suitable room in the area? She looked around the room where so many people had told her their secrets. Her gaze settled on her father's painting of water lilies – her favourite of her father's paintings. He admired Monet and was influenced by his style. It was a gentle painting in delicate colours with the lustre and translucence of Monet's work. He had not been in favour of her attending university. He wanted her to have a practical career and her decision to study psychology displeased him. He pointed out to her that the long years of study would be costly. With his stern look, he said emphatically that she would have to find work to pay her way. She wasn't discouraged and worked as a waitress in a wine bar throughout her student years. With her earnings and the help of a bank loan, she managed to pay for her studies.

A phone call from Sabine, a nurse at an aged home she visited regularly interrupted her thoughts.

"Sorry to disturb you, Carla. Please come around today, if you can. We need you." The woman spoke with a lilting European accent, her words punctuated by short breaths. "Do you remember Mrs Greenblatt, the ninety-year-old lady who had a birthday party last week?"

"Yes, Hannah Greenblatt." A stab of alarm shot through her.

At her party, Hannah was the happiest she'd been for ages. What could have happened to her in just a week?

"The night nurse found her sobbing, hiding under her bedclothes," the nurse said.

"Have you called her doctor?"

"He's already been to see her and gave her a shot to calm her, but it hasn't had any effect. She's still crying and restless. She's asking for you. Maybe you can help to settle her."

Carla thought of her long day with her list of clients and sighed. "Sure, I'll be there on my way home."

The brick building was much like other retirement centres she visited. The only difference was that a huge blue *menorah*, or Jewish candelabra, adorned the side of the building. The receptionist waved as Carla passed the communal lounge where residents sat in armchairs around a blaring television set. Some were asleep, others chatting. Only a few appeared to be watching the programme. A powerful aroma of calming lavender clung to her nostrils as she made her way up the stairs.

Sabine, the nurse who had phoned, rushed to greet her.

"Thanks for coming, Carla. I think Mrs Greenblatt had one of her nightmares about the concentration camp again last night. She was screaming so loudly that she woke most of the residents. What a night we had to get them all back to sleep!" She wiped her brow. "The residents forget some things, but it's always their terrible experiences that they dream about." Sabine looked concerned. "Hannah didn't say a word to her doctor about her nightmare and hasn't talked to any of us about it either, but she's asked to see you."

Sobs in the narrow hallway led Carla to Hannah's room. Hannah faced the wall, her white hair usually wound in a tight coil at the nape of her neck lay like silk threads on her shoulders.

"I'm here, Hannah."

The old woman stopped sobbing and turned slowly. "I'm so pleased to see you, Carla. You never let me down." Her speech was rasping.

"Something must've upset you badly, I haven't seen you like this for ages," Carla said as she took Hannah's hand.

"They came for us again last night. It was terrible, horrible, *fruchtbar*" she muttered, drifting into German.

"Shush, shush," Carla said reassuringly as she groped for the box of tissues that had fallen under the bed.

Hannah's eyes grew large, her lips quivered. "We were hiding behind the false bookshelf Papa built to keep us safe They didn't find us," she whimpered. "I was only six and Werner four and we were so frightened."

Carla had hoped that after many sessions with Hannah, her dreams about the SS marching into the house, dragging her parents away and sending them off to a concentration camp had stopped, but it seemed these memories were too entrenched to leave her.

Hannah's stare was unfocused.

"The soldiers were shouting. Mama and Papa were screaming as they were dragged down the stairs," she said between sobs. "I didn't see my parents again."

"You're safe here now, Hannah. All that was years ago. Nothing like that can happen to you now." Carla put her arm around Hannah and passed her a wad of tissues. "I know that your memories of that time are scary. Try to remember some of the happier things. You told me that a Catholic lady who owned a bakery cared for both you and Werner throughout the war."

"Yes, we were very lucky," Hannah said smiling weakly. "Elsa Schmidt, God bless her memory. She didn't have children and told the Germans that we were her children. She was kind and looked after us like a loving aunty."

They talked until Hannah's eyes began to close. Carla covered her with a quilt and tiptoed out of the room.

During the drive home, Carla's thoughts were about Hannah but she had trained herself to stop thinking about her clients when she turned into her driveway. Mostly it worked, but thoughts of people in crisis often stayed with her. When she walked into the living room Steve was asleep in front of the television, with his empty plate and glass on the floor near him. She didn't wake him. He had eaten the leftovers in the fridge. Too tired to cook, she made a sandwich and went to bed.

Chapter 3

Carla tugged at the stubborn curtain cord to allow sunlight into the room. Her appointment book was open on her desk and she scanned the entries. It would be another full day. The solicitor's letter lay on her desk like a nagging sore. She felt a stir of panic as she looked around the high-ceilinged room with its endless cupboards and bookshelves. Would she look for other premises, join another psychologist or a group of doctors? A glance at the clock stopped her questioning. Her first client was due to arrive soon, an older man, originally a refugee from Bosnia.

It was Friday, and she would have a break from work over the weekend. She was about to check her emails when the phone rang. The deep voice was Basil Parker's, a doctor who often referred clients. As he talked, she scribbled on her notepad.

"I know you see clients who are new to the country and Holocaust survivors and their descendants." He hesitated. "I'm hoping you will have time to see Josef Martinsen, a depressed, young man with a Danish background. He emigrated to Australia when he was a child. He's an architect. I think you'd be the right person for him with your broad background."

"I've had a few Scandinavian clients. I'd be happy to see him."

"Could you fit him in urgently? He's in bad shape."

Dr Parker had referred several of his patients to her in the past and besides, she liked him. She consulted her appointments for the following week and agreed to fit him in. Before leaving, she phoned the retirement home for an update on Hannah's progress. Sabine told her that Hannah was eating well and had not complained of nightmares again.

At last, work was over for the week. With her head down and her coat turned up to avoid a spring shower, she rushed to the car. A quick swipe freed the bonnet of clumps of pink blossoms and she drove away. The traffic crawled all the way home. Once her car was parked in the garage, she breathed a relieved sigh. She grabbed her briefcase and glanced at her watch. She was running late. Her family were coming for Sabbath dinner. Zoe, her cat was waiting as she opened the front door. The cat began her welcoming ritual of high-pitched meows and enthusiastic rolls on the carpet. There was always time for Zoe's tummy tickle. Carla draped her coat over a chair and placed her briefcase in its corner. Then she hurried to the kitchen. Her daughter Deanne, son-in-law Brad and her grandchildren would be arriving soon.

The kitchen was quiet apart from leaves scratching on the roof and the clink of forks and spoons against steel as she worked. Fortunately, she had set the table the night before and prepared most of the meal in advance. The Sabbath family meal was a ritual of love, attention and individual tastes that she cooked in the same way her mother and grandmother had prepared it. In her youth, Friday nights were the highlight of the week. Parents, in-laws, aunts, uncles and cousins dressed in their best squashed around her grandmother's large table. The images of the Sabbath that lived with her were precious memories. She could still taste sweet cashews, horseradish that made her cough, homemade pickled gherkins, dark chocolates and candied ginger. They were all placed in decorative dishes on a lace-edged tablecloth. Fitting cooking into her work schedule wasn't easy, but she considered it important to provide her children and grandchildren with rich memories they could draw on later. As she carried platters of food to the table, she sniffed the variety of aromas and smiled. Even if she had taken short cuts, the food was tempting.

The candles! She had almost forgotten them. The sun was

melting into the horizon. She placed two candles for herself and Steve in the silver candlesticks she inherited from her grandmother, and as was the custom in the family, another two smaller candles in candlesticks for her two children. She lit the candles, closed her eyes and spread her hands over the flames, encircling and drawing in the warmth as she whispered the ancient prayer to welcome the Sabbath. The flames in the darkening room and the familiar smell of molten wax was a comforting connection with all those who had gone before.

Then she concentrated on the meal. The family favourite, a crusty apple strudel baked earlier that week and defrosted, followed Tanta Emmy's recipe exactly. The strudel evoked memories of the diminutive woman who wore lily of the valley perfume and spoke in fractured sentences. She thought of her parents and how much she missed them – her mother who died eleven years ago and her father who followed her mother five years later. It was on the Sabbath, that she felt the loss most keenly. After her mother's death, the Sabbath had become more important than ever for her father. It allowed him to hold on to his memories. She recalled how much he enjoyed Emmy's strudel and could have eaten half in one sitting. When she baked a strudel to please him, he regularly complained that she had added too few *mandeln und rosinen*, almonds and raisins. On rare occasions, he lapsed into German to describe food or recall his childhood. Early after his arrival in Australia, he chose to struggle with English rather than speak German, the language associated with the enemy. She often wondered how he continued to go to synagogue and keep the Sabbath after he had been forced out of his homeland and so many of his relatives were killed during the Holocaust. However, his feelings about the war were forbidden topics in their home.

When she heard her husband, Steve's key turned in the front door, the dinner was almost ready. His kiss brushed her cheek as he placed a bunch of flowers on the kitchen table. Only a few words passed between them. Then he went into the dining room to make final touches to the table, moving platters to preferred positions and adding clumps of fine, dark chocolates that were kept in a drawer of the sideboard. He poured celebratory, red wine into a crystal decanter and placed it next to the *challah,* or plaited bread, at the head of the table. He rubbed his hands with pleasure as he gave the table a final glance.

The doorbell chimed and Steve rushed to the door.

"*Shabbat Shalom!* Lovely to see you all. It's cold out there, so come inside quickly!"

With a tug, Carla removed her apron and rushed out to greet her guests. She bent to kiss her grandchildren, smelling their sweetness. How she loved them and their shrieks of joy when they saw her. Coats were peeled off and her family gathered around the table waiting for Steve to make the Sabbath blessing. The children eyed the laden table hungrily but had learned to wait for the basket of sliced *challah* to be passed around. They picked at the raisins in the sweet bread and nibbled the crisp, outside edges. Nuts and chocolates were more appealing than a plate of chicken and vegetables. While the adults ate, the children collected chocolates and sweets in their pockets. Restlessly, they squirmed in their seats and kicked each other under the table. Deanne occasionally issued futile commands in a soft voice. Brad uttered sterner warnings and waggled a finger at them for reinforcement. Though Steve's brow clouded, he made no comments. At their age, he'd sat at the table without a word, but that was in the past when fear ruled. At least, his grandchildren were not expected to be little puppets, old before their time. Watching their free, confident speech and play gave him a burst of joy.

She placed cake, coffee and weak tea for the children on the sitting room table, but they were already curled up asleep on the couch. The adults caught up on family news, but it was past the children's bedtime and they woke them to dress them for the cool outdoors. Deanne yawned and glanced at her watch. Brad's eyes were about to close. Deanne gave him a disapproving look, but he turned away and sank lower into the armchair.

"Come on Brad, wake up," she said as she dressed ths children.

Brad grumbled as he collected toys and clothing. Hurried kisses and they were gone.

Carla sighed. Lately, she hardly talked to Deanne. They had quick phone calls enquiring after each other's health and discussed the children, but they hadn't chatted over a cup of coffee for months. She unwrapped a chocolate in a gold wrapper, sucked its sweetness and licked the dribble from her lips. She thought of Leo their oldest child who lived in England. He was divorced and had virtually cut himself off from his family. Steve stopped mentioning him and Deanne didn't talk about him either, but Carla missed her son. She had learned to accept his occasional phonecalls. All she wanted to know was if he was well and managing. It was late and she was too tired to mull over what had gone wrong with Leo's marriage and taken him overseas, or wonder if he would eventually return. She sighed. Now that she and Steve were alone at home, the hollowness of their marriage was declaring itself. Without their family, they had little to say to each other. She watched him unfurl the carpet and then flick crumbs off the table. He was slightly taller than her, his greying hair wiry and full, but his once sinewy, taut body had softened.

For a moment, she stopped tidying and allowed herself snatched memories of their year of enchantment after the honeymoon - their early lovemaking. She smiled. Then, he wanted her in seconds. A teasing flick of her long hair, the site of her bare shoulder, a honeyed tone in her voice, and he was aroused. They hadn't made love for over a month and she missed it. If only they both weren't so tired.

She set a glass platter down with a bang and frowned at her clumsiness. Thankfully, it was not broken. Steve glanced in her direction, grunted with tiredness and went to his study. The dishwasher had completed its cycle and the final tidying could wait until the morning. She poured herself a second cup of coffee, carried it to the sofa and stretched. The building tiredness she'd ignored all evening enveloped her as she sank into the softness. In the stillness, she relaxed after an evening of entertaining and a day of listening and problem-solving. A collage of her client's faces intruded and then drifted past her.

Chapter 4

Steve burped and rubbed his stomach. He'd eaten too much as he did when Carla made a Sabbath meal. Her cooking was excellent and always had been. The bright lights in the sitting room revealed shiny sweet papers strewn over the carpet. He bent to collect the wrappers and smiled as he removed a sticky mess stuck to a platter. He recognised his eldest grandchild's handiwork.

I love 'em but I wish they weren't so wild. Brad and Dee let them do what they like.

While gathering cushions the children had tossed about the room in play, he hummed a tune that accompanied a Sabbath prayer. It reminded him of Friday nights at Aunt Rita's when he was one of five, young cousins around the table. His aunt, his father's sister-in-law, was the only Rosen wife of four sons who could afford not to work. She made up for her easier life by preparing lavish Sabbath meals for the entire, extended family of about thirty.

A sound from the children then and his father, the eldest brother, lashed out with an elbow jab that hurt. After the meal, and with full pockets gleaned from the table, they ran to the back of the old house to play. The area was a storeroom for furniture, paintings and bric-a-brac from a series of family members who had passed on. His grandmother had been a hoarder who refused to give any item away.

He rubbed his stomach again and went into the kitchen for a glass of soda water. After a quick check that windows and doors were locked, he made his way up the stairs to the bedroom. Carla was asleep on her side of the bed. It had been a heavy week with a long case he had won at court. Usually, he hung his trousers neatly in the cupboard and stuffed his dirty underwear in the laundry basket, but that night he piled his clothes on the chair. In bed, he glanced at Carla's dark curls making a delicate pattern on the pillow and at the lump beneath the covers where the cat cuddled next to her. He longed to hold Carla.

Even after all these years, she was a beauty. How long was it since they had made love?

Turning away from her, he thought how remote and self-contained she had become. Muttering about the cat having taken his place, he clicked off the bedside lamp. As he waited for sleep to overwhelm him, he recalled meeting her at university. Her long, dark hair, her eyes that shone when she talked and her sinuous body caught his attention. She was not like the other girls hanging about in groups eyeing each other when they expressed opinions. It was her independent mind and her way of caring for people in trouble or suffering that he found appealing.

First hot and then too cold, he turned his cushion over and groaned restlessly. He had noticed how tired she looked. Lately, she was withdrawn. He had tried but he was unable to break through her barrier. Flowers, dinner at a restaurant or concerts she'd once enjoyed did not help. Her work devoured her energy and he wondered how she managed to listen for so long to clients' stories that were rarely happy. She possessed extraordinary patience and tolerance and he appreciated that quality in her. Just as well he could hide behind the law with the people who sought his help. Listening to their agony for too long distressed him. She had the habit of deflecting questions about herself and she was still doing it - smiling and nodding when he asked if she was well. Something was bugging her. Silently he ran through the possibilities. Had her hard work burned her out, were their children upsetting her, or was she unhappy in the marriage? Any or all those factors could be bothering her. Lately, she was preoccupied with her past and had asked him to recall incidents and occasions they had spent with her parents. Tiredly, He rubbed his head, sighed and fell asleep.

Chapter 5

Josef sat in the narrow hallway as he waited for his appointment with Carla Rosen, the counsellor. This was his first visit to a psychologist or counsellor as Dr Parker called her. Psychologists were not his thing, especially after all he had heard and imagined about them. At least with a doctor or dentist, he knew what to expect. Three times that morning he'd picked up the phone to cancel the appointment but replaced it. He wouldn't have been there at all if his doctor hadn't insisted he talk to her. Talk. He was not much of a talker. And what was talking going to do to fix him? How could he explain to her or anyone how wretched he felt when he failed to understand it? Even if she made sense of his ramblings, what could she do to help him?

At last, the door opened and he heard voices – one from a woman who sounded Australian and another from a younger woman with a foreign accent. Was it Spanish? A tall, bronzed teenager with a floral smell rushed from the room. When she noticed Josef, she bowed her head and scuttled past him. The door closed and after a wait, a woman of medium height, round, with dark hair stood before him.

"You must be Mr Martinsen...Carla Rosen," she said, extending her hand. "Let's talk in my room." Inside her room, she indicated an armchair scattered with cushions. "Make yourself comfortable."

"Josef, please call me Josef."

"You were born in Denmark, Dr Parker told me." Her voice was soft and plying.

"Yes, my family are Danish. We came to Australia when I was nine."

She nodded, scanned the doctor's email referral, placed her hands on her lap and looked at him.

"So how can I help you, Josef?" Her generous smile made him feel more at ease.

"I guess I'm here about my family... my grandfather, Erik, who died three months ago. Since then... I've been..." He threw his hands in the air.

"I am so sorry about the loss of your grandfather. Losing someone deeply loved can hit hard."

The tap Josef had vowed not to open would not close. He heard himself talking from a distance. "I've been a wreck since *Farfar* died." He explained that the Danish name for grandfather was *Farfar*."

"A delightful name for a grandfather."

He took a deep breath before continuing. "Nothing could've prepared me for the sadness of losing him, even if he was eighty-eight and not all that well." He swallowed hard. "But why do I feel like this, not able to think straight or work? I should be over it by now." He fiddled with the chain around his neck.

"Life doesn't work according to shoulds and musts."

His eyes swooped across the room - a wooden desk cluttered with papers, wall to wall shelves crammed with books, a carpet with an Asian design, a few ornaments of cats and a large vase of flowers.

What could he say about *Farfar*? How was he going to explain to her what his grandfather meant to him and the ache since *Farfar* died?

He thought of how his grandfather had cared for him when his mother went back to work soon after he was born. It was his grandfather, and not his parents, who watched him play football at school. For a moment, he was caught up in memories. It was summer in Copenhagen and *Farfar* was playing ball with him while Lars played indoors. A flash of the old man's face was wreathed in wrinkly smiles. A snatch of his voice - a voice that praised him when he kicked a long ball or ran faster than usual. It was *Farfar* who noticed his talent for building and design and later encouraged him to apply for the architectural course at university. Suddenly, his throat tightened, and he felt like a fish gulping for air.

"Are you okay?"

"Yes, yes...I'm fine."

"Please tell me more about your grandfather," she asked gently.

He looked at his hands before answering. "*Farfar* was seventy when we arrived in Australia. Everything was different for him. His English was too poor for him to work in his profession as a quantity surveyor. Instead, he became a handyman. He said he liked the work and made no complaints. I was stronger than I looked and good with my hands. After school, I helped him. I liked him saying that he couldn't do without me, even if it wasn't true. I enjoyed being around him when we worked. While we fixed broken doors, painted a wall or mended fences, I talked. I could say anything and he would listen. When mum came home, she had housework to do and was too tired to talk. My father...he and I had little to say to each other. Well, that's another story." He felt a hot tight ball rising from his gut.

"Did *Farfar* get along with your father?" She asked.

He shook his head vehemently and stared at the carpet.

She glanced at him as she asked about his family's move to Australia.

He heard himself speaking too fast as he told her that his mother had been ill in Denmark and that the long, cold winters worsened her condition. When his father was offered work in Australia, he decided to emigrate with the family to the warmer climate. Neither his grandfather, his brother Lars, nor he wanted to leave Denmark. His mother managed to smooth things over by saying that they were all going on an exciting adventure. Though the warmer climate suited her, she developed heart trouble after a few years. The doctors tried everything they could, but she died ten years after arriving in Australia.

Josef's eyes misted. "I wish I'd been there for her at the end," he said as his hands formed a fist.

He wasn't going to tell her how his mother became a virtual invalid by the time he was in his late teens. That the shock of her illness stopped him from visiting her as often as he should've, and that it was too painful to watch his once beautiful mother deteriorate into helpless flabbiness, puffing for air on her special adjustable chair. No longer was she aware of the changes in his life or able to advise him on minor problems. She was in her own bubble of illness. When she was hospitalised and needed his love and support, he was unable to give it. 'I'll be here for you,' he told her, squeezing her hand, but he was not there. When he knew that his mother was dying, he could not go to the hospital. Instead, to distract himself, he worked longer hours and filled his spare hours with his mates at the pub, leaving drunk enough to fall into bed. He was stunned when his father called to tell him she had died.

"Do you have anyone close? Are you in a relationship?"

"There's Greta, but things are not going too well." He was aware of covering his face and his hot tears with his hands. He wished he could melt into the chair.

Twenty-six years old and whimpering like a baby.

"It's okay, Josef. Take a few deep breaths," she said gently.

A pressure lifted as he wiped his eyes and took a deep breath.

She was quiet and waited for him to talk. Rain pattered on the iron roof and the room became darker. She turned on the light and smiled again. Their discussion moved on to Josef's work as an architect, work that had once been his passion. When she asked about his interests, he mentioned sailing, but he had not been on the water for months.

He stared at the pattern on the carpet, wondering what she would ask next.

"You must be feeling awful to have decided to visit me."

How could he explain his lost feelings.

"I guess it's more than grieving by now. Am I depressed?"

She nodded and made notes on her computer.

He stared at the door longing to leave, to end her questioning about his eating, sleeping, loss of energy and whether he could concentrate and finish a task.

"Is there anything I can do now... to make me feel right...feel like I used to?" he heard himself plead.

"Be patient with yourself. You'll need to work through your feelings and face them slowly. Then you'll move on."

He looked puzzled.

"It's a slow process but I'm here to help you and make things clearer as you go through this. There's a lot of work that you'll have to do, but you can move on and come out of it."

His inner voice drummed with uncertainty.

She rotated the ring on her finger. "You could write down your feelings and memories about *Farfar* and Greta."

"Uh-huh. Like a journal?"

She nodded. "It will help a lot." Unobtrusively she looked at the purple plastic clock on her desk. "We'll have to stop now, but I hope to see you again so that we can talk more."

He stared at the dots of rain on the window. Commit himself to another appointment in the following week or the one after that. He would have to think about it.

Chapter 6

Rain pelted down as Josef drove up the cobblestone driveway, a steep incline to his ecologically, sound house. He had designed the house and set it on a slab of rock facing the Dandenong Mountains. Instead of following the current architectural trend for geometric starkness and steely tones, he chose organic forms and earthy shades. He prided himself on his manly sensitivity and appreciation of art and design. But since *Farfar's* death, design and architecture failed to interest him. Nothing much interested him.

In the fading light, the inside of the house was chilly. He turned on the solar heating and flicked on the CD player to Bach's *Prelude No.1*, a piano piece he found calming. His taste for music had changed from rock to pop, then to jazz. Now it was the classics that he most enjoyed. He grabbed a few beers from the fridge, hoping to shut out the vision of the psychologist, her room and the chatter inside his head.

The music receded as images of the session rolled furiously. He was outside Carla's office on edge again, waiting for her door to open. As he thought about her, he nibbled the froth of his beer. There was something different about her? A pleasant woman who knew the right questions. She had to be experienced. Not a spring chicken but then who could tell with women. She seemed to care. If only she would stop nodding her head so often and twisting her ring around her finger. He had told her the truth about being a wreck since *Farfar* died. What would she have thought if he had told her what his father was really like? That that they had no real connection. A vision of his father standing near him at *Farfar's* funeral, assuming a mock solemnity that he set aside for sad occasions, appeared and then faded. He stared out of the window at the wet pines swaying in unison.

Soon the trees blended into the landscape and he was once again at his grandfather's funeral. A larger than expected crowd were there. His father's business friends, some of his work colleagues and fellow architects attended. Carers from the retirement home who had helped his grandfather to shower and dress each morning were there as well as his friends from the social club he played cards with twice a week. The social club members in their 'Sunday best', supported by walkers and sticks clung together. They talked of those who had died recently and others who were likely to join them soon. A Lutheran priest handled the service. In his eulogy, the priest painted a picture of his grandfather as he knew him –a self-educated man with strong moral values who had changed his career in his new country. The priest focussed on his grandfather's work for the community and how much he would be missed. In comparison, his father's brief speech was pathetic with insincere comments about his perfect father when in truth he hated *Farfar*.

Just as well he had organised the catering. If it had been left to his father, there wouldn't have been enough food at the wake. His father wouldn't have cared. The Danish-owned hotel prepared an authentic Danish buffet, a *smorgasbord* of thinly sliced open sandwiches and fluffy pastries with Danish beer on tap. Friends stayed on to drink to his grandfather until the hotel staff lifted chairs onto the tables. His father rushed off early with excuses.

"Give me a ring and we'll get together soon son," he called out.

Howling wind carried Josef back into the room with Carla. He rubbed his temples. How could he explain to her how much his grandfather meant to him? He kicked the table in frustration. If only Greta was still with him. She had complained that his dark moods were unbearable. At least if he could go to work he would see her there. As a talented draughtswoman, she assisted the company's architects with drawings for clients.

The walls seemed to squeeze and shift. To calm himself, he opened another can of beer and placed a bowl of pretzels on the table near the couch. The remote lay next to him and he clicked it to change the CD. The music soothed his thoughts, and he began to reason more clearly. He knew that needed to see Carla again.

After several beers, the room became a blur, and he was back in the past again. Now, he was enjoying the sunshine with his grandfather on his small front veranda with its striped awning. His grandfather prepared the same meal they ate for lunch in Denmark - fried bread with an omelette filled with leftover meat, onion and tomato. As a treat, he was allowed a beer shandy. His grandfather talked longingly about the soccer team he'd played with in his youth - the members of the team and coaches. Though Josef knew all the stories, in each telling there was a new twist or humorous incident.

A memory of his grandfather's smiling face distracted him.

You're out there *Farfar*, I sense it. You have no idea how much I miss you. It was you who listened when I was in a jam or scared. Now I'm going to this woman, this 'headshrinker', you'd call her. But I realise now how little I know about you. It was always me we talked about. I should've nagged you to tell me more about your life but it's too late now.

He nibbled at a few pretzels, stretched on the couch and piled up cushions to support his head. Then he slept.

Chapter 7

Greta ran her hand over the bathroom's white surfaces and sniffed the air in the fresh-smelling room. The result of her cleaning satisfied her. When she was younger her mother stressed the old story about cleanliness being next to godliness so often that she believed it. She walked through her small house with a smile. Everything was in its place. Just as well she refused to rent the house while living with Josef. The money would've been useful, but her independence was her main consideration.

Josef wanted to meet her for coffee or a drink, but she wasn't ready to see him. They had been separated for three months and she was enjoying time to herself. He needed to sort himself out before she would consider meeting him. Though the familiarity of her house and her possessions were comforting, she missed him. Not the pathetic child she had left behind, but the man she had met at the Danish Club – tall, interesting and sexy. His recent pining for his dead grandfather, an unremarkable old man, much like her uncles, was inexplicable. In her family, they mourned the dead briefly and then moved on. Josef's lurching emotions demanded more patience and understanding than she could muster. She understood physical complaints, but his dark moods that lasted for days and cast a pall over the house were intolerable. One moment he was clinging to her, the next he was gloomily mooching about the house ignoring her. Depression, he said the doctor called it. No one in her family had suffered from depression, whatever that was. He asked if she'd like to accompany him to the psychologist, but why would she? It was his problem. She had done all she could for him – made his favourite meals to tempt his appetite but he had left the food untouched. She had tried to arouse him sexually, but her naked body no longer excited him. Even teasing him with see-through, black lingerie was useless. He was not interested. When he refused to go to work because he claimed he was struggling to concentrate, she was unable to condone his laziness. Her parents had taught her that busy hands and a busy mind were sound medicine. Leaving him for a while was the best thing for her to do.

When she arrived home from work the emptiness of the house bothered her. There was late-night shopping that night, so she left for the shopping mall only a short drive away. The old couch could do with a lift she decided, as she piled a colourful throw rug and cushions on the shop counter. Not an impulsive buyer, her actions surprised her. Afraid that she might extend the shopping spree, she hurriedly packed her parcels into the boot of the car and drove home.

Before bed, she unpinned her long hair. Her image stared at her in the mirror. She smiled at her naturally blonde hair and even features. She was aware of her attractiveness. Some even called her beautiful. She thanked God often for not having created her ugly, though she was tired of the swarm of men drawn to her and the women who resented her. She thought of Josef again and their only argument. She had called his depression a sham, a cover for laziness. He responded that she was superficial. His comment had hurt. What if she liked what she liked, didn't enjoy his heavy music or want to delve into the meaning of things for hours. He had no right to criticise her.

Rearranging the sitting room to incorporate the new items she had bought and some old ones retrieved from back cupboards took her all of Sunday afternoon. The result of the new look pleased her. That night she gazed at her clothes in her cupboard. She had a meeting with one of the firm's partners the following day and needed to look efficient. A grey suit and pink blouse were perfect. She placed the clothes on the chair for the following morning.

The news of her breakup with Josef had spread, and her phone rang with invitations. As much as Josef had irritated her, and pushed her patience to its limit, she hoped that he would recover so that she could return to the man she had fallen in love with. Right then, she had no interest in other men.

Chapter 8

Carla's head tilted to one side as she listened.

"Let's talk about your move from Denmark to Australia. It couldn't have been easy."

"You have no idea! No one could. Everything was so different from school in Denmark, but I guess I got the hang of it and caught up."

He cursed softly as he wiped his eyes. "I don't know why talking about this is making me so emotional. It isn't like me at all."

"Upsetting memories. Did you make any friends?"

"Not at junior school. Coming from Denmark I was too different, and it took me ages to blend in. I had no friends at school. I was small for my age, skinnier than the rest. They went for me like a magnet, chasing me through the schoolyard. When they caught me they pulled my yellow hair that was much longer and thicker than theirs. I put up with sticks in the spokes of my bicycle too. It took ages to pull them out." He swallowed hard and tried to focus on the row of cats on her cabinet near the window. "I begged mum to take me out of that school and she did, but my grandfather was against me leaving. He kept on like a broken record. 'You'll never be a man if you don't learn to fight your own battles, he'd say.' Josef paused, remembering. "I refused to eat and mum was so upset that she put me into an expensive private school but I didn't fit in there either. There were bullies there too but not as many. *Farfar* refused to talk to her for days. He believed that giving in to me would make me soft."

"Was he right?" She turned her ring as she waited for his reply.

"Maybe. I was scared and didn't know how to stand up for myself. Well, look at the mess I'm in now?" He ran his hand through his hair.

"You're tough on yourself," she said.

"I grew taller and stronger. Then I fought off the bullies. Later, in high school, I made a few friends. My drinking mates haven't clue about the way I'm feeling, and I wouldn't tell them."

He looked down at the pattern in the carpet.

"I know I'm sorry for myself but not everyone cracks up when their grandfather dies."

"Your grandfather was such an important part of your life and his death hit you hard. He was more of a parent to you than a grandparent."

He stared at her unable to answer and wiped his moist eyes.

Both were quiet, travelling along their paths of contemplation. Then he was speaking again, telling her how sad and tired he was. She talked about eating well and exercising, but when she repeated the suggestion she'd made on his previous visit about writing his memories and feelings in a diary, his body stiffened with irritation.

How could a diary help? He needed answers now.

Then she surprised him.

"Do you have a dog?"

He frowned and shook his head.

"A dog would be excellent company. You'd have to feed it, play with it and take it for walks. A dog could help."

He nodded and then shifted restlessly. He looked at the clock. It had been a long session. When Carla stood, he thanked her and rushed to the door. Sitting in the narrow reception area waiting for Carla was a tall man. Josef wondered fleetingly why the man was seeing Carla and what his problem was.

As he walked towards his car, the impact of the session took over. Talking to a stranger about private thoughts made him uneasy. It was as if he had eaten a large meal. Nothing about the session leapt out at him. He was aware that it had affected him at a deeper level, but he struggled to define it. He turned the key in the ignition, but instead of driving home, he stopped at a park and pulled up under a tree.

Walking will fix it, he thought. He looked at the lush grass spotted with a variety of weeds - stubby ones that spread out and devoured the ground, tall, spindly ones and short flat leaves with yellow pincushion heads. Blossoms were about to fall from the trees and a gentle wind teased the clouds. He walked faster until he was almost running, hoping to erase the ache inside. After scrambling up a steep incline, he stopped to blow a blast of air that gripped his chest. With knees clasped, he sat on a rock and allowed the wind to ruffle his hair and clothes.

A woman and her dog strode past. She was talking to the dog, telling him to stop sniffing and to hurry up. He watched them enviously. Carla was correct, a dog was a good idea. He thought of his mate Terry whose brother raced greyhounds and was on the lookout for good homes for his retired dogs. He promised himself that he'd give Terry a ring.

The call to Terry was disappointing. Terry's brother had no greyhounds to rehome, but he came up with another idea.

"I have a four-year-old miniature Dachshund, Ben, who needs more care. They are one-person dogs and with my job and the kids to look after, Ben's not getting the attention he needs. If you take him, you'll do us both a favour. Try him for a few days."

"They're small dogs, long and squat. Not exactly what I had in mind."

"You'll fall in love with Ben, I promise. He has a brave heart."

"You've talked me into taking him. I'll come round to pick him up."

The black and tan dog whined during the journey back to the house.

"I hope I haven't made a big mistake with you."

He pulled up in the garage, gathered the dog in his arms and went into the house through the back door.

He placed the dog on the kitchen floor and it followed him on a tour of the house, stopping to sniff at doorways and corners. Joseph eyed his muscular body as he waddled on stumpy feet. He should've been ugly and yet he wasn't, Josef thought.

"First thing, food and water and then a place to sleep." He filled a bowl with milk, tore up pieces of bread and added a bit of left over chicken. "This will have to do until I can go to the shops for doggy food."

The dog consumed the food in minutes, licked his lips and stood staring at Josef expectantly. His dark eyes flecked with amber gave Josef the impression of complete understanding.

He bent down to pat the dog.

"You're a little sausage, half a dog high and one and a half long. With luck, we'll get along but we'll have to find another name for you. Bjorn. Yes, you'll be Bjorn." The dog wagged his slim tail for the first time.

Chapter 9

Once Kumar, Carla's last client left, she placed her head in her hands and closed her eyes. He was one of the thousands of Sudanese forced out of their villages by Arab militia with no other place to go to other than to the notorious Darfur Camp. She sighed. Half his family had been killed, his mother and sisters were raped, and he witnessed atrocities that he struggled to talk about. He came to Australia as a refugee and was battling to adapt - trapped between his culture and the Australian way of life. He had learned to speak English and hoped to find permanent employment. The ringing phone interrupted her thoughts with a request to visit Hannah on her way home.

Hannah was thrilled to see her and appeared to have forgotten her recent nightmares. After a check with Sabine, Carla left with a promise to return the following week.

Carla checked her watch. She was running late and would have to hurry to make her appointment with Mike, her case supervisor. Monthly supervision of her cases was just as much a requisite of her job as attending professional development seminars and keeping up to date with journals. Though she was convinced that she no longer needed supervision, she had no choice if she wanted to maintain her professional credentials. Mike had been one of her university tutors who was now a professor. She liked and respected him and asked him to be her supervisor.

Students poured out of lecture theatres in the building devoted to Psychology and queues of students waited to take their place. In the passage near Mike's room, a group of students chatted. His door was open.

He put down his book, glanced at his watch and greeted her. He studied her for a few seconds before speaking, "You look done in."

"A day off work and a long sleep and I'll be fine."

"You've had that look for months."

She made a dismissive gesture with her hand. "My landlord notified me that I'll have to move to new premises. Since then I've been thinking of cutting down my hours, but I haven't got around to organising it yet."

"There are no medals for exhaustion."

She shrugged and fumbled with her iPad to log onto cases for discussion.

He moved his chair closer. "A selection of this month's troubled souls," he said.

Their case consultation did not take long. Mostly he agreed with her approach and made only minor suggestions. She valued his opinion and after noting his ideas, she placed her iPad in her briefcase.

"We have fifteen minutes left," he said.

"I'd like to chat, but I've got some urgent shopping to do," she lied.

She didn't want Mike to elaborate on her tiredness.

After her shower that evening, she looked in the mirror, still foggy from the heat. As the mist disappeared, she saw her shiny hair and her face with only a few wrinkles around her eyes. Her eyes betrayed her tiredness, but she told herself that she was still reasonably attractive. After two children, her breasts were no longer as firm as they once were and her stomach protruded slightly. Exercise could tone her muscles but there was no place in her schedule for visits to the gym. She ran her hands down the length of her torso and sighed as she wondered what had happened to her once passionate sex life. Steve worked hard, but that hadn't stopped him before. Only a year ago he was easily aroused.

She opened her drawer and found her blue negligee, the one Steve liked. The satin clung to her body and lifted her breasts. She slipped between the cool sheets and waited for Steve to join her.

Chapter 10

Josef grimaced as the morning light streamed into his bedroom through a chink in the curtain. He had no memory of the night before. From his crushing headache, dry mouth, the empty, whiskey bottle on the table next to his bed and beer cans on the floor, he concluded that he had wiped himself out. Once he had opened the curtains, he noticed a thick layer of dust on the furniture. He'd have to get around to cleaning, vacuuming and dusting, but he didn't feel up to it. His hand hovered over the phone. He was about to dial Carla's number to cancel an appointment with her. What was the point of seeing her again? What would she say or want to know this time? Someone had told him that psychologists could read one's mind. Well, she asked too many questions for him to believe that. He resisted his impulse and put the phone down. He rubbed his eyes. A long glass of water, breakfast and hopefully he'd be in shape for the session that afternoon.

He was about to leave when the phone rang. It was Tim, one his firm's senior partners urging him to consider returning to work.

"Thanks for ringing, but I'm not ready for work yet, mate." There was an edge to Josef's voice.

"I'm sure that being around people again and a few hours of work would do you good. And we need you."

"Look, Tim, I can't concentrate! Wish I could."

"We all want you to know how much we miss you. You are our most talented young architect by far. Anything you design has pizzaz and the clients want you and no one else."

With eyes shut he tapped the table.

"I wish I could come back," he replied tersely.

"I'll leave the timing to you, then. We'll all be pleased to see you when you're ready, mate. Take care of yourself."

Josef put the phone on the kitchen benchtop with a relieved sigh. Tim was the partner who supervised new projects and reading between the lines, Josef could tell that work was pouring into the office. All that pizzaz stuff was nice, complimentary. The reality was that they were short-staffed. At least for the moment, he didn't need to worry about holding onto his job. He missed the busy office. He pictured his colleagues saying the odd word to each other in the lift to the office or the reception area. There was little contact after that apart from discussions at meetings. All their socialising waited for late Friday afternoons when everyone met up for a drink, and even then, not all of them could make it. Like all creative work, it was carried out alone and his draughtboard, computer and phone were his essential tools. When he thought of the demanding clients and difficulties he had encountered with suppliers of materials and tradesmen, he knew that he wasn't ready for that sort of pressure yet.

It was a cool, windy afternoon when he turned into Carla's street. The previous night's storm had tossed fallen blossoms onto the grass and flattened gardens. At least the old houses with their white walls and red roofs appeared welcoming. He walked up the slippery, privet-edged path and climbed the stone steps to Carla's office at the side of the building. When her door opened, she looked in his direction, held up her hand and walked past him supporting an elderly man along the passage and down the stairs.

She was back in minutes.

"Good to see you, Josef, let's go into my room and talk."

He waited for her to speak.

"So, how are you?" She asked, glancing at her computer.

"Today's been a lousy day," he mumbled. 'But there were a

few days when I felt a bit more energetic, went for walks and cooked a meal."

He fingered the cuff of his jacket.

"That sounds positive."

He dropped his head and glowered at her through his eyelashes.

"Not really! It's so slow...endless," he said and swallowed. "Maybe I would've handled *Farfar's* passing better if Greta hadn't left me." He threw his hands up and shrugged. "I don't know if I told you that we work in the same office and were attracted to each other from the start." Then he told her about a Sunday *smorgasbord* lunch at the Danish Club where they had almost collided while stretching for the smoked salmon.

He drifted away from Carla and was with Greta at the Danish Club. How they laughed as their eyes met. He recalled moving from his group to sit with Greta and her friend Jacinta, who was embarrassed by their giggles, piled food on her plate and ate with other friends. After he and Greta had gorged themselves with the delicacies offered, they left the club and walked along the marine parade. They were too wrapped in each other to notice the high tide or dark storm threatening on the horizon.

"We saw each other during the week and spent weekends together," he told Carla. "She's a beauty and resembles my mother when she was a young woman. Initially, we had a lot to talk about – music, architecture, art, and we had similar backgrounds." He smiled wistfully. "She was born in Austria, migrating to Australia with her parents at twelve years old. She has a Swedish grandparent and some Danish cousins. Our decision to live together in my house came naturally."

He followed a thread on the carpet with the toe of his shoe.

"I thought I'd found my soul mate." His eyes shone with tears. To control his surge of emotion, he focused on the window opposite and the row of cypress trees swaying in the breeze. "When she said she wanted a break, I couldn't even tell her that I loved her. I was like a block of wood." He recalled his desperation, his fruitless search for words to stop her from leaving. "She told me that she couldn't handle my dark moods, that I'd ruined everything and packed her things."

Carla nodded.

"She should've noticed that I was depressed. I wasn't working, I'd stopped gardening and wasn't even interested in sex."

Carla's eyes were liquid with empathy.

"I haven't seen or spoken to her since she left."

He placed his hands on his lap and looked at her.

"Do you think that we could ever get together again?"

"Are you ready for that?" She asked dodging his question.

He looked down. He longed for the sound of Greta's laughter echoing through the house, her steps as she tidied and her touch on his skin.

Chapter 11

Carla tried to switch off from her work, but the clients she had seen that day were still on her mind. She was concerned about Sergio who was severely depressed. According to his family, his depression had worsened. She made a note to phone his doctor in the morning. Then there was Mary Ann, an elderly woman whose recovery was swifter than expected but she had no family support and Carla worried about a relapse. A call to the community social worker might be helpful, she thought. Then she thought about Josef. With his background, a mother working and later bedridden and an autocratic father away from home much of the time, no wonder his grandfather had become his most important adult. His childhood struggles to be accepted in a new country, his sense of loss over his grandfather's death and then his lover's lack of understanding and rejection, had tipped him into depression. He was so brittle and yet in a hurry for results

She sat on the couch, stretched and yawned. The cat noticed her vacant lap and jumped up hoping for cuddles. As Carla caressed the cat's favourite spots, she talked to her. The cat purred as its eyes closed. A quiet evening lay ahead as Steve was attending a Rotary meeting. Barefoot, she padded to the bedroom. She slipped between the crisp cotton sheets, shifting until she found a comfortable position. A book was lying open next to her, but she pushed it aside, too tired to concentrate. She gazed around the room and more specifically at the alcove that she and Steve created when they moved into the house. The alcove contained her mother's favourite porcelain vase filled with roses from the garden. As she breathed their fragrance, she closed her eyes. The scent of roses reminded her of earlier years of marriage when she and Steve planted a rose garden and renovated the house. Perhaps they could do some renovations again - a weekend project to draw them together. She was lonely in the marriage and if she hadn't been committed to her work, her days would have been empty. Her thoughts drifted to her childhood when she longed for a sister to share her dreams and secrets. As a child, she sensed all her parents' disagreements, but she knew that their squabbling meant nothing. They loved, even adored each other. They loved her too, but the gleam in their eyes, their longing looks at each other, spontaneous hugs and touches confirmed that their closeness was out of bounds to her. As an only child and the third member of the triangle, she was in a shifting position – sometimes smothered with affection, others ignored or told to go out and play. She remembered at five, sitting under shady trees in the garden with her mother. She was about to start school. Her mother was telling her about the school uniform she would wear and the routine she would follow. Quickly, she changed the topic to the one on her mind. 'Mum, when am I going to have a brother or sister?' she asked. Her mother smiled at her. 'Sorry, my darling. There'll be no brothers or sisters.'

Chapter 12

Josef was in his pyjamas seated at his computer. Though Carla asked him to make notes of his thoughts and feelings each day, he hadn't written a word. Knowing she was there, made him feel secure. She was a crutch for his emotions. Though he became despondent at times about the slowness of his recovery, he believed her when she said his mood would eventually lift. She appeared to know a lot about depression, and he sensed that she was genuine.

The warmer weather eased the intensity of his despair and he left the house more often to go to the shops for food or beer, and short morning walks. Exercise, especially walking, was one of Carla's suggestions that he followed.

He bent to pat the dog curled around his feet and fed him the remains of his sandwich. Then he leaned back against the chair, put his hands behind his head and closed his eyes. Thoughts of his grandfather hadn't left him, and as soon as he relaxed memories of *Farfar* slipped back.

When he raided his memory, he was able to access precious moments spent with his grandfather, but he was left with some unanswered questions. As a child, he didn't question his grandfather's stories about the past, but lately, inconsistencies flew up at him. He wondered if time had embroidered *Farfar's* stories. Josef began to doubt whether his grandfather had been a member of the Danish King's regiment at the start of the war, as he'd claimed. There were no photographs of his grandfather dressed proudly in the regiment's uniform with its pomp and ceremony, or papers to support it. Even if his grandfather's account was true, the king's army failed to hold out against the Germans when they attacked Denmark. The Danish Government capitulated within about two hours. It was common knowledge and nothing like the story of glory and heroism that his grandfather fed him. And then, there was the Danish Resistance. Was it true that his grandfather joined the Resistance, or was it a fictional account of the old man's involvement during the war to impress his grandchild? What Josef had once accepted as indisputable facts were now shaky. He longed for more information.

He began to dissect his memories, memories that had not occurred to him until he visited Carla. His thoughts stuck at Sweden, and the refrain of Sweden, Sweden, Sweden hammered his brain. He could pinpoint the day he heard about his grandfather's stay in Sweden for the first time. It was on Christmas before the family left for Australia. The tree in the window of the house sparked and quivered with lights and tinsel. The table groaned with delicacies. His mother intended this Christmas, their last one in Denmark, to be unforgettable. While the adults drank coffee and sipped schnapps after their meal, Josef left them to play with his new toys. As he picked up his gift of an aeroplane, he overheard them talking about the war. The war was a topic so often discussed in the house, that it bored him and he usually didn't bother to eavesdrop. He was about to play outside when he heard his mother mention his grandfather's visit to Sweden during the war. This was new, interesting information. He placed the aeroplane on the floor and moved closer to listen. He heard his grandfather's angry voice, insisting that his family knew very well that his visit to Sweden during the war was brief. Josef was puzzled and he asked *Farfar* about his stay in Sweden.

"Well, my boy, you know how flat Denmark is, and that Sweden has mountains, lakes and forests. It is a beautiful country, but it is nothing like living at home," was all he said at first. After Josef nagged for a precise answer, his grandfather finally told him that he had hidden on a boat that crossed the channel to Malmo at the start of the war and stayed in a rented room for a few months. Josef recalled his grandfather's final comment. "I moved away to escape being conscripted into the German army when they occupied Denmark."

It was a sharp memory and Josef scratched the side of his unshaven face. He was certain that the Danes did not join the German army during the war. Most Danes loathed the Germans and the occupation of their country. While some joined the Resistance, others put up with the situation. Only traitors joined the Germans. He learned at school about collaborators who returned to Denmark. His grandfather's story that he had accepted at face value for so long did not make sense.

He recalled Greta's pointed remarks about his grandfather's charming manner. 'He smiles often and tends to gloss over details. I've seen him with women. He must've been a lady's man when he was younger.' Then her cynical comments wounded him, but now he wondered if she was correct.

CHAPTER 13

Josef woke early to drizzle and a brooding sky. His breakfast was a few mouthfuls of cereal. Bjorn wolfed down his dog biscuits.

"At least someone's hungry around here," he said to the dog, giving him a quick pat. Bjorn jumped onto the couch. Despite Josef's commands to "get down", the dog had a mind of his own and Josef found that trying to dissuade him by placing him on the floor, saying "no" loudly, or even locking him out was useless. The small head rested on his knee and waited for affectionate strokes.

After breakfast, Josef followed Carla's suggestion and made a list of tasks for the day. Eventually, the list became so long that he put it aside. He glanced at the wall clock with its hands seeming to click the passing of time louder than before. Only a month or two ago he was at work by now. That was where he belonged instead of lounging around at home. A group housing project was waiting for him on the drawing board in his study, but he ignored it. The council management would be demanding its completion soon. He thumped the table in annoyance as he thought that someone else might finish it. His partners had been understanding, until now, that is. How long would they make excuses for him and put up with his absence?

The drizzle stopped and a pale sun fringed the clouds casting an uneven light in the room. In the mirror, a flickering image of a tall, old man with piercing blue eyes stared at him. At that moment, he imagined he was looking at his grandfather. As brighter light streamed into the room the vision disappeared.

I'm cracking up, he muttered and rushed outdoors to take a deep breath.

After a miserable two days, Josef woke early, feeling unusually energetic. He dressed fast and rushed outside with Bjorn on a lead. He promised himself that he would clean the house later. His grandfather's insistence on tidiness and neatness were as automatic as were his unbending rules of reliability, punctuality and frugality. Some of his grandfather's training had rubbed off on him.

During his down days of focus on his misery, he didn't care about his surroundings. But that day, he noticed the sky streaked with a glorious shade of peach, and sharp green shoots of leaves poking through the soil. Under a gum tree, he noticed massed bluebells as bright as *Farfar's* eyes in his mother's photos. Instead of dragging his feet, his step was firm on the crisp earth.

"Come on!" He admonished the dog who stopped to sniff every bush and tree. "Let's get going." The temperature was rising and after his energetic walk, he stopped to rest on a tree stump conveniently placed to view the mountains. Bjorn was pulling on the lead keen to be free. He unclipped the lead and watched the dog run. Delighting in the warmth and the view, he leaned back and relaxed. He hadn't enjoyed a walk so much for ages. He felt so well that he toyed with cancelling his counselling session with Carla that afternoon. Perhaps his renewed energy was a break in his mood.

He called out to Bjorn, but initially the dog ignored him and it took several, long whistles for him to come bounding back. As Josef walked on, his thoughts returned to his grandfather's fabrications. The little he had discovered about his grandfather's visit to Sweden bothered him. He gathered some stones and threw them in the air. Surely *Farfar* wouldn't have omitted a huge chunk of his life intentionally. The more Josef told himself that his questions were unimportant and that the answers belonged to the past, the more he sought the truth.

As they neared home, Bjorn barked at four boys playing in a garden. Though the boys were only about five years old they ran fast. He watched the bigger boys pick on the smallest one. With shouts and whooping laughs, the bigger boys edged the smallest boy into the flowerbed. They held him down in the mud and plants and left him crying. Josef's spontaneous inclination was to rush into the garden, pick the child up and comfort him, but he was a stranger. How could he burst into the garden? He shook his head, shocked that overpowering and hurting of the weak began so early! The episode he'd just watched reminded him of his first year at school in Australia. His heavy, European clothing must have looked odd to the other children. As his parents could not afford to buy him the school's uniform, one of the teachers kindly took him to a room near the principal's office where previously worn uniforms hung on racks. She estimated his size and handed him a blazer and pants. Though he now looked like the others, he was not accepted as part of their class. Insulting names he did not understand flew over his head. During class, he was kicked under the desk and jabbed in the ribs in the playground. Soon he learned sufficient English to make himself understood and grasp the lessons, but being brighter than some of the children born in the country was no benefit. He became known as a "smart ass". The bullying continued. He was attacked in the toilets or corners of the playground.

He recalled his fear of attending school. One afternoon, he arrived at his grandfather's with blood on his shirt. Once his shirt was off, his bruises were revealed.

"Sit down my boy," his grandfather said in his serious voice. "It's time you learned to defend yourself."

A week later, a man-sized punching bag appeared in the back room. Fafar's demonstrations on the bag were delivered with the thrusts and deft moves of a man half his age. Josef watched amazed at this new side of his grandfather. He encouraged Josef to punch the bag with all his strength. It took weeks until he was satisfied that Josef moved quickly enough and punched hard enough to protect himself. After this training, Josef managed to fight off his bullies, but the experience did not provide him with the pleasure of dominance. He was happier when unnoticed.

Bjorn barked and wagged his tail as they reached home. A quick cup of coffee and then Josef cleaned his house thoroughly, ensuring that the bathroom glistened. While vacuuming, his questioning voice throbbed in ruthless harmony with the buzz of the vacuum cleaner.

Find out if Farfar was telling the truth! Find out!

With little appetite for lunch, he pushed his sandwich away.

"You might as well finish it, Bjorn. It's a pity to throw it out." He broke half of the sandwich into pieces and fed it to the eager dog waiting next to his foot.

He recalled Greta telling him that he was becoming obsessed with the past and he couldn't disagree. She suggested that he talk to Anders Hansen, who they met at the Danish Club. Anders was a history professor at one of the prestigious universities in Melbourne. Josef and Anders enjoyed sailing, so there was a lot to talk about. They became friends and on weekends they often went sailing together. Greta was probably correct, if anyone could answer his questions, Anders could. He phoned his friend and they arranged to meet at the Danish Club over lunch.

Anders was early and chose a table in the corner where they could talk freely. He drank a glass of beer while waiting. When Josef arrived, they were pleased to see each other and caught up on their news.

Then, Anders tapped the table impatiently. "When you phoned you said that you wanted to discuss something about the last war with me. I have to admit that I'm curious."

Josef didn't know where to begin with his questions and had scribbled a few notes as a guide.

He began haltingly, "I've been home a lot, not feeling that great and I've remembered some of my grandfather's stories about the war. They don't add up, so I'm confused and asking for your help."

"I'm sorry that you haven't been well. You don't look your tanned self. Tell me what bothers you about the stories and I'll try to help if I can...and by the way, anything we discuss is confidential. You don't need to worry about that."

Josef began by asking Anders how he could find out whether his grandfather had belonged to the King's regiment when Denmark was attacked by Germany.

"There are lists of names on the computer. If you give me your grandfather's name, I'll look it up while you fetch more beer."

"Erik Martinsen," he replied.

When Josef returned with two beers, his friend threw his hands up in the air and shrugged.

"There is no listing of anyone by that name in the King's Guards before the war, during or after."

"Well, that's one lie I no longer need to worry about," Josef said cynically.

"Can you check if my grandfather joined the Danish Resistance? He talked a lot about it."

"That will take me a bit longer as I'll need to check the archives, but I'll do that and come back to you as soon as I can."

Their conversation turned to sailing and sport when Anders looked at his watch.

"It's been great catching up, but I'm late already." He gulped down the remainder of his beer and stood. "My wife is expecting me at home. It's my turn to look after the children while she takes a break."

"Thanks, mate, there's lots more of our Danish history I'd like to hear about. I'll give you a call and maybe we can chat about it another time."

Chapter 14

Josef stayed on at the club and continued drinking as he tried to digest what Anders had told him. He nibbled peanuts and thought about the Germans in Denmark who had volunteered to join the enemy. They disgusted him. With Germany on their border, there were many Germans living in Denmark. Before he and his family left for Australia, Danish was their main language, but he learned to speak German as well. He could remember most of it. Having a German culture and language didn't automatically make those Germans living in Denmark Nazis. He thought of friends he had played with regularly who had German-speaking parents. They welcomed him into their homes and he liked them. He closed his eyes and shook his head. Joining the Nazis was too awful to contemplate.

Anders had not come back to him yet with information about the Resistance as he had promised, and he wondered why. Anders was a man who was true to his promises. Now that his suspicions about his grandfather's stories were aroused, he was determined to find out more.

The idea of phoning his father came to him as unexpectedly as the rain clouds banking up on the horizon. Whenever possible he avoided conversation with his father. The last time he phoned his father was to inform him that his grandfather had died. If anyone knew what his grandfather had been up to in Sweden, his father would.

As his father's phone rang, he hesitated, expecting a gruff response.

He swallowed. "Hello, Dad...it's me...Josef."

"Josef?"

"There's something I must ask you."

"Good to hear your voice! A welcome surprise! Yes, certainly, ask."

"I need to know...the truth."

"Ah hah."

"It's about *Farfar*."

"I don't know that much about your grandfather."

Josef ignored his father's comment.

"What I want to know is why he went to Sweden during the war and what he did there."

Josef heard his father breathing heavily before he answered.

"You won't like what I have to say, but since it's the truth you're after." He sighed before continuing. "Your grandfather sided with the Nazis during the war."

"What!"

"You heard what I said, and it's the truth. Your beloved *Farfar* supported the Nazis during the war."

"The Nazis!" Josef's hand on his phone weakened and he almost dropped it.

"I'm sorry to shatter your dreams, son. His friends were a small group of pro-Nazis in Copenhagen who met and drank at the Phoenix Bar. They were not a dangerous or subversive group as far as I know, but they made their feelings clear about the King and the Jews. As you can imagine, that he and his friends were in their element when the Germans invaded."

"I thought that the population was fully behind the King and supported the Jews. Perhaps I've been naïve never questioning what I was told."

He heard his father's sarcastic laugh.

"It's time you found out the truth and grew up. Your grandfather was no angel."

Josef's throat tensed. "Okay, but why did he leave Denmark for Sweden?"

"It's quite simple. During the occupation, his neighbours noticed that he was friendly with German soldiers and openly drank with them. Most Danes hated the Germans. After all, they were occupying our country. His neighbours turned on him, went as far as throwing bricks at his house and placing manure outside his front door. They viewed him as a Nazi sympathiser – a traitor. I doubt they went as far as notifying the authorities, but they made their feelings clear. I knew, but what could I do about it. I couldn't have made my disapproval and disgust more obvious. We weren't close, and his Nazi tenancies set us even further apart. From then on I had nothing to do with him."

"Okay, but you haven't answered my question, the full story about his visit to Sweden?" Josef persisted.

"We weren't talking, so how could I know what he was thinking. One night he disappeared and later I heard he'd turned up in Sweden. He stayed there longer than he admitted."

"I don't believe any of it!"

"Well, it's the truth, whether you like it or not.

Weak with shock, Josef sat on the stool next to the phone.

"So, he was in Sweden but what did he do there?" He insisted.

"That is something I'll leave for you to find out. He left you all his stuff. You can go through it. Heaven knows what you'll find."

"I haven't touched it. I couldn't. Not yet."

"Well, I reckon now's the time to look at it."

Josef put down his phone and rushed to the toilet. After vomiting, he wiped his face with cold water. His head swam. As he retreated into a fog, he watched his legs walk to the small cupboard where he kept the whisky and glasses. He poured one whisky and then another, and then he couldn't remember how long it took him to empty the bottle, or how he spent the rest of the evening.

The next morning, his hangover equalled only his heavy drinking, university days. Cans of beer and empty whisky bottles were strewn over the carpet that he had cleaned so carefully.

Bjorn was hiding under the bed and when Josef called, he refused to come out.

"You don't like the smell in the room and the way I smell, eh?" Josef muttered.

A shower, two glasses of soda water, followed by strong coffee, and he began to put together his conversation with his father. His father had left out important details. He was sure of that. But what were they? Had *Farfar* befriended the enemy in occupied Denmark? What his father had told him about *Farfar* was impossible to accept. His grandfather had told him that he ought to be proud to be Danish. He repeated his grandfather's reasons for pride like a mantra. 'We have our wonderful democratic way of life, our King and Queen, the Norse gods, our beautiful old buildings and Hans Christian Anderson's fairy stories.' Then he'd add, 'We are a caring people and don't forget we were the only country to save nearly all our Jews from the clutches of the gas chambers.'

Josef was unsteady as blood thumped through his head. Later, he picked up a pile of photos he'd extracted from the album and placed them on the coffee table. He flicked through them until he found a portrait of his grandfather with smiling eyes. This was his loving grandfather. Roughly he pushed the photos away, spilling them onto the carpet. He closed his eyes and tears rolled down his face. He hadn't cried like that since he had broken his arm as a nine-year-old.

Chapter 15

Carla parked five blocks from her practice to have some exercise. As she walked briskly admiring the blossoms and flowers in the gardens she passed, she thought of her father, and how much he would've enjoyed the morning walk. Her mother adored flowers too and would've picked armfuls of blossoms to fill all the vases in the house.

A sudden shower brought her back to the present with a shudder. She pulled the hood of her jacket over her head and rushed to her practice. When she reached the main door of the old house where she rented her room, her clothes were wet and heavy. Shivering, she spread her wet jacket over a chair. Once the heater warmed the room, she logged on to her computer. Her first appointment was cancelled. Pleased to use the time, she began writing a report.

The ringing phone interrupted her.

"Sabine speaking, sorry to disturb you. Hannah collapsed in tears after her shower this morning. The doctor visited and said that she is fine physically but it was her nerves. She's asking for you. I'd like you to talk to Anna Lisa the lady two doors down from Hannah as well if you can manage to come. She's been screaming in her sleep. "

"Of course, I'll come. These poor women have suffered so much, I can only try to make things a bit easier for them. I'll be there over my lunch break."

After greeting Sabine, she found Hannah in bed watching television.

"Thank you for coming, Carla. So good to see you."

Carla took Hannah's trembling hand.

"What's been happening? I heard you weren't well this morning."

"While I was in the shower my mind took off and I was going to the showers at the camp to be gassed. I haven't thought of that for months."

Carla gently stroked Hannah's hand.

"What happened to that magnificent embroidery you were doing and the knitting for your great-grandchild due soon? You were feeling much better when you were busy."

"I finished them both at night when I couldn't sleep."

The old woman opened the drawer next to her bed and removed a tablecloth and baby's cardigan rolled in tissue paper. She spread them over the bed cover.

"How magnificent, Hannah! Your embroidery is exquisite, and the cardigan is adorable. Now that you've finished them both you're bored, and when you're bored all the unpleasant memories creep back."

Hannah gave Carla a wry smile.

"You're correct."

"If you let Sabine know what you want to embroider or knit next, she'll go to the shops to buy it for you."

Hannah clapped her hands. "That's wonderful, I'll tell Sabine."

Carla left Hannah in a more positive mood and knocked on Anna Lisa's door. She found Anna Lisa sitting on her bed in the darkened room.

"Let's open the curtains and the windows and let in light and warmth. The light will destroy the nasty memories you've been dreaming about."

After a long chat, Anna Lisa was calmer. Carla left with a full afternoon of clients awaiting her.

After her last patient for the day, exhausted, she placed her head in her hands and lowered it onto the desk. After sitting for a few moments, she gathered her bag and jacket and was outdoors in minutes. She took deep breaths as she walked to her car. The walk she called her unscrambling time. The weather forecast had signalled a mild summer's day. That morning, she dressed optimistically in a long cotton skirt and sandals, but the temperature plummeted and light rain fell. Just as well she always carried a jacket to work. Three schoolgirls, arms linked under a shared raincoat, giggled past. Boys in school uniforms cycled home as fast as their pedals allowed. She avoided the splash of their wheels and hurried on. At last, she was inside the warm car.

Carla and Steve had searched for an older house near her work for months. Heritage houses, old paintings and antiques fascinated Carla. Steve shared her interest but not as passionately. When Carla found an old house in Manningham for sale, she fell in love with it. Its two-tone brickwork with a wraparound veranda and slate roof had been popular in the early nineteen hundreds. The cottage stood on a rise with a view of tall pines, a forested gully and misty mountains in the distance. A tall hedge formed a front fence while nectaries on both sides of the property almost blocked out all their neighbours. The trees were a privacy plus and she enjoyed their fruit which each season she bottled. The high rose ceilings, the arch into the dining room and the deep fireplace delighted her. In what remained of the Victorian garden, she insisted she would plant flowers and shrubs of the long-gone era. She was set on living in the old house and Steve's arguments about practicalities were useless. He was horrified about the condition of the house. Apart from painting inside and out, many of the floor tiles were cracked and leaky copper plumbing needed replacing. As Carla was set on living there, he signed the papers with gritted teeth, trying to make light of the time and cost that would be involved in the renovation.

The history of the suburb interested Carla as well. Thousands of years before European settlers staked their claims, Aboriginals of the Wurundjeri People had lived on the land. She researched their confrontation with the early settlers. It pleased her that historians were working with the Wurundjeri Elders to acknowledge some of the known Heritage Sites of Significance - early walking trails or special planting ceremonies. On this land, the European settlers established pubs, churches and schools as well as acres of fruit orchards. It intrigued her that small amounts of gold were first found close to the house in 1851. Eager prospectors still searched the land for gold.

Carla and Steve spent many weekends and holidays renovating the house and replanting the garden. Working together brought them as close as the heady days in their marriage before their children were born. They planned their activities together during the week, bought materials and worked every weekend. The result was a magnificent home. But that was six years ago. Now they hired a gardener and maintenance person on a regular basis.

Carla had a morning off work and was determined to use it well. Immediately after Steve left for work, she was in the garden. Dewy grass wet her bare feet as she inspected the garden. The blooms cried out for a loving touch. She promised herself that she would prune the garden over the weekend to her liking as the gardener cut back the plants too harshly. Roses her favourites, were in bloom. She decided to pick tall, pink roses for the house. As she bent to cut them, she sniffed their perfume. The perfume carried her back to her younger days of holding Steve's hand as they ambled towards the beach through a meadow of wildflowers. He picked a bunch of the flowers and presented them to her with a flourish. Kisses were followed by laughter. At the beach, they stood on a dune overlooking the sea, her shirt flapping in the breeze, her hair wild. She threw each flower into the wind hoping it might reach the water. Then they tumbled down the dune to the beach. Breathing fast, with their bodies wet from exertion they kissed. Though she was filled with yearning, she pulled away from him. Her mother had drummed into her head what nice girls did not do.

Carla was back in her garden again as Zoe's tail swished through the plants checking her territory. She placed the bunch of cut roses on the grass and looked at the distant hills, purple in the sunlight. She thought of Steve. It was a pity that he wasn't with her to enjoy the view. Absentmindedly, she tugged at a spiked weed that cut her finger. She cursed and licked away the dot of blood. With the flowers in her hand, reluctantly she went indoors, where report writing awaited her.

Chapter 16

Josef answered his phone to a familiar voice.

"Hi Joe, How are things?"

"Much the same...and you? "Yep, all good," he replied quickly."

Anders coughed before carrying on the conversation. "Sorry, it has taken me so long to get back to you. I can tell you definitely that your grandfather was not in the Resistance."

"I've gathered that. To my disgust, I found out he was a Nazi sympathiser."

'Hmm," was Ander's reply.

Josef was silent.

"He's not with you any longer so it all belongs in the past. Try not to let it upset you, my friend."

"I'm trying, but so far, it's not working," Josef said.

"We can catch up again to talk if you want to."

"Thanks, mate, I'll give you a call," Josef replied softly, embarrassed that his friend had found out the disgrace his grandfather had been.

The next morning, he tried to convince himself to find an excuse and cancel his appointment with Carla. Talking about his discoveries about his grandfather would be embarrassing, but there were no reasonable excuses and he knew that he needed to see her. Reluctantly, he yanked on his jeans. He assured himself that he would avoid talking about his grandfather and try to avoid talking about Greta too. He missed her Greta lying next to him, her hair, silken against his body, the touch of her breast and even her chatter when he wanted to sleep.

When his mood was negative as it was then, he returned to

asking himself if he was in the wrong place, the wrong country. Did he truly identify with Australia and everything Australian? Would he have been happier if he had remained in Denmark eating and drinking with people he knew well? Visiting his Australian friends and working with them had become part of his life, but in his sour mood, his thoughts switched to the flat Danish landscape, the ancient, cobbled streets of Copenhagen, its seaports and beaches. He missed the Danish camaraderie and cosy lifestyle called *Hygge*. Anywhere that could carry him away from his inner ache seemed preferable.

Carla's door was open when he arrived and she beckoned him to join her. She smiled her full smile as he sat in the familiar cushioned chair. He began to relax. They went through the ritual of her questions he had become accustomed to about his general wellbeing and whether he was eating and sleeping. Then she asked about his parents.

Why is she asking about my parents when it's my grandfather she should ask about?

"Dad worked late and often travelled interstate and overseas, so he wasn't home much. When he was there, he was in his study and might as well have been away. He hardly talked to me except when I'd mucked up. Then he yelled. He had his rules, not that they were unreasonable – keeping my room tidy, not swearing and that sort of thing. If I bucked against them there was trouble - punishment. I switched off during a belting after a while ... didn't feel it that much. I hated him for it, but I was young and stupid. I'd do anything to upset him even at my own cost - playing music when he wanted quiet to work, smoking when he had forbidden it. Annoying him made it worthwhile."

"And your mother?"

"She was a softie and tried to teach me to avoid the beltings by doing the right thing, which amounted to doing what my father wanted. She tried to stop him but couldn't. I guess if she'd been home more it could've worked out better for me. After her work at the laboratory, there were chores to attend to - food to buy too and there was cooking. Lars and I did our bit to help, but there was too much for her to handle. I knew she loved me, but I rarely had her complete attention. She listened while she was doing something else – cooking or cleaning. When I was young, it was different with my grandfather. He sat down and listened to me, and only me."

"I can see why he was so important to you. You felt totally loved by him."

He drummed his thighs with his fists.

He wasn't going to talk about *Farfar*.

She placed her hands together and waited for him to continue, her dark eyes knowing about his sadness. They knew a lot about sadness.

"My grandfather wasn't who I thought he was," he blurted out.

She looked up at him expectantly.

He fumbled in his pocket.

"I have a small photo of him in my wallet. I'll show it to you."

He watched her scrutinise the photo.

"A handsome man."

"There was an ugly side to him. Very ugly."

"When did you discover this...ugly side?"

He looked at his feet and felt a cold shiver creep up his back.

"Recently." At first, his unspoken pain choked in his throat. Then his words stormed out. "How would you like to find out that your grandfather who pretended to be a model Danish citizen was a Nazi sympathiser during the war?"

He watched her blink and an almost imperceptible frown cross her face.

"That's a big one. No, I wouldn't like it one bit, but are you sure?"

"Unfortunately, my father confirmed it," he replied with a grimace.

She flexed her fingers and moved forward to hear more.

"He left some of his belongings to me in a trunk. I haven't got around to opening it yet. I'll have to tackle it if I can find the courage," he said as he grasped his knees.

She nodded.

Then he threw up his hands.

"His lies have freaked me out."

"The person whose love you felt certain of died. That was devastating enough and now he's let you down. You're even questioning your memories," she said gently.

The room became misty, and she seemed to be talking to him from a distance.

"Yeah, he's let me down alright. And what about Greta? Another one who doesn't care."

He noticed her glance at the clock. The end of the session hung in the air. He clung to those final seconds and would've liked to sit with her for a while longer in that calm place.

"It's been a full session. You'll have quite a bit to digest," she said slowly rising from her chair.

Chapter 17

Carla sighed with relief as the door closed behind Josef. After a day of listening to her client's anguish, fear, despair, and accounts of hurt and rejection and trying to find ways to help them, she was exhausted. Josef was her last client that day. She had allowed their session to continue for longer than the usual hour, as she knew how crucial it was for him to tell her his worrying discovery. His story lingered with her. She hoped that her face did not betray her shock when he told her that his Danish grandfather was a Nazi supporter. She was confused. Denmark was occupied by Germany during the Second World War, and to her knowledge, the population were not known to be Nazis. On the contrary, the Danes were the people that saved most of their Jews by ferrying them by sea to neutral Sweden.

She had to admit to herself that Josef's discovery was a jolt, especially as many of her relatives had perished at the hands of the Nazis – uncles, aunts and cousins on both sides of her family. The Nazis and the barbarity of the Holocaust were constant themes in the minds of most Jewish people, whether they had lost relatives during the period or not. Even after seventy-five years the loss and pain lingered. How could she wipe that out? Besides, she visited elderly wounded survivors like Hannah and others at the aged home, who would never recover from their ordeals in the concentration camps.

Did she have a conflict of interest she wondered? Would Josef suffer due to her feelings? She doubted it. She was concerned about this intelligent, fragile man who would battle to come to terms with his findings. Possibly, he would discover many more disturbing details about his grandfather if he was prepared to dig further. Whatever happened, whatever he discovered, she would do her best to help him to realise that he was not in any way to blame for his grandfather's actions.

The dusk sky was patterned with pink clouds as she walked to her car. The double-story, corner house with a red turret was her sign that the parking area was nearby. The traffic light changed to green and she crossed the road to her car.

Steve was home when she drove into the house. He greeted her and instead of rushing off to his study, he dawdled watching as she went through her ritual of petting the cat.

At the kitchen door, she sniffed and smiled.

"Fish and Chips? What a great idea! I couldn't have managed dinner tonight," she murmured. "I'll throw some greens together for a salad and we can eat."

After their meal, Carla stacked the dishwasher, tidied the kitchen and gave the benchtop a spray with an antibacterial cleaning aid. She then carried her coffee to the second bedroom that served as her study and logged on to her computer. No messages. She picked up a book she had been reading but found concentrating on the story difficult. Steve came up behind her, touched her shoulder and hovered but did not speak.

She turned around and smiled.

"How're you doing darling?"

"Good, but far too busy at work."

"Same here. I'm done in."

Uneasily, he moved from one foot to the other.

"I have some work for tomorrow and then I'm off to bed." He brushed her forehead with a kiss.

"Don't work too late," she said touching his hand.

Chapter 18

Constant knocking on the front door and Bjorn's barking woke Josef. He put his hands over his ears. The knocking became more insistent.

"Open up, Josef. Your car is in the garage and the window's open. I know you're in there."

"Shut up, dog!" Josef shouted at Bjorn as the knocking continued. When Bjorn stopped barking, he recognised his friend,Terry's, voice.

"You don't have to break the door down, I'm coming," he yelled.

He ran his hand through his dishevelled hair and pulled on a tee shirt.

"So, how're you doing, mate?" Terry asked as he strode into the room.

"Bjorn's kicking up a din."

Josef nodded.

"Not a word from you. No answer on your phone and no sign of you at the footy, so I thought I'd check up on you and the dog."

"Sorry, I should've phoned but I've been..." Josef shuffled his bare feet.

Terry nodded. "I've heard you've been doing it tough." He placed a cardboard box on the kitchen table. "Jean sent you some of her meat pies. She knows how much you like them."

Joseph coughed and looked away. "Yeah, a bit of a rough spell. Please thank Jean for the pies. They're delicious. Good of her to think of me."

Terry pointed to Bjorn. "So, mate, how're you two getting

along?" He clicked his fingers for the dog to come to him. "He's looking well and happy."

"I wasn't sure I'd like him. I wanted a Greyhound, but he's got a big heart, smart and good company, even if he's stubborn as hell. You won't be getting him back."

Terry laughed. "So, you called him Bjorn! ABBA days, eh?"

"Yeah, I still like ABBA when I'm in the mood."

Terry laughed again and cupped his head in his hands.

"Tell you what, I feel like getting out. Let's go for a beer later."

"I don't know if I want to go. There's plenty beer in the cupboard."

"Come on, it's just up the road. I'll pick you up," Terry said giving Josef an encouraging grin.

"Okay, mate, you win. We'll go but I'll have to clean up first."

"I'll pick you up around 6.30."

The sky was almost dark when they found a quiet table towards the back of the beer garden. They chatted about friends and football. Then Josef looked up at the stars, pulled the tag on a can of beer and took a gulp.

"My grandad's death has mucked me up. Life can be a bummer!"

"Don't I know it!" Terry said kicking a leaf on the concrete. "Things haven't gone well for me either in the last four months."

"Oh? I had no idea," Josef said with a frown.

"The company was going under and the management pressured the staff to pull it out of the water, meet impossible goals with long hours and poor pay. Finally, there was a takeover. I was one of the bunch squeezed out. When the security guards marched me out of my office I cracked up, went berserk yelling and chucking things. I haven't worked since then."

"I'm so sorry, mate."

"It's not the sort of thing one goes about broadcasting," Terry said opening another can.

"Yeah." Josef touched his friend's arm.

"I dragged you here to cheer you up and I'm talking about my hassles."

"That's okay. We're friends, right! We share stuff. We'll both get over it."

Suddenly Josef's head was spinning and the moon and stars were out of focus. He drained his can of beer.

"I've had enough booze for tonight."

"Let's have something to eat and a strong coffee before I drive you home," Terry said as he gathered up their empties.

An hour later, Terry stopped outside the entrance to his friend's house. Outside the house they clasped each other roughly, followed by pats on the back.

"Thanks for this Terry," Josef said.

"We'll catch up...do this again soon," Terry agreed.

"Yeah, we must."

Josef thought about his friend. Though he wished Terry well and hoped he would find a job soon, part of him was pleased that he was not alone in his misery and that someone else close to him was struggling.

Chapter 19

On the way home, Terry hit the traffic banked up as far as he could see. He opened the window and took a puff of his cigarette, only the second that day. Proud that he had cut down, he promised himself that soon he would give up smoking completely. Heaven knows what has happened to Josef, he thought, as he exhaled. He's turned into a skinny, sad-sack with all the juice squeezed out of him. As he crawled forward in the traffic, he squashed the half-smoked cigarette in the ashtray.

Terry reminded himself that he had once been jealous of Josef, dressed in svelte gear with expensive sunglasses – a young architect on the make and women crazy for him. He was jealous of Joseph's artistically designed house too. It was constructed from dark brick and erected on a huge rock with angles cutting into one another with precision. The view of the mountains from Josef's sitting room was breathtaking. Terry had not seen a house like that before.

What was the use of fine clothing and an outstanding house if one was miserable in it? Look at him now. Depression has him by the balls.

He'd had it with Greta, moving out and leaving Josef when he needed her most. She was a beauty, he had to admit that, but she lacked something – kindness possibly. He drew a breath as he visualised her taut body, sexy walk and swinging, blonde hair, but she couldn't have cared much for Josef, the way she walked out on him.

The traffic was unbearable. He gave the horn a blast. Would he ever get home? What was Joe mumbling about after he'd had a few drinks and loosened up, he wondered. Something about his grandpa and the Nazis. It didn't make sense. *I didn't like that old bloke – something cold about him, but his death certainly stuffed Joe up.*

As the car moved a few spaces forward, he thought about Josef's serious side they didn't share – architecture, art and classical music. When he was well, Joe knew how to have fun, went to clubs and restaurants regularly and they both enjoyed sailing. Now he'd dried up inside. He and Jeannie often talked about asking Joe to visit to cheer him up.

As he neared home, he remembered that he was due to attend another job interview the following day.

Perhaps this one will work out if I'm more enthusiastic about the work and the company.

Chapter 20

The university student's face was bathed in relief as she left Carla's room uttering her thanks. The student was Carla's last client for the morning. She stretched her neck, flexed her tense shoulders and rubbed her eyes. She decided to treat herself to a lunch of a gourmet sandwich and cappuccino at a café a short walk from her practice.

She was sipping a cappuccino when a young couple sat at a table near her and removed their heavy backpacks. Initially, passing traffic drowned their conversation but after a lull, it was clear that they were visitors speaking a mix of English and a Scandinavian language. Her mind created a snap connection, and her thoughts flitted to Josef's concerns about his grandfather. There was a bad smell about his grandfather. She wondered if Josef had the steel to persevere until he unearthed more information about him. After scooping up the last of the froth of her coffee, she placed the cup on its saucer and groped for her bag on the floor. As she walked away, the young couple's babble merged with the traffic noises.

She was back at her desk when the phone buzzed.

"Josef Martinsen speaking."

She heard the shakiness in his voice and a gasp followed by fast breathing.

"I'm sorry to bother you like this."

"You're not bothering me. I told you that you could ring me if you needed to."

"I'm feeling...dreadful." He was speaking in a little boy's voice.

"What's up, Josef?"

"I'm a bit better now than I was fifteen minutes ago. I thought

I was dying. My head was spinning, my heart thumping and my chest was as tight as anything. I thought I was going to collapse, have a heart attack or a stroke."

"It sounds like a panic attack."

He interjected, "I had lunch early and fell asleep on the couch. I dreamed that I opened my grandfather's trunk and masses of snakes wriggled out of it. Horrible, long, slimy things rearing up at me and flicking their fangs. I was sweaty and scared. My head kept telling me that I would find something awful in the trunk, something I didn't want to know about. I'm not imagining how horrible I felt."

"Panic is real and very scary. Some sufferers feel so bad that they rush to a hospital emergency department with a suspected heart attack, but they recover and are released an hour or two later."

His breaths came more slowly now.

"Feeling better?"

His voice was stronger, "Much better than I was."

"It's fear, anxiety that sets it off. Anyone would be scared by a dream like that. We talked about the trunk and you told me how afraid you were of opening it."

"I've been putting it off. *Farfar* has turned out to be such a mystery that God only knows what I'll find. I suppose I'd better get on with it, then I'll know if I have anything to freak out about or not," he said waiting for her comment.

"Open the trunk when you feel ready."

"I'll follow your advice, and thanks for talking to me."

They talked a little longer and then she replaced the receiver. It was strange, she thought that Josef had been on her mind over lunch.

She liked to believe that she left her thoughts about her clients behind when she closed her office door. In moments of self-revelation, she admitted to herself that they left their imprint and she worried about her clients on the edge or going through a particularly taxing experience.

Sabine phoned earlier to ask Carla to visit Hannah and Bertha, another resident at the Home. After finishing her counselling for the day, she left in the rain. The cloudy sky had been grumbling all day. Now it fell so heavily that driving to the retirement home was slow and demanded all her attention. She was relieved when she reached the Home and found parking near the entrance.

Hannah was waiting for her at the top of the stairs.

"Sabine shouldn't have asked you to come in this rain."

"I'm fine, Hannah. Don't worry, a bit of rain won't hurt me."

"It's not me so much, but my friend Bertha that I'm worried about. Her family hasn't been to see her in months. They left her here like a sick dog. She hasn't anyone to turn to and she's suffering," Hannah said looking distressed.

"It's kind of you to be concerned about her. What's troubling her?"

"The same old story – terrible dreams about the past."

"I'll speak to her after we've had a chat."

Sabine provided tea and sandwiches and they talked about how Hannah was coping. Hannah was still having bad dreams. She was managing to tell herself that she was safe now. Her horrors lived in the past.

Bertha's room was further down the corridor. She was slumped on her bed and barely looked up when Carla entered her room. Carla talked to her gently. Memories of two of Bertha's children, both girls under the age of ten, who had died in the gas chambers of the camp, triggered her nightmares and bouts of sobbing. Carla listened to Bertha's story, tried to comfort her and promised to visit her again.

The rain had passed when she left the Home. While she battled through the late afternoon traffic, she tried to stop herself from thinking about the two women. If only she could do more – remove their pain, make their horrific memories easier.

She unlocked her front door and with the cat at her heels she made for an armchair, intending to close her eyes for a few moments before facing the kitchen.

"Wake up!" Steve's voice penetrated her weariness. She felt a jerk as the cat jumped off her lap.

"Your body is sending you a message about your tiredness," Steve said softly. "You need an early night."

She nodded and rearranged her clothing. "I'll make quick meal now and we'll eat soon."

Repetitive chopping and slicing salad vegetables soothed her. Assembling the parts of the meal was a simple task. They ate in the kitchen and other than an occasional word, barely talked. Thinking only of bed, Carla quickly tidied the kitchen.

Chapter 21

Josef woke to a brilliant sky and warm day. Pieces of himself that were previously shaky now felt in place, but not in the same place as before. He had no idea how or when the shift had occurred, but the feeling was too new to be natural or comfortable. He wondered if his talks to Carla were behind this change.

He moved his foot to the end of the bed, to a lump.

"It's you, is it, Bjorn? I thought I told you not to come onto the bed."

The dog lowered his head and turned away sulkily.

"You're sulking already and it's not 8.00 a.m. yet. Come here my sausage." Bjorn ignored Josef for several minutes and after repeated requests approached him keeping a slight distance.

"Silly dog," he said picking him up. "I'm getting fond of you," he said, stroking the dog's long nose and silky ears.

Josef did not lie in bed daydreaming. The opening of *Farfar*'s trunk awaited him. He dreaded opening it, being confronted with the smells and feel of his grandfather, but he had no other means of finding the answers he sought. For some reason, *Farfar* had wanted him to have the trunk and its contents.

His usual lengthy shower was a quick affair and he hurried over his breakfast. He locked Bjorn in the yard ignoring the dog's indignant howls. Down the passage Josef raced, past the bedroom to the back storage room. He sniffed at the musty smell. The trunk lay on the carpet where he had dumped it months before among old books, files and papers. It was huge, the sort of trunk once used on sea voyages. Labels from Hungary, Rumania, France, Germany and Denmark were plastered over it.

Uneasy about invading his grandfather's private possessions, he ran his hands over the pitted surface. He dragged the trunk out to open its catches. They sprang back releasing a potent smell of mothballs. Layers of yellowed newspaper lay under the lid. Beneath were hard objects swathed in white tissue. He tore at the tissue. Gently, he touched the treasures that had once adorned the antique cabinet in *Farfar's* living room: an exquisitely embroidered Turkish, spectacle case; a glass goblet with a swirl of red and cream; a glass candlestick in green and yellow that opened like a flower; a wooden box studded with lapis lazuli; a blue, glass elephant, a set of babushka dolls and a tiny, silver Viking ship. He had played with the dolls more often than he could remember. There was more in the trunk under a further layer of tissue paper: a framed photograph; two European landscapes; a flower painting that once hung in his grandfather's bedroom and a framed photograph of himself as a baby with *Farfar* holding him and smiling indulgently. The photo protected with glass was one he had not seen before. It must've been precious to his grandfather. Their two happy faces and the love between them was obvious. He stacked the paintings against the wall and put the photo aside. He looked at each ornament carefully searching for a clue about his grandfather's past but found nothing. Then he carefully deposited the delicate objects on the bed. Under further layers of tissue paper lay clothing still in cellophane wrapping, all gifts to his grandfather that had not been opened. As he aged, *Farfar* was more comfortable in his old clothes. He would find a charity to donate the unused clothing. The bottom section of the large trunk contained books that were on shelves in *Farfar's* house. He shook each one for a hidden letter or message. When nothing fell out, he hastily returned the books to the trunk. He banged it shut and shoved it in a corner. Disappointed, he took the photo of himself and *Farfar* and closed the door. Once cleaned, the photo would join his other family photos on the dresser.

Days later, he was tidying plates and cups on the dresser, when Bjorn strolled in wagging his tail. As Josef was about to move a cup,Bjorn brushed past his legs demanding attention. When Josef did not respond immediately, the dog tried to jump onto the dresser. His short legs let him down and he dislodged the baby photo of Josef with *Farfar*. It lay on the floor with its glass covering smashed.

Josef scooped up Bjorn, locked him out and swept up the glass. As he shook the frame for hidden bits of glass lodged in its corners, something slid onto the floor. It was a small photo of four middle-aged men, their arms linked. Immediately, Josef recognised his grandfather and Willie, a man he recalled meeting years ago, who had died. He did not know the third man, older than the rest, though the fourth one looked familiar. Josef gazed at the old photo puzzled until he realised that the fourth man was a young Kristian Hansen, his grandfather's closest friend.

Why hide a picture of yourself and your friends? Another one of your secrets?

He took the photo of *Farfar* and his friends to the window where the light was sharper. On each man's jacket lapel was a small blob. With a powerful magnifier that he used for his work, he examined the photo more closely. What he saw was four identical brass lapel pins. The magnifying instrument recorded the image and within seconds he saw an eagle in flight on a circle decorated with a swastika.

He sat stupefied. After two whiskies, he told himself not to jump to conclusions. Later that night, he searched the internet and found a matching lapel pin called a Veteran's Pin worn by supporters of Hitler. His anger surged, his head felt as if it would explode. An image of his grandfather smiling with the pin attached to his lapel dominated his thoughts. He kicked the wastebasket and screamed obscenities.

Just so you know it, I've discovered that you belonged to an old boy's Nazi club. To think of the lies you told me about the poor Jews, to cover what you believed. What a lesson in lies you taught me - not to believe or trust what I hear or see. Why couldn't you have told me the truth about yourself, even if it stank? You must've realised I would find out about your past. The trouble is that I sense that this doesn't end with your pro-Nazi sentiments. Heaven knows what I'll discover next.

Josef spent the following day indoors insulating himself from his misery by drinking alcohol and watching mindless television. He thought of phoning Carla, but what would he tell her – that he was freaking out because he had discovered more dreadful things about his grandfather. He was too ashamed.

Late that night, a spell of near panic chased him out of the house. With no plans, he drove towards the city passing through familiar streets near beachside cafés. At a traffic light, a woman posed seductively. Further down the street, other women tried to catch his attention. He had not come to this part of the city in search of a prostitute, but when a slender, young blonde who resembled Greta smiled at him, he stopped.

"Want to spend some time with me," she whispered, flicking her hair back and attempting to sound husky. Without discussing her charges, he opened the door for her. She gave him directions to an old building two blocks away.

"Park here and let's go upstairs," she said.

He followed her in a rickety lift, through a barely lit passage to a room. All he noticed in the small room was a large bed with coloured cushions and a satiny bedspread. When she began to undress, he was aware of the broadness of her back and shoulders. Her heavy breasts were nothing like Greta's pert rounded ones. When she pointed to the shower, he turned about shocked as his fantasy disintegrated.

"You look like my ex-girlfriend," he said struggling to explain himself. "I'm sorry, I made a mistake," he muttered.

"What did you think was happening? That we were going to

take a walk along the beach together. Your mistake is my time and money!" she replied tersely.

"I'll pay for your time," he answered quickly.

She quoted a figure.

Fortunately, he had enough cash in his wallet and he placed the notes on the bed.

"Right, best get going, then," she said as she counted the money.

As he walked down the passage to the car, he shook his head.

I'm not thinking straight. I should've stayed. I paid after all. She isn't Greta but quite attractive. A year ago, I would've jumped at the opportunity for some extra sex. I couldn't get enough of it then. This depression has destroyed the man I was.

Chapter 22

Carla checked the clock and tapped the desk with her fingers in annoyance. Her next client was always late for her appointments. While she waited, she looked at a restful landscape her father painted in his fifties. His hair was black and luxuriant then and his skin was barely lined. A tall, handsome man, quite dapper when he was dressed in his suit and tie. When she was out with him it was clear that she wasn't his only admirer. Everyone said that she resembled him. He had a European appearance and his slight accent was discernible. But he chose to struggle with English rather than speak German, the language he associated with the enemy. In so many ways he bore the stamp of his history. It didn't make sense to her that though he was proud of being Jewish, occasionally the Germany of his early recollections still represented everything he believed to be excellent. He complained about Melbourne trains being unpunctual and launched into his memories of the railways or the post that had run so smoothly in Germany. It was clear that at that moment he had forgotten about Hitler and his Third Reich. In his pursuit of excellence, everything had to be correct, or as he perceived it to be correct. She was nothing like him. Perhaps she took after her grandmother who tossed ingredients into her cooking rather than measure and follow recipes. Both her parents were loving and generous. She knew that she was fortunate in not having any complaints about them. Their ways and customs were European, and she was certain that their souls were buried with their kin in Europe. She looked at the painting again and frowned. She ought to have insisted that her parents answer her when she plied them with questions about their past.

A rosy, dawn light embraced the room. It was too late to go back to sleep and too early for her shower. As she lay in bed, her father was on her mind again. Over the years, she had gleaned scattered jewels of information about his past. He was born in Regensburg, a German, medieval town on the Danube, surrounded by mountains and forests. His eyes misted when he talked of glorious summers spent with friends walking through the shady forests, tips of tall trees breaking through into the sunshine. They swam in crystal streams or climbed the mountain peaks. In winter, they would ski across the lower hills or race down the tall slopes. Remembering, he'd close his eyes and smile with longing. 'I lived for freedom after school and my friends. No one could grow up in a more beautiful place. And there was a rich Jewish life there when I was a child.'

Once when Beethoven's fifth symphony played on the radio, he patted a spot on the sofa for her to join him. He told her how much he had enjoyed symphony concerts as a young man, while the opera with the voices surrounding him was magic. Then his face grew sad. 'It was Germany at its best in those days...until the bastards started hounding us.'

There were facets of information she gleaned at different times. Like pieces of a quilt, she had assembled them to tell his story. His talent at art was discovered early. Though his dream was to become an architect, money didn't stretch to a university course, so he studied art at the Polytechnic. Once he took a job, within a short period, he worked himself up to a senior position as a commercial artist, but his future that seemed so secure crumbled as the Nazis gained a stronghold.

He talked of Anti-Semitism that was always present in German society. 'In the 1930's Jews enjoyed relative prosperity and there were Jewish leaders in the community. When Hitler was elected as *Reich Chancellor* everything changed,' he said. 'Guards stood outside Jewish owned stores preventing people from entering. Then it got worse. Ugly placards with anti-Jewish propaganda were everywhere. In the street, people spat at me and called me names. We couldn't go to a Jewish doctor, lawyer or Jewish butcher. Soon we weren't allowed to practice our professions and Jews were no longer considered German citizens.'

She knew that he had always been a proud German and upheld German values, but survival was everything. She thought how dreadful it must've been to be forced out of his country like a rat scuttling onto a ship to a place of safety. How unpleasant it must've been squashed into a small cabin with strangers. He made new friends on the ship and they kept in contact - unlikely bonds forged in sadness and fear. He was young then, wrenched from all he'd known on an adventure, to a new life. The ship docked in Melbourne and he was one of a group of refugees, none of whom spoke much English. Did people laugh at his accent? It must've been difficult to adjust to a different culture and learn the language, but he found a place to stay and a job. Then he met her mother. They were married for a year when the war broke out and he volunteered to join the army.

She thought of her beautiful mother who worked as a secretary until she was born. Then she became a devoted mother and housewife as was the custom in those days.

Steve's voice interrupted her thoughts. "Aren't you getting up this morning?"

She showered and dressed quickly. She had an early appointment with Mike, her supervisor. Difficulty finding a parking spot made her late and she rushed to Mike's office. Breathing fast, she fell into the chair.

"Sorry I'm late, Mike."

He made a dismissive gesture with his hand.

She rummaged in her large bag for her iPad. After scrolling through documents, she looked up at him.

"This is the client I want to discuss today," she said pointing to her iPad. "His name is Josef."

Talking fast she described Josef's background and his discovery that his beloved grandfather had Nazi leanings.

Mike raised his eyebrows.

"That won't be easy to come to terms with. He'll have to talk it out until he can see it in perspective. No matter what his grandfather was up to there must be a loving caring part of him to remember and cherish."

"Josef's revelations have stirred me up, with the suffering and devastation the Nazis caused. They hounded my father out of Germany and murdered many of our relatives. It has been on my mind."

She looked through the window at the darkening sky, the sun low on the horizon, as she tried to control her emotions.

"I feel such anger for Josef, as well as for my father and our people, for the endless suffering through the generations. I'm still seeing survivors of the Holocaust and I feel their pain. It's like an ulcer that doesn't heal. I've tried to tell myself that it all happened years ago and I should put it aside but I can't."

They were both lost in their thoughts. The whirring of the fan was the only sound in the room.

"My father, a refugee joined the army and spent four years fighting the Nazis in Italy, in the desert. Apart from injuries to his back, my mother says it changed him – made him moody."

Mike listened without interruption. " Your father was a brave man. He was a German Jew who took the risk of fighting against the Germans. If he'd been taken as a prisoner of war he would've been killed. You can be proud."

"I'm concerned. Do you think my feelings could compromise Josef's recovery?"

"I doubt it. You're an objective and caring counsellor. You feel for him, and with him, so I am sure you can help him."

"I hope you're right."

Mike rubbed his chin thoughtfully.

"I don't see why your history would change your relationship with him. In the past, you've had clients who were anti-Semitic, and you told them that you were Jewish and they were free to go elsewhere for counselling if they wished. If I recall correctly, they chose to stay with you and you helped them to resolve their issues."

She nodded. "You're right, of course. I guess I needed to talk it through."

They discussed Josef's predicament for a bit longer and after making notes, she slipped her iPad into her bag and stood to leave.

"Thanks, Mike."

"It's Friday, the weekend. Relax and try to put this aside," he said as he put his arm around her shoulder.

She smiled. "Let's welcome the Sabbath."

Chapter 23

When Josef opened his eyes the room was flooded with light. Bjorn was licking his face and he winced as he covered his head with a pillow. It was Saturday morning and he lingered in bed. Previously, when the weather was fine, he would be sailing on the bay.

He lay in bed and once again pictured the photograph of the four men – the four Nazis. One of them, Kristian, he had visited recently. As hard as he tried to remove it, the picture was stamped into him.

He bent to fill the dog's water bowl.

I won't be calling my grandfather the affectionate name Farfar, any longer. I have no love for him now and he doesn't deserve that special name.

He reminded himself that he wanted to talk to Carla but making an appointment would have to wait until Monday. His thoughts returned to Kristian.

I should go back to the retirement home and talk to Kristian again. A chat with him could add substance to the photograph. He hasn't told me all he knows, I'm certain of that.

The retirement home was a short drive away. Kristian wasn't in his room or watching television in the resident's shared lounge, but in a back room playing poker with his friends. Josef watched Kristian. The once tall man with an athletic build had shrivelled. Now he was an old man with sloppy muscles. He stood a distance from the table observing the tension build as the cards were placed and expert moves made. The prize was a king-size slab of chocolate. Each of the six men had deadpan expressions. A smirk passed Kristian's lips as he turned up his cards – a straight flush. One of the men pushed the chocolate in his direction.

"You'll get sick with all that chocolate you're winning, Kristian," the man said scornfully.

"I doubt it, chocolate still loves me."

Kristian slipped his prize into his pocket and rose slowly, stiff from sitting in the one position for too long. He patted his silver hair and placed his glasses in their case before giving Josef his attention.

"Sorry to keep you, my boy."

Be polite. You need him, Josef told himself.

"Not at all. It was interesting to watch the game," Josef replied attempting to be polite despite his feelings of disgust for the man."

"We're stuck in this place but at least we haven't lost all our marbles...yet."

"You're well, I hope?" Josef asked as they stepped away from the table.

"Ja, ja, as well as can be expected at my age."

Josef continued the forced conversation as he watched Kristian open the slab of chocolate he had won and peel back the shiny covering. He broke off the top line.

"Have some," he said pushing the slab towards Josef.

Josef shook his head.

"So then, what brings you here this time?"

"There are a few things I would like to ask you. To clear up. If you don't mind."

"Anything to pass the time. Life in this place is boring." He beckoned Josef to follow him. The panelled reading lounge was empty, and a scatter of books lay where their readers had left them. Josef picked up one of the old leather-bound books and ran a finger over its title.

"Ah, *The Scarlet Pimpernel*, an old friend," he said softly before replacing it.

"Too many books and not enough action doesn't build healthy young men," Kristian said as he pulled out a chair.

He shifted on the hard chair until he asked Josef to pass him a cushion. Once comfortable, he leaned back and was silent as if gathering his strength. When he began to talk, his words flowed as he reminisced enthusiastically about his exploits with Josef's grandfather, his friend Erik.

Josef nodded and smiled as if on cue. He could remember feeling unsure of Kristian on their first meeting many years ago. 'This is my oldest and dearest friend,' his grandfather had said, insisting Josef shake Kristian's hand. He spoke of Kristian often quoting his words and regaling their adventures.

After about ten minutes of polite attention, which Josef considered more than ample, he produced the photograph of the four men and slid it across to Kristian.

"Have a look at this."

"Oh my! Where did you get hold of this?" Kristian asked sharply as his cheeks paled.

Josef felt his throat tighten.

"It fell out from behind the glass of a framed photograph. I doubt I was meant to see it."

"This is an old photo and it all happened so long ago. By now, you have the right to know the truth. Your grandfather should have told you. Now it has been left to me."

Josef looked at him expectantly.

"There we are, the four of us – Hans, Willie, Erik, your grandfather and me. All four of us were friends."

"In the photo you are all middle-aged men dressed in jackets and ties and wearing identical badges. What's that about?"

The old man turned his head away and rubbed his hands.

"Why worry, it's all in the past. Willie and Erik have gone to greener fields now. As for Hans, I'm not sure." He scratched his head. "He might have gone too. I haven't heard from him for ages."

Josef thumped the highly polished table with the palm of his hand.

His voice was loud and demanding. "I know that my grandfather supported the Nazis during the war but I want to know more. The truth. What he was really up to. I've heard enough lies."

"Don't get so wound up, Josef. The badge is nonsense, a nothing – a membership badge, that's all. We were all members of a club."

"That's not the truth, Kristian. I looked at the badges under a high-definition magnifying glass and saw the eagle and swastika."

"So, what! We were pro-German and we wore a German club badge. What of it. We weren't the only ones."

"Pro-Nazi before the war and after it too!"

"We all had German blood and it was natural for us. It was hard to break our ties."

"German blood? But my family is Danish."

Kristin sniggered. "Oh, so, you don't know?"

"Know what?" Josef demanded.

"Come, let's go for a little walk" He grimaced as he stood. "We need to have a long talk. The subject needs air," he said, pointing to the louvre door leading into the garden. Together they walked slowly into the fragrant garden lit by insect encrusted lamps. Kristian scanned the murky outlines of flower beds, shrubs and the enclosing hedge. Satisfied that they were alone, he nodded to himself.

"What do you mean by German blood?" Josef insisted.

"Your family are not Danish. Erik was as German as I am. Your grandfather's father, Paul, was born in Germany, in the Black Forest of Bavaria, in a small town in the mountains. I forget which one. In the 1930's all us boys were members of the *Hitler Jugend* or Hitler's Youth."

Josef felt his stomach lurch at the image that began to form of youngsters in their brown shirts, knobbly boots and black short pants, all obedient to Hitler.

"It was a way of hardening us for our future role as soldiers, teaching us basic military skills. We were a ready-made division."

"How horrible," Josef muttered.

"Generations of your family lived in the Black Forest, the *Schwarzwald,* but when Erik was twelve or thirteen the family moved to Denmark, to Copenhagen."

"Why?"

"Some hullabaloo or another, but I've forgotten the reason." He threw his hands in the air. "You know *Vesterbro,* the old slum area in Copenhagen? That's where the family moved to."

Josef's expression changed to distaste.

"My God! The old haunt of prostitutes and druggies?"

Kristian nodded.

"And how do I know? All four of us in the picture lived there later. Our parents decided to move there too. They liked to keep together." He looked up remembering. "We were all in senior school together in Vesterbro. It wasn't the best of places that's true, but we didn't know better, didn't even notice the narrow streets and old houses."

"Tell me more about my grandfather," Josef said trying to mask the impatience in his voice.

"You know how charming Erik could be when he was in the right mood. And he was a bit of a lady killer too," Kristian said with a chuckle. He told Josef more about his grandfather's exploits. "We were jealous of his way with the ladies. One night after work, we four met for a sandwich and a few drinks. Erik spotted a young woman he fancied. What a beauty Agathe was with her amber hair in a coil and her figure like a bottle of Pepsi. She came from a rich family too." Kristian explained how his grandfather had charmed her into giving him her address and then courted her lavishly. "We knew how to treat a lady in those days. Erik was madly in love with her and we expected a wedding any day, but the war broke out and relationships fell apart."

From the little Josef knew about Kristian told him that the old man was still trying to cover up the truth. There was so much more he needed to know.

His next question was direct.

"That's a lovely romantic story about my grandfather, but please tell me when he decided to leave for Sweden?"

The old man looked flustered and coughed.

"I'm not feeling well. I must go back to my room now."

Josef took Kristian's arm and they walked silently towards the room.

At the door, Kristian's face was creased in concern.

"I hope I haven't upset you."

"I am here to learn the truth."

"Of course, I understand," Kristian replied, but I'm an old man and need to rest."

"I'll visit again if that's okay with you?"

"Excellent idea. I like seeing a young face. My grandchildren are always busy and hardly visit."

"Anything special I can bring you when I visit again?"

"Chocolates - the best Belgian ones. Not this rubbish," he said pointing to his pocket. "And I love Schnapps. I'm not allowed it now, but a small glass won't hurt."

They shook hands.

"Grues Gott," Kristian said with a pat on Josef's back.

Josef stared at him blankly.

"Don't you know the Bavarian greeting?"The old man didn't wait for a reply. He entered his room and closed the door.

Chapter 24

As he drove, Josef struggled to concentrate on the road. He tried to push his feelings of revulsion about Kristian away but couldn't.

He's a German and a Nazi who doesn't hide his background. He speaks with a German accent and it doesn't bother him either. At least he is true to himself.

The information about his grandfather was a shock and he hadn't begun to come to terms with it.

I was born in Denmark and thought I was Danish, but under my Danish skin flows tainted blood.

Images of Nazi rallies he had seen in countless documentaries flashed through his mind. He envisaged the *Hofbrau*, the beer house packed with beer-swilling SS officers singing during the *Oktoberfest*.

At last he was home. He pressed the automatic control of his garage, drove in and turned off the engine. Once he had freed himself from the safety belt, he placed his head on the wheel and sat in the dull light, his head throbbing. The grandfather he had adored and missed all these months was unworthy of his love.

I've been grieving for you, and now I find out that you are a hypocrite and a liar! You taught me to be honest and face the consequences of my actions, but you've left a legacy of betrayal. I doubt Kristian gave me the full story. After the war, you couldn't get enough of Hitler. Why did you identify with him, wear his badge? Bastard Nazis the lot of you!

That night, he drank beer followed by whiskey and turned up his music to try to obliterate what Kristian had told him, but it didn't work. Right then he loathed Germans, all Germans and thought they were a bunch of humourless, arrogant and pedantic people. Their once blind following of Hitler was unfathomable to him.

The next day he stayed in bed until the late afternoon and hardly ate. He didn't bother to shower or change his clothing. Instead, he drowned his wretchedness with more beer. In a haze, he looked up at the only decoration on the wall in his living room, a poster of the Little Mermaid.

"Who am I", he asked her.

He covered his body with a throw rug and reached for another cushion? "I'm Danish but I've lived in Australia for most of my life. The Danes I know tend to be genuine and worthy of trust, irritatingly punctual and precise, but when they relax they enjoy themselves. I'm too miserable to want to know myself now. I guess those characteristics describe me now too." He felt like a wolf howling but he couldn't even cry.

Chapter 25

It was the Jewish New Year, and Carla and Steve were taking a long weekend off work to celebrate. It was a break from work and an opportunity to catch up with family.

The Autumn wind was up as they walked to the synagogue past neighbourhood driveways and gardens littered with fallen leaves. Curious eyes peered from behind net curtains at the stream of men in suits and the women dressed in their best heading in the same direction.

They passed people milling outside the synagogue. She left Steve to enter the front of the building. She climbed the steps of the side entrance of the nondescript, brick building to the women's balcony. She squeezed past women she knew, nodded and smiled before removing her coat. Her usual seat close to the edge of the balcony, allowed her to look down on the men praying. The service had already begun. Amongst the women's faces, she recognised many. During a lengthy prayer, she looked around at the other worshippers. Some she knew were struggling with illness, personal sadness, financial woes or family problems. An old, arthritic woman sitting next to her struggled to turn the pages of her prayer book. A young woman battled to quieten a crying toddler. What was important was that they were all there, together.

The mumble of prayer rose as the cantor intoned the ancient chants. A calm spread through her. The loose fragments of her being were somehow whole again as she connected to her roots - all that had gone before, and what was spiritual for her now. As always, when she attended synagogue she thought of her parents, her large extended family, and friends who had all passed on. They were memories now and missing them was part of her life.

She tried to listen to the Rabbi's long, complicated sermon but her thoughts drifted to the previous Sabbath when her children and grandchildren had come to their home for dinner. It was one of the most successful evenings they had shared in years. There were no arguments, and the children behaved surprisingly well. The family enjoyed her meal and there were leftovers for her and Steve. After everyone had left, Steve threw his arms around her and kissed her. He hadn't done that for ages.

A person coughing sharpened her focus. She reminded herself that after synagogue, her family were coming to their home for lunch to celebrate the New Year and she hoped it would be another enjoyable meal spent together.

A period of prayer passed and everyone stood as the Rabbi lifted the *shofar*, a ram's horn, to his lips. This was one of the most important aspects of the service. The sound was primitive and piercing. The message was delivered in nine blasts – of biblical significance, and for her a reminder to look inward and make positive changes in the New Year.

She left the synagogue before the end of the service, while Steve stayed on. There were last-minute preparations to attend to for the family lunch. Earlier in the week, she didn't have the energy for more than grills and salads. With more time now over a break, she threw herself into cooking a delicious lunch. The table was laden and once Steve added wine and chocolates for the children, it looked festive and inviting. She relaxed while waiting for the doorbell to chime.

Deanne kissed her mother and handed her a bouquet of her favourite pink and mauve flowers.

"A happy and healthy year, mum."

"They're gorgeous. Thanks, my darling, and the very best to you," Carla said kissing her daughter. The rest of the family followed and kissed and hugged her and Steve.

"Happy New Year," the children said in unison.

"I know you children are hungry and we'll eat soon," Deanne said glancing at the tempting food.

When all were seated, Steve poured wine for the adults and grape juice for the children.

"*L'Chaim*, to a Happy New Year!" Steve said as he and Carla clinked glasses.

There were so many dishes to choose from that they were tried one after another. All complimented Carla's cooking. There was talk and laughter. The lunch was another success.

Then the phone rang, and Steve answered, "It's Leo," he called out to the others.

Carla jumped up excitedly and Deanne followed. Leo was phoning from London with good wishes for the New Year. They all spoke to Leo and caught up on news until Steve raised his hand.

"This call must be costing Leo a fortune!" he said. "We'll call him back tomorrow."

Over dessert, they discussed Leo and his news. It was late for the children and Deanne and Brad helped them dress for the outdoors.

Though the children had been unusually well behaved, Carla and Steve were relieved when their family finally left. Once again, Steve kissed her to thank her for making the lunch. As they sipped their second cup of coffee, Carla eyed the uncut cakes on the benchtop.

"I'm cutting the cheesecake and having it with ice cream," she said to Steve.

"I'm full, but I'll find a place. Cut me some, too," Steve said rubbing his belly. You can freeze the fruit cake but leave the chocolate and cheesecake for the two of us."

"Why not, let's enjoy it! It's the New Year!"

Carla had put on weight and was hunting for some of her clothing from a previous size increase. Clothing she no longer wore was stored in a suitcase in a top cupboard of the study. As she tugged at a suitcase, a pair of brown boots were dislodged with an avalanche of once-loved possessions that flew to the floor. A metal box containing her school geometry set just missed her head. She managed to retrieve the suitcase and put it aside while she tidied the forgotten remnants of her past. Among the fallen items was a large, round cardboard box. Inside the box smelling of mothballs, she found her mother's crumpled, satin wedding dress and her father's top hat. Her parent's wedding photograph that stood on a dresser in the lounge, told how happy they were on their special day. As she tidied the odd postcards and books that had fallen, she found a stained, yellow cap. She swung the cap on her finger, remembering that her father wore it when he painted outdoors. She sniffed the hat. Turps and cigarettes lingered.

She accompanied her father as a child during his summer painting expeditions. He wore the cap and a paint-spattered, brown coat when he painted outdoors. After an early breakfast, they packed the boot of the car, his first car, a grey Chevy. He was so proud of the car that it shone from frequent washes and buffing. In the boot, were his easel, stool, brushes, paints, and for Carla, a cushion and rug. She was little then and found the back spacious enough to move around without disrupting his driving. His 'personals', as he called them, a bag with cigarettes and a slim bottle containing brandy were out of bounds for her. He drank the brandy only when his paintings pleased him. On the front seat of the car sat their sandwiches and a flask of coffee. For Carla, the best part was that her mother decided not to join them. She had her father to herself. Watching him paint was always enthralling - the way he interpreted a scene with colour laden brushes. As well as his paintings in her office, one graced the wall in the dining room and another occupied most of the wall in the main bedroom. The rest remained piled up in the storeroom. Carla smiled as she placed her father's cap on a shelf in the storeroom with the rest of his belongings.

What memories, and all in one day! I can't recall a day as nostalgic. If only I knew more about my ancestors.

The night was warm and a full moon tempted her onto the patio. She inhaled the smell of garden's pungent soil and the flower's scents as Zoe brushed past her and dashed into the bushes. The desire for coffee drove her indoors. Though it was earlier than usual for bed, she was tired.

During the night she tossed about so much that she woke Steve. The next morning, she recalled only fragments of her dreams.

"What's up with you? You were writhing and moaning in your sleep," Steve asked looking concerned.

"I'm not sure. I think it could've had something to do with my dad. I can remember dreaming of us painting together. I miss him."

"Missing them never goes, but I needn't tell you that," Steve said.

"I think I should be spending more time on finding out about my family," she replied.

Chapter 26

Josef woke with the conversations with his father and Kristian on his mind. Angrily, he left the house and drove to the beach at high speed. In the cool breeze, he took a familiar path in the soft, golden sand. As leaves and debris swirled around him, he stumbled towards a dune away from other walkers. While agitatedly tugging at the rough grass he muttered to himself.

You idiot. You should've known the old man was up to something fishy to do with the Nazis in Sweden. You didn't want to see it, to acknowledge that what he showed you were façades and lies.

When a gust of wind began to cover him in sand, he quickly resumed his walk, past the main beach, the holiday houses and towards the cliffs. The overhanging rocks formed a natural marina where small boats were moored. He missed sailing and the sea, but his boat needed cleaning before he could consider taking her out, and in his present mood, the task seemed too tiring. The sun was about to drop into the ocean when he reached his car.

That evening, he tried to watch television, but he could not concentrate. His thoughts were about Kristian. The little he knew about him was that he had been a commercial traveller in Denmark who gambled away much of his money at poker. He remembered his grandfather telling him that Kristian had followed him to Australia. He dredged his memory to recall the reasons his grandfather had given for Kristian's migration. He was almost certain that his grandfather had said that the warmer climate and open spaces had enticed him. How Kristian had made his money in Australia remained a blank. A sudden heart attack had forced him to sell his home and move into a retirement village.

Josef's memories took him to his childhood and late afternoon visits to Kristian's large house where Kristian and his grandfather sat on the tiled porch sipping lemon tea and playing cards. While the adults played, he fought monsters in the shadows of old trees decked with wisteria. When he became bored, he slid down the ornamental balustrade.

The shrill ring of the phone jolted him back to the present. The caller was Tim, the firm's senior partner. Josef glanced at his watch. It was late, for Tim.

"We've been waiting for you at the office, hoping you'd come in. You haven't touched that project you were working on."

Josef's mouth felt dry.

"The client must be pushing to see it finished," Josef said. "What's the time frame?"

"No huge rush. They won't even look at it for a few months."

"I don't know if I could."

"You could finish it at home, relax as you go, Tim added.

"We...ll."

"Come on, mate. I'll be round after work tomorrow. We can talk about it then," Tim's voice was encouraging.

Josef hesitated. "Okay, see you then."

Josef's heart thumped, and his throat was tight. Carla's calming voice in his head melded with his own as he told himself to take a few deep breaths and then have another look at his design. After a while, his throat muscles relaxed and his heart resumed its usual rhythm, but his calm was temporary. Dread swamped his thoughts. How would he be able to concentrate, focus sharply enough on the design when he found reading a newspaper taxing? Would his sagging energy provide him with the juice to see it through to completion? He paced, his body tingling with adrenaline.

He hoped that a late snack would soothe him. He boiled the

kettle for coffee and made toast. It was all he could stomach. Aching with exhaustion he flopped onto the couch.

The following morning, he woke in a more positive mood. He was due to see Carla later that day. It had been a long wait. She had suggested exercise to still his anxiety, but he hadn't followed her advice. He kicked his runners from under the coffee table and laced them. In the garage, half the space was taken by his second-hand BMW. The other half was a gym. He had admired the expensive, luxury car from a distance in magazines and car sale windows. When he heard that a friend was selling his BMW, he had to have it. In the year since he'd owned it, the car had become an extension of himself. When he drove he was puffed with confidence, every bit the young successful architect.

The garage was chilly and he shivered while unhooking the tarp protecting his gym equipment, and brushed away a dead spider and debris before rolling it up. He had not been in his gym since his grandfather's funeral, though he had threatened to exercise for weeks. He told himself that he ought to work out, become fit again. After moving some half-empty paint tins to the side wall, he wiped each piece of gym equipment with an old tee shirt. Once the rower and the bike were clean, he was warmer and his excuses had ran out. There was just enough time for a quick workout before showering and dressing for his appointment with Carla. Perched on the saddle of the bike felt strange at first, but he surprised himself when the pedals whizzed. Ten minutes on the bike and he turned to the weights. The lighter ones were an easy lift, but as he progressed to the heavier dumbbells he battled. Sweat poured from him, but the workout had a way of burning his nervousness. At least he could tell Carla that he had followed her advice and started exercising.

Apart from the empty vase on the bookcase, Carla's room hadn't changed with the season. It was the room Josef dreamed about. He was soothed in her presence despite some of her provocative questions.

"So, Josef, what's been happening since I saw you last? It's been a few weeks."

He was aware of his crowding thoughts.

"I have a lot to tell you."

Her hands opened as she leaned forward.

Josef began by telling her how he had opened the trunk containing his grandfather's possessions. He explained that he found a photograph taken many years ago of his grandfather and three other men, one of whom he recognised as his grandfather's friend Kristian. He explained that each of the men wore a badge with a Nazi emblem - an eagle and swastika.

"I was blown away when I realised that my grandfather was more involved with the Nazis than I thought. It is hard to believe it of the man I knew."

"Not a pleasant find at all." Her voice had a serious tone.

His head dropped as he nodded.

"I wanted the truth, no matter how ugly it was, so I visited Kristian at the retirement home, where my grandfather spent the last days of his life."

"How did the meeting go?"

"When I showed him the photo and asked him about the badge, he was cagey." Josef's voice rose in anger. "He told me that the four men were members of a veteran's club. Can you believe it, a veteran's club? Finally, he admitted that they all belonged to a Nazi group. I prodded but he said nothing further."

"Some new information, but not easy to deal with," she said gently.

"There's more. He told me that my grandfather was not born in Copenhagen as I'd always thought. Both my grandparents were born in Germany, in Bavaria." He put his hand to his forehead. "My mother was part Danish, part Swedish."

"I can imagine your surprise."

"I hate the idea. What bastards those Nazis were...what they did!" He said, staring at the carpet.

"Not all Germans were evil," she said softly.

"I've heard it before. They were just following orders," he said with clenched fists.

When he looked up at her, she didn't appear to be concerned about his revelations. He had worried about revealing his discoveries to her as she was Jewish, and anything to do with Nazis was a tricky subject. As they talked, he relaxed. He didn't know how it had come about, but he felt that they had developed a bond of some sort.

"I don't understand why my mother didn't tell me about my grandfather's past. She must've known. One night we were warming ourselves before the fire and she mentioned *Dragor*, a fishing village close to Copenhagen, where generations of her family once lived. When I asked what she knew about my father's family, she told me abruptly that I'd have to ask my father or grandfather about my ancestry. I remember being puzzled by her bitter tone. I should've pushed her for more information, but I didn't." His eyes shifted to the ornamental cats on the cabinet.

She nodded.

"Why was she so secretive? It is better to get things out in the open," he said with a sigh.

"Perhaps she was trying to protect you."

"If only my mum was here now, I wouldn't be in this state. I miss her even though we didn't spend a lot of time together. Occasionally, we went on nature walks or into the old parts of the city and she took her camera along. Losing her to cancer was tough." He coughed awkwardly.

"It must've been tough." She waited a few seconds before continuing. "What happened to your family in the fishing village?"

"My grandparents on mum's side died before we left Denmark and I haven't seen my father's brother since he moved to London."

She nodded again.

He shuddered. "Sometimes I wish I hadn't started digging into my grandfather's past with all the disgusting stuff that is coming out now."

"Well, the past doesn't always smell of roses." Her eyes brimmed with knowing.

During the remainder of the session, he talked about his work, his fears concerning the architectural design he'd begun before he took leave and was expected to complete.

"I can't even imagine working on it."

"After being away from work for so long anyone would feel uncertain."

"But I can't imagine ever being able to do something like that again."

"You could try," she said with a smile.

"Yeah, I guess I should get stuck into some work."

"You don't have to tackle it all at once. How about starting with a bit at a time. If that works out, you can do more when you're ready."

"I suppose I could try. At least, I'm having more good days than bad, though this morning was miserable. One positive thing, I started exercising."

"That's good!"

'I've been meaning to ask you if you have a hobby. As an architect, you must be good at drawing and making things like models. Hobbies can be fun and help concentration too," she said.

"I've thought about making a model of a ship, but not done anything about it."

"Just a thought," she said with a shrug.

He glanced at the clock on her desk. The session was almost over. He hadn't told her how panicky he'd been all week.

"Anything else before we close?"

"No, not really," he lied.

Carla tidied her desk and smiled to herself.

It is strange that our families both come from Bavaria and that we are both seeking information about our family backgrounds, but for different reasons.

Chapter 27

Bjorn's loud barking alerted Josef. He peeped out.It was Jean, his pal Terry's wife.

"I won't stay, I've brought you more meat pies," she said with a grin. "I doubt you've been cooking, and I know how much you like them."

"That's kind of you to think of me. They're delicious."

"You need feeding up. Put them in the freezer and heat them as you need them," she said with a laugh.

He felt her eyes on his unkempt appearance. Bjorn jumped up on her lap and wagged his tail. She stroked his head and when he rolled over for a tummy rub she made a huge fuss of him.

"I was sorry to let him go and I miss him, but he wasn't that good with the kids – jealous and sulky with the attention I gave them. I hope you're happy with him."

Josef put her mind at rest about Bjorn and shared the dog's exploits.

She looked up at him and hesitated before speaking

"So, how're you going?"

"Much better than I was. How is Terry?"

"He's started looking for a job. Of course, I want him to work again, but I'm worried about him getting stressed."

Josef nodded. "Stress is always a problem."

She was quiet for a few seconds.

"I haven't even offered you a cup of tea." Josef said as he walked towards the kitchen.

"Thanks, but no, I must be going."

"I'm sorry you won't stay but great to see you, Jean, and thanks again for the pies – a lifesaver."

"I make them often for our church functions so there's more where they came from. Just ask." She lingered holding onto the doorpost.

"Have you thought of sailing? Terry was talking about it the other day. He loves the water."

"I've been thinking of taking the boat out even though the weather isn't the best. She's in the trailer where I left her months ago. Tell Terry I'll give him a ring when I've washed her and rigged up the sails."

"I'm glad things are working out well with you and Bjorn," she said with a wave.

After Jean left, he stood at the closed door gripped by an unusual feeling – a mixture of gratitude for her kindness and pleasure that someone cared about him.

He recalled that when Terry and Jean were newly married they went to Church together regularly, but nowadays Terry spent Sunday mornings riding his bike. Thoughts of Church triggered a shadowy memory for Josef of singing hymns in Melbourne's Lutheran Church with his grandfather next to him. His hair was straw blonde then and he wore short pants and his school blazer.

How could the old man have taken me to Church and at the same time lied to me about his past?

He shook his head in bewilderment.

The clouds hung low all day and when night fell, the sky was without a moon or stars. Joseph went from room to room to draw the blinds. The front room looked out onto the porch, and as he stretched to pull the cord, he thought he saw his grandfather, an aura shimmering around his silver head and his eyes pleading. Josef turned his back on the image and switched on the lights. The image disappeared.

With the heating warming the room, a few cold beers and his

CD playing loudly, he relaxed. If there was a ghost out there, he hoped it had left.

Chapter 28

It was Saturday and instead of lounging in bed or reading the morning paper, Carla followed her internal nudging, her quest to know more about her family. After feeding the cat, she went into the sitting room, to her only genuine piece of antique furniture, the secretary desk that had belonged to her grandfather. She hadn't looked inside the drawers for years, but now she was driven to discover all she could. The top drawer held a velvet pouch that had belonged to her father, a folder containing his letters and a leather photograph wallet. She began with the pouch. Before pulling the cord, she stroked the velvet. Her father's war medals filled most of the pouch. Slowly she extracted the long pin that held the medals. Each medal that hung from coloured striped ribbons recognised his participation as a member of the Combined Commonwealth Forces. With the edge of her skirt, she rubbed the dull medals until they were brighter.

I wish you had told me more when I asked about the war, she muttered.

She held each medal up to the light, remembering him in his dark suit with the medals pinned to his lapel when he left home to march on Anzac Day, the day that commemorated the Australian and New Zealand Army Corps, that in April 1915 formed part of the allied expedition that set out to capture the Gallipoli Peninsula. Now the special day honoured the contribution of Australians and New Zealanders who served and died in all wars, conflicts, and peacekeeping operations.

She could hear her mother's angry voice, 'He volunteered and left me, a new bride alone for four years, while many of his friends didn't join up. Every day I expected that dreaded telegram but thank goodness it didn't come.'

An image returned of an afternoon after the march when her father met up with his army mates at the local pub. He came home late, his face rosy from alcohol. It was the last march he was well enough to attend.

When she asked him why he had volunteered, he replied, 'The bloody Nazis hounded us out of our country. I was lucky, but there were members of my family who stayed in Germany and died in concentration camps. How could I live with myself if I did nothing? So, I joined the army and fought for what was right.'

One ribbon that held a medal was twisted. She straightened it before replacing all the medals in the pouch. After stroking the pouch once again, she kissed it and returned it to the desk drawer. Then she picked up the photograph wallet. She hadn't opened the wallet before, and though she felt uncomfortable about viewing her father's private photographs and letters, she was driven to learn all she could about his war.

Black and white shots were of the desert's shifting dunes, sandstorms and the wind snaking the sand. There were snaps of him and his mates next to crippled or burnt-out planes and large unexploded bombs left lying in the desert. On the back of each picture were handwritten names. She assumed that a line drawn through a name meant the worst. He had traced his journey with pictures of the places and armies where he fought, first the Italians and then the Germans. There were photos of his battalion marching, as well as disturbing images of soldiers running through smoke and grotesquely blackened remains of human beings lying at the side of a road.

Before returning the wallet to the desk, she kissed it too. She wasn't ready to read her father's letters and left them in their folder. She explored the side drawers of the desk and found faded photographs of her maternal grandfather who died before she was born. He had fine features. He wore a white linen suit and was smoking a pipe. His smile was shy, she thought, and she recognised in him her mother's slightly distant but defiant eyes. A photo of her maternal grandmother as a young woman showed her as a beauty with dark hair and a tall, erect stature she had retained into her old age. Her grandparent's photos deserved fine frames.

That night, as she chopped carrots and threw potatoes in the pot for dinner, unexpressed tears of regret mingled with the steam of the cooking vegetables. She reminded herself that the past was a hidden territory for her parent's generation, and they didn't talk about it. She wished she'd asked more questions but wondered if they would've told her the truth.

Chapter 29

The lit house was welcoming when Carla returned after a full day. As she opened the front door, her Siamese cat, Zoe, came bounding out to greet her with meows and rolls on the carpet. Steve was seated at the kitchen table, his head in his hands. Her daughter, Deanne, sat opposite. With one look at his posture and the tired young woman with red-rimmed eyes, she could tell that they had argued. Carla greeted Steve with a kiss and rushed to Deanne to hug her.

"What's up, Dee?"

Deanne wiped her eyes.

"She arrived with Jason and a suitcase an hour ago. I'll leave you two to talk," Steve said as he leaned on the table to pull himself up.

"You needn't go, Steve."

He had already reached the door and was walking towards his study muttering.

Deanne lifted her head, patted her eyes with a crumpled tissue and looked at her mother.

"I'm sorry to crash in on you... and now I've upset dad. I should've phoned, but I was scared the two of you would talk me out of leaving. I had a big row with Brad, so I decided to teach him a lesson. l packed a bag for Jason and came over. He's asleep thank goodness. David refused to come, so I left him with Brad."

Carla's face was creased in concern. This was the second time that month that Dee had arrived with one or both her grandchildren.

"You're walking out after a row again! What's going on, Dee?"

"It's about money. He accused me of spending too much."

As her daughter whined, Carla's shoulders tensed. Deanne spent money easily, but it wasn't for her to judge and comment.

"What about some tea and cake and something for Jason?" She suggested.

"No thanks, mum." Deanne wore a teenager's dissatisfied pout. "All I spent on was a few extras for the kids and one or two items for me – hardly anything. But please don't start with the psych talk."

Carla listened and then put her arm around her daughter's shoulders.

"I'm pleased that you can talk to me, but I can't give you answers, darling. It's for you and Brad to discuss and work out."

"We love each other but it's not that easy, mum!"

"I know...but try to sort it out. Money is important for a couple."

"It's easy for you to talk," Deanne snapped.

When Jason began to cry, Dee tried to pacify him, but he began to wail.

"I'd better take him home. I think he's hungry and David is alone with his grumpy Dad," she said.

Carla nodded.

She decided that it was best not to comment.

There was no goodbye kiss for her mother or a farewell to her father as Deanne hurriedly collected her belongings and left.

When Steve heard the door bang, he joined Carla in the kitchen.

"So, she's gone home?"

"Yes, thank heavens."

"When will she grow up?" Steve said shaking his head.

"They're both young and need to sort things out."

"Let's not go into that." He scowled. "I'll get back to my work for tomorrow."

"I'll call you in a while when I've made dinner," she replied.

The air between them was heavy with unexpressed emotions.

Carla made a cup of tea and sipped it slowly as she sat at the table. Only a few years earlier they shared the events of their day during the evening meal. Back then, Carla regularly discussed Steve's legal cases with him. He often ran through his argument with her before appearing in court the following day, but all that had gone now. When she joined a team at the hospital to work with a group of suicidal teens, their relationship became strained. It meant an hour and a half two nights a week extra after work, and then there were the emergency calls at home. The team rescued many teens from the brink, but it wreaked havoc in their marriage. Late phone calls interfered with her sleep and she was tired. Steve argued that the team sucked too much out of her and left him with not much more than the bare bones of their relationship. She couldn't even summon the energy for sex.

When she became chronically tired, she reluctantly decided to leave the team, but it had left its mark. She and Steve no longer argued. Nothing seemed to matter enough to warrant an argument. They existed together in a vacuum.

They were both asleep when Deanne phoned to tell them that Brad had been pacing the driveway waiting for her and Jason to return and that they agreed to talk the following evening.

Chapter 30

The ringing phone woke Josef.

"Hi Jo, Anders. I rang to catch up...find out how you are."

"All okay," Josef said sleepily.

"Sorry, did I wake you?"

"It's time to get up anyway. I'm awake now. How are things with you?

"I've been crazily busy at uni with lectures and exams. Just as well I have my dog to take for a walk, Juscinta to talk to and my ship to keep me sane."

"Ship? What ship?"

"It's a long story. My dad's been sharing his research stories of our Viking past with me. I liked the idea and started collecting some ancient Viking stuff I picked up in salerooms. I saw a magnificent model of an authentic long Viking ship but it was hellishly expensive, so I started building my own Viking ship. I'm enjoying it. It's complicated – but relaxing."

"That's great. I was thinking of building a sailing ship but one of those long Viking ships would be much more fun to make. I used to enjoy making models as a kid and later as a student, I made models of buildings as part of my course. Maybe one day I'll have a go at it."

Suddenly he remembered Cara's suggestion of model building. Well, he'd think about it.

"The idea of being a Viking is hilarious!" Josef said thumping the side of the boat and laughing.

"You might have a touch of Viking with your name ending in 'sen' but a Viking past is hard to trace."

"My real name is German, Martin, but my mother's family is part Swedish and part Danish. They are Rogersons, and she told me that they once lived on the island of Shetland."

"Well, I have to tell you, mate, Rogerson is one of the top Viking names and Shetland is a place where they once lived." Anders said.

Josef laughed again and threw his hands in the air.

"A warrior on a long ship! I love it," Josef said with a laugh. 'If I have some Viking ancestry I'll be an incredibly unusual mix."

"There's more to being a Viking than being a warrior, but when we meet up and I fill you in. There's a Viking restaurant in Melbourne, in the city. Hardware Street or Lane, I think. We could meet there."

"What do they eat?"

"You'll find out. I'll text you the address and we can settle on a time to meet."

After the conversation, Josef smiled and slapped his thigh.

"I haven't had such a fun chat for ages," he said to Bjorn and patted his head.

Bjorn wagged his tail and stared at his owner.

"Okay, breakfast. Coming up!"

It was cool but with no winds or rain it was pleasant enough for Josef to tackle the overgrowth in his garden. It hadn't been attended to for months. At first, he was overwhelmed by the tall grasses, wild shoots and rambling branches. Light from windows was obscured, stems and leaves crept up the steps. Josef began by cutting back branches, creeping stems and roots. He then attended to weeding and cutting off dead flowers. It was a task that was taking longer than he thought it but at last the garden looked more controlled but natural.

A text from Tim offering to help Josef with his project propelled him indoors. After initial panic, he told himself sternly that if he had started the work months before, now all he would have to do was pick it up where he had left it. It was an important assignment and knowing that Tim was there to call on was a relief.

He forced himself to sit at his desk. All the files he had spent months working on earlier were labelled and in order. He began tentatively with the first file, *Introduction: Group Housing for Twenty Individuals (sixty-five years and over)* It stared at him in bold type. He read the words "draft copy" stamped on each page in shadowy capitals. It looked unfamiliar. As he read the introduction he wrote months earlier, he became more comfortable with the material The clarity of his simple but functional concept surprised him. He nodded to himself. This was the healthy confident part of himself before he broke into pieces.

Half of the introduction took him three-quarters of an hour to read. Concentrating was a problem and he was so weary that he almost fell asleep at his desk. He panicked until he listened to the voice in his head reminding him to follow Carla's advice of 'a little each day to start with and build from there.' He took a few deep breaths and closed his eyes. After a nap, he felt more positive and logged onto his computer again. Bjorn was in his basket nearby as Josef worked in spurts followed by brief rests. He was working slowly, but he was relieved that at least he was on his way to recovery.

The following week, he revisited the building site. He had forgotten how well-placed it was, close to shopping centres and not far from the city. The view of forested hills as a backdrop ensured that each house would have a pleasing outlook. He was delighted with his choice. Before he left, he made some notes about necessary materials and checked the surveyor's figures.

Back at his desk, he took another look at the council's recommendations. He was almost ready to move on. His original design had created comfortable houses to suit the pensioners who would live in them. Each house of two rooms with a living area, kitchen and bathroom would be a home and not just a living space with a roof. Being cool in summer and warm in winter was a basic requirement.

Whether he was in the shower, cleaning his house or eating his lunch, he visualised ways of nutting out a problem with an architrave or oddly shaped window. Once he had completed checking all the plans and preliminary estimates on specifications, material, costs and recommendations, some of his earlier confidence melted. It was all very well working with ideas and notes. How would he pull his concept together in a final computer image? While he was off work, the partners had installed new computer programmes. He had no idea how to operate them. He sighed as anxiety and negativity overwhelmed him once more. While he was away from the office they had moved on.

Josef's appointment with Carla was in the late afternoon. A sharp wind cut the air and the trees cast long shadows on the pavements as he walked towards her office. He did not have to wait. She ushered him into her room immediately. Proudly and dramatically, like a child telling his mother he had won a sporting trophy, Josef told her that he was working on his design. Carla's delighted grin and her voice bubbling with congratulations was the recognition he craved.

He knew it now. She did care.

The moment of pleasure suspended in the space between them vanished as soon as he mentioned the firm's deadline for the completed design. His expression of joy at pleasing her changed as he looked absently at the carpet.

"How on earth will I finish it in time and do it well?"

"You've designed many buildings. You managed to do that successfully or you wouldn't be a junior partner in your firm," she said.

"I guess so."

"You haven't lost the ideas, knowledge and skill. It's your

confidence that's dented, and that will come back. Surely you don't have to finish it alone? Your firm wouldn't expect that."

"Tim, one of the partners has offered to help, but pride gets in my way sometimes."

Her eyebrows lifted in response.

"Okay, I'll call him."

It seemed as if Carla could look into his soul and sense that he expected too much of himself and rarely asked for help.

When he dialled Tim's number the phone rang several times before it was answered.

"Tim's extension, can I help you?"

He recognised Greta's voice.

"Is that you, Josef?" She paused. "If you're after Tim he'll be out all day. Do you want to leave him a message?"

"No, it's okay, I'll phone tomorrow." He closed his eyes, as he had when making a wish as a child. *If only she didn't put the phone down.* "It's great to hear your voice, I've missed you." The touch of her hair and peachy fragrance of her skin floated back to him.

"I've been thinking of you. How are you?"

He felt a stab of abandonment, but this wasn't the moment for recriminations. The initial tension between them eased with bantering chatter. There was so much to catch up on since they had last spoken that they agreed to meet for an early dinner after work the following day.

Josef drove to the city fringe, parked at the market where there were spaces and took a tram to the city centre. The tram edged through the crowds and homebound traffic, passing forgotten buildings and tall constructions of massed steel, concrete and glass. Some were ugly, he thought, but there were a few architectural gems for him to feast his eyes on. He had avoided the crowded city for months, but now the excitement of anticipation rippled through him. Soon he would be travelling to and from meetings with clients on trams and trains again. At a traffic light, he jumped off the tram to join the throng that propelled him to the bridge across the river that bordered the business end of the city. A short walk and he was in South Bank, a popular area lined with bars and restaurants. At the bistro where they had chosen to meet, he found a table facing the river and waited. He was early and had time to think. His yearning to be with Greta again began with a quiver, a flutter of nervousness. He hoped she was looking forward to their meeting too, but his longing to see her again was tinged with uncertainty.

Would she find me changed? How can I blame her for finding my dark moods and irritability objectionable? I drove her away. If only I could be with her, and only her. I'm moving forward, but who knows if I'll be okay and the depression will leave me in peace.

He knew that all he could hope for was a renewed friendship with Greta though he wanted much more. To distract himself from his unease, he checked his watch and observed how fast the tables around him were filling. A tour boat passed and the image carried him back to the picture-postcard suburb of *Nyhaven* in Copenhagen when he and his brother enjoyed ice cream while his mother took photographs of the boats and painted wooden apartments that faced the old harbour. Lost in the past, he was unaware of Greta standing watching him.

"Hi there, dreamer. Where are you?"

"Right back with you now." He stood quickly and bent to kiss her.

Awkwardly she presented her cheek.

She was setting the limits.

"Sorry, I'm late. I had to stay back to work with Barry. He wanted me to change a design for him. He's battling with a difficult client. You know what it's like."

He thought of the burly partner who had built up the practice with his attention to detail and service to clients.

"Yeah, sure," he said softly, as he swallowed.

I hope to be battling with clients soon too.

"Sorry, it was a bit insensitive of me talking about work."

"It's fine. Your work is reality and you can't walk on eggshells around me."

While she removed her jacket and carefully placed it over a spare chair, he looked at her pencil skirt, high heeled shoes and hair tied back in a knot. He remembered her nude with her hair skimming her shoulders and her breasts round and high.

Their faces were hidden behind tall menu cards and until the wine arrived, they talked stiltedly about mutual friends, and members of her family. The topic of his return to work remained a barrier between them. While waiting for their food, wine relaxed them enough for talk to flow more easily. Tentatively she asked after his health.

"I'm getting there. At least the fog is lifting." He noticed she avoided mentioning the design he was meant to complete. "The project ... I guess you want to ask about the project but you're being tactful."

She smiled and nodded.

"Tim has offered to help me."

He explained that the new computer software in the office was complicated and the older, longer method of constructing three-dimensional models he was accustomed to , was easier for him.

Their desserts arrived and they giggled over their enjoyment of the sticky richness. Without realising it they moved closer to each other, touching now and again.

Greta had been looking at him when she picked up his hand and stroked it.

"I'll help you with the computer graphics starting next week after work but no strings attached."

He nodded. "Thanks, I'd much rather work with you than Tim," he said with a grin.

He accompanied her to her car. Rather than take a tram he continued walking through the city. He had been given a reprieve. She was holding her hand out to him, testing whether he would burn or cherish it. It was his last chance.

Chapter 30

It was one of those early spring days with the iciness of winter forgotten. Josef put his hand up to feel the breeze. It was ideal for sailing.

He phoned Terry.

"Hey, mate, it's a great day for sailing, so let's take the dinghy out later. I cleaned and polished her. She's ready to go. "

"Great idea! I'll meet you at the jetty in an hour," Terry replied.

When Josef arrived, he found Terry sitting on the stone wall surveying the scene. The beach was already crowded with sunseekers. Sailing boats and crafts of all sizes were dotted on the bay. The waves, perfect for surfers, encouraged them to move further down the coast leaving the waters free for swimmers and children wading.

They carried the dinghy from the roof rack on Josef's car to the ramp. As they rolled it into the water, it splashed unsteadily. A burst from the motor and they were in deep enough to sail.

"I don't know why we waited so long for this, "Terry said waving his hat in the air.

Josef breathed in the air, looked into the distance and sighed happily.

"Isn't it great?"

"Just like the Vikings, eh Joe!" Terry said with a grin.

"Maybe you know my mate, Anders? He called to chat and we ended up talking about Vikings. He's into his Viking background big time, and he thought I could have some Viking ancestors. It's fun, but who knows."

"Wow!" Terry said thoughtfully but made no further comment.

As they sailed, they drank beer, smiled and grunted with pleasure.

Each was in his own space. There was no need to talk.

❦

Carla watched Josef enter the room. His previous sad slump was replaced by a firm step and a smile.

"Good to see you again, you seem chirpy."

"Some good things have happened."

"Excellent news!"

"It's Greta. I think there's a chance of having her back in my life. That's if I don't muck things up again," he said speaking fast.

"Hey, slow down and fill me in."

He told Carla about his phone call to the office, his subsequent meeting with Greta and her offer to help him. His smile vanished when he repeated her "no strings attached" request.

"It'll be difficult keeping to that, not saying anything romantic or touching her, but I'll stick to it if that's what she wants. Anything to have her around again."

The rest of the session was spent discussing the way Greta was encouraging him with the project and his progress with his work. He laughed at her warnings that he was pushing himself too hard. His energy was returning and he was keen to use every drop.

Chapter 31

The session was over, the door closed behind Josef and she heard his footsteps disappear down the passage.

He was showing signs of improvement, but his enthusiasm waned when he talked of his fear of his depression returning. Would Greta reject him if his mood slumped? He was ashamed of his depression. He kept it to himself and this prevented Greta from understanding what was happening to him. Perhaps she still had little idea about the seriousness of depression and its consequences. Being vulnerable, he could easily snap if rejected by her. She had dumped Josef before. Would she be there for him now?

As Carla tidied her desk, she thought of Deanne and Brad and dialled her daughter's number.

"I was going to ring you, Mum. We talked and sorted out our finances. Things should be okay now."

"I'm pleased to hear that."

"Mum..."

"Yes, darling, what is it?"

"I'm worried about Jason. He's crying a lot, more than before."

"Is he healthy?"

"Oh, yes, but I think the two of us yelling at each other was upsetting him."

Carla was silent for a few seconds.

"Now that things are easier between you two, let's hope he settles down. Lots of affection should help."

Carla was early when she knocked on Mike's door.

His smile was welcoming.

"It's good to see you, as always."

They discussed her clients briefly, and then Mike stretched his arms above his head to alter his position in his chair.

"We've been through all your patients except that Danish young man. Josef, Is it? How's he doing?"

Carla told him about Josef's reunion with Greta and his progress with his work.

"What about that stuff about his Nazi background?" Mike asked.

Carla ran her hand over her skirt slowly before meeting his gaze.

"He didn't discuss it in our last session, but it's still there, of course."

He looked at her quizzically.

"And how have you been? You were tired last time we met. All this talk about Nazis seems to have triggered memories of your family and especially your father."

"Yes, Josef's story has made me more conscious of my background." She pursed her lips and sighed. "I've been reliving times I spent with my father and snippets of conversation I'd forgotten. The more I remember of those past days, the less I seem to have known him. Unfortunately, we didn't know our parents as people but more as caregivers. I've been thinking of his life in Germany and his struggles with anti-Semitism that led to his escape from Hitler. He knew that he was one of the lucky ones and felt impelled to enlist in the army."

Mike was quiet as he twirled his pen and looked at her. "Any thoughts of slowing down?"

"I'm thinking of making changes to my work schedule. I'm already taking a few hours off, and intend to cut back on some late afternoon appointments as well. I want to keep one morning free each week."

"That's a huge change. What brought it about?"

"You were right as usual," she said wryly. "I had trouble admitting how tired I was."

He nodded.

"I want to spend more time with my grandson, Jason. He and my daughter need me now. I haven't devoted enough of myself to them, so I will try to do as much repair work as possible."

In the car driving home, she smiled to herself. Mike was more than a supervisor. He was part friend, part therapist.

Chapter 32

Squawking birds under the eaves woke Josef at dawn. Cursing the noise, he rolled over onto the other side of the bed and fell into a dreamy sleep. He was transported to Copenhagen harbour in the dawn light. A scene unfolded of Greta, a coppery beauty, seated on large rocks. She stretched her limbs and flicked her hair. She was perfect, from her hair that kissed her shoulders to the curve of her calves. As he ran towards her, his vision became misty and she disappeared. He called out to her as he scoured the sand and water. He was about to turn away when she reappeared at the water's edge with her feet in the foam of incoming waves. She ignored his call and stared out to sea. He woke to find sticky sweat trickling down his chest.

Bjorn eyed him from the end of the bed. After patting the dog, he headed for the shower. In the warm water, he thought of the meal he would prepare for Greta that evening. She had promised to look at his project after they had dinner and make suggestions about adapting it to the new system.

He recalled his mother's joking comment that one day the women in his life would be grateful that she had taught him simple cooking. What would he cook? He knew his grandfather's basic recipes and a few of his mothers. After some thought, he decided on Danish meatballs with potato dumplings served with a crisp salad and red wine. He knew that she liked meatballs. It was a simple recipe he made well. He pictured his grandfather tenderly rolling a ball of meat in his hand and placing it into boiling water. Then quickly he pushed the image away.

He collected the ingredients for the meal and started with

the potatoes. 'Potato dumplings mustn't be raw or overcooked. Just boiled long enough to be tender.' Josef heard himself laughing. 'And how long is that, then?' he remembered asking his grandfather. As he listened to the potatoes bubbling in the pot he was overcome with sadness.

He tossed a poorly formed meatball into Bjorn's plate. The dog ate it greedily and stood waiting for more.

"One more and that's it," he said to the dog.

After mixing the salad, he glanced at the old man's photograph. They last ate dumplings together about two years ago. Those were precious memories before he learned about the ugliness and lies.

An hour before Greta was due to arrive, Bjorn began to fart.

"Out, out!" Joseph shouted waving him into the yard. "Sorry little fella, the meatballs must've been too spicy for you."

By 6.30, a green salad waited in the fridge and the meal was cooked. He turned the air-conditioning on to warm the house and checked all was tidy. A last thought was to add fresh fruit with lemon sorbet to the heavy meal. He gave the meatballs a final stir, hoping that Greta would enjoy his cooking. When the doorbell rang, he restrained himself from greeting her with a kiss. Their talk was business-like, and they ate almost immediately.

She had two helpings of meatballs, patted her stomach and smiled.

"Delicious, Josef! The fruit and sorbet were perfect. You have hidden talents, ones you kept secret when we lived together."

"We all have our little secrets," he replied with a smile.

He opened the back door for Bjorn.

"Bland chicken for you and you should settle down," he said to the dog as he placed a bowl of food on the floor for him.

After the meal, they moved to the study, where a printout of his earlier plans and notes lay on the desk.

"Coffee please", she said as she flipped through the pages. "We can have a closer look at how to put your design onto the software later. Meanwhile, talk me through the path you're taking, and I won't say a word until you've stopped talking."

With her experience, he looked forward to following her suggestions.

He showed her his initial sketches and as he clarified concepts, she listened. She had been an architectural draughtswoman in his office for many years and worked with computer-aided design software to create designs and drawings for the architect's projects.

When he stopped talking, he placed his head in his hands.

"I'm wiped out. Just talking about it takes the guts out of me. You can see why I can't go back to the office yet."

She nodded sympathetically.

"I understand what a huge commitment this is and that it exhausts you. I'm not an architect, but from your drawings and what you're telling me, your concepts and design should make a great project."

"I'm glad that you approve, but I'm not finished reading through all the notes and sketches that I made earlier. I'll get there. Luckily I'm feeling a lot better even if I haven't got my full tank of energy back."

"You seem more like your old self." Her voice was soft and encouraging as her eyes probed his.

For that moment, he was reminded of the searching way Carla looked at him, seeking answers.

If she wants to know more, to understand, I'll tell her more.

"I've been seeing a psychologist, an older woman. She's smart and caring. She doesn't say much but what she does say has helped me to help myself." He said smiling nervously.

"That's good."

Their hands touched for a moment. Then they talked about office gossip and mutual friends. There was so much more he had to tell her – his discoveries about his grandfather and his family's German background, but not then. She promised to return later in the week. He walked with her to her car, opened the door for her and waved as she drove off.

I can only hope that we can have a relationship again. It will take time and I'm such an impatient person.

Chapter 33

With Greta's support and knowledge, Josef was able to move back into a daily routine of a few hours of work followed by relaxation. Hungry to return to the office, he struggled until his energy levels improved and his skills flowed back. Each of his drawings he scrutinised carefully, asking himself if all the spaces he designed were necessary and worked functionally as well as aesthetically. He took into consideration the use of natural light sources and energy. The council's requirements were checked and rechecked until he was certain that he had created a complex of comfortable and functional homes. His efficiency increased and within a month the project was almost completed. Greta was delighted that he was mastering the new software. Occasionally she asked if he was handling his work more energetically and he would answer that he was certain that soon he'd be back in the office.

After her help was no longer necessary, they continued eating out, visiting old haunts and new ones. Like a courting couple, they walked along the river before the first stars greeted the sky or shopped at late-night tourist haunts. It was a move to a new place in their relationship, a friendship underpinned by shared interests. They avoided sex despite their mutual attraction. In the past, sex rather than friendship had been of prime importance.

Despite the cool air, one night after a meal, they drove to the beach and took a leisurely walk. Passion for each other that they had controlled over weeks, suddenly drew them into an embrace so consuming that they battled to separate. Neither talked as they walked back to the car holding hands. They drove to Greta's home as it was nearest. They rushed to the bedroom. A tender kiss and then they hungrily made love. Afterwards, she pulled away from him. At that moment, the space between them spoke the loving words they could not. When she found her voice, she talked of *time,* a word Josef hated. They needed *time* to be able to discuss their feelings and to develop trust in each other again. She was afraid to risk another round of anguish. He listened and nodded. All he wanted right then was to be with her again.

Though Greta assured Josef that his proposal was excellent, he checked it again. Finally, he was ready to present it to his colleagues. With his laptop in his briefcase, he drove to the firm's offices. When he parked in his old spot and took the lift up the two floors, he felt a pleasant anticipatory tingle. The firm had a new, young receptionist, Sharon, a redhead who sat with her legs crossed under the desk. When she mistook him for a client, he corrected her. As he walked down the short corridor to Tim's office, he passed his office and put his head around the door. Nothing had been moved and even the waste bin was in its place next to his desk. The room smelled musty and was far too tidy. It seemed dead, rather than empty.

Tim, the senior partner, had a large, corner office with a view spanning the river, the sea, city and the suburbs in the distance. He gave Josef a welcoming, bear hug and then rushed out to call the other partners to join them. Soon they were all around Josef, slapping him on the back, shaking his hand, genuinely pleased to see him. The noise brought the secretaries and Greta. The torrent of enthusiasm and pleasure at his return was unexpected and he revelled in it. When everyone returned to their desks, he followed Gerald, one of the partners, to his office. With a flourish, he placed his proposal on the desk. Gerald nodded enthusiastically as he looked at the images and text. He rubbed his hands together and smiled.

"I'm sure our client will approve." After viewing Josef's

entire proposal and discussing his concepts in detail, the date and time to present the project to the client were scheduled. Gerald's support was a strong indication for Josef that he would be returning to work on his terms.

"You have nothing to worry about, I'm positive the client will want to start preparations for building immediately," Gerald said.

The presentation went well with smiles on the client's face. The following day the call came. The proposal was accepted. When he clicked on his computer the screen was full of congratulatory emails from Gerald, Greta, Tim and the others. He had landed the firm a huge contract. It meant that he would be back at work within days.

The partners were delighted that he was returning and left the timing to him. At first, he worked for only four hours a day. Even that short period was an initial struggle. He wasn't accustomed to phones ringing and people around him after months of being at home. Most of all it was interruptions from others about whether he wanted tea, coffee or a request for some record on his computer that bothered him. When his clients learned he was back they phoned and emailed him. With all the interruptions and his flagging energy, he struggled to work.

When he grew stronger, he increased his work to six hours, but by mid-afternoon his concentration was fuzzy and he was extremely tired. Though Tim and the other partners were disappointed, he had no option than to wait for his strength and concentration to return before considering working a full day.

Josef invited Greta to dinner at one of the best restaurants in the city. They followed the waiter to their table, with a view of the river and the city. Once the waiter lit the candle on their table, Josef hoped for the romance suggested.

After their first sips of wine, Greta took his hand.

"We haven't talked about ourselves since you've been back

at work. There have been days when you've looked tired. I was worried that it's too much for you, but I didn't want to ask."

"It's been a bit of a strain, but I'm pleased to be back."

Her eyes probed his.

"I'm feeling better even if I haven't my full tank of energy yet."

"You seem happier, more energetic," she said moving closer.

"I have to watch out for pressure or the depression will be back, but so far so good." It seemed strange saying the "D" word, even acknowledging to her that he suffered from it.

"I need to know exactly what's happening. I've never been good at reading tea leaves," she said and kissed his hand.

He avoided a direct answer and their focus changed to the food. Over sips of wine, they touched and there was a warm stillness between them.He still had so much more to tell her. He had not mentioned his discoveries about his grandfather.

The wait for Carla to open her door seemed endless. He wasn't used to her running late. The extra time allowed him to mentally tick off all the items he wanted to discuss with her. He was bursting with news about his blossoming relationship with Greta and there was his completed work project to tell her about. He knew she would not be pleased to hear that he had experienced spells of extreme fatigue. Excitement over Greta's reappearance in his life, his involvement in work and his investigation of his grandfather's past, was a lot to deal with. It tired him and flattened his mood for a short while but relaxation helped and he recovered faster than previously. He checked his watch. She was half an hour late. He moved to one of the lower, softer chairs and felt in his pocket for his phone.

He might as well make more notes about his grandfather, he decided. The heading was ERIK. His first point was that he ought to visit Kristian again. The old man's account of his grandfather's past had been too glib. He was sure Kristian had omitted some important details. Then he would phone his father. He was certain his father knew far more about their German background.

When Carla's door opened, she escorted a tearful patient to the front entrance. Josef pretended not to look at the quivering man or listen to what was said. Then she stood before him, smiling apologetically.

"Sorry I kept you waiting for so long."

He followed her into her room.

"That's a sick guy," he commented.

She looked away.

"So, tell me what's happening in your life?"

Josef talked with enthusiasm about Greta, his project and his return to work.

"I'm pleased that things seem to be going well but don't rush it." She was concerned he was working too long and too late. "Only six hours tops," she insisted.

He admitted that some days he worked a little longer and it tired him.

"I had a few down days last week, but I think I'm okay now. Could I slide back into the shadows?"

"It takes a while to stabilise. Try not to put yourself under too much pressure."

"Uh-huh." He sighed. "So, it's easy does it, but they won't like it back at the office."

"You have almost completed a project, and by the sound of it very successfully. Of course, they're going to urge you to do as much as possible. Stand your ground, your health comes first."

"I find saying 'no' difficult. It is something I need to learn to say more often."

She nodded.

"Is there anything else you want to discuss?"

He noticed a slight edge to her voice. Perhaps she was tired.

"I have been chasing up my grandfather's past but I'd like to do further digging. I'll leave telling you about my progress in another session."

"Try not to rush with your digging up the past. It's been buried for so long that if you find the answers you were looking for a little later it won't matter. "

"You're right."

He scratched his jaw.

She can be irritating, coming out with such simple, obvious comments about not rushing at work or about finding out more information about my grandfather. I shouldn't need her now. She's not telling me anything I don't know.

A black European car was parked in Josef's driveway. It was Tim.

"Hi, Joe, glad I caught you."

"Come in and have a beer," Josef said with a smile.

Tim sipped his beer slowly.

"You're looking good, mate. How're things going?"

"Improving."

"You won't believe how well that design of yours went down with Bradshaw and his group. He's a huge developer and the big news is that he wants you, and only you, to design an even bigger housing venture," Tim said grinning.

"It's great news but I can't see myself doing it right now."

"Why not? We'd provide all the support you need, even find someone to do all the hack work."

"Look, Tim, I can only manage six hours a day... and that's it. I can't do more and this new project is huge. It would require full-time attention."

"You could try."

"I won't risk it. And the project I'm working on hasn't been completed yet."

Tim rubbed his forehead and grimaced.

"Sure, but it's big bucks."

"Tell Bradshaw that I'll discuss the new project with him. I'll listen to what he says, give him some ideas and estimates, but I'll have to tell him that if he wants me to supervise the project it will have to wait."

"We could do that, but who knows if he'll be prepared to wait that long. We could lose the deal," Tim said with a sigh.

"Of course, I want to do more, but my health comes first. I can't risk falling in a heap again. Maybe Bradshaw will consider using one of our other architects instead of waiting. Or I could consult with one of them. Let's hear him out."

They talked a little longer and Tim finished his beer.

"I'll get back to you soon."

The sleek, black car screeched off like a panther.

Bjorn hid under the bed. He had seen suitcases and lots of them. Suitcases meant that someone was leaving him. But this time the suitcases, parcels and bags were arriving. Greta was moving back.

Chapter 34

Carla was running late and dressed hurriedly in pants, and a black top and coat she had worn all season. There had been no time to shop for new clothes. After coffee and a slice of toast, she rushed out to the car. Deanne was expecting her to care for Jason that morning.

When Deanne opened the door to greet her mother, Jason waddled out from behind his mother's legs towards Carla.

"Gran Car, Gran Car, you late," he said, his little face in furrows.

"Yes, darling, sorry."

She kissed Deanne and then Jason.

"Go, do your shopping, Dee. We'll have fun together, won't we little one?" she said as she bent to scoop the child into her arms and hugged him.

"Play, play," he said giggling with delight. She placed him on the carpet and he pointed to the back room where a colourful rayon tent had been erected. "Play tent."

For over an hour, crawling in and out of the tent, Carla joined Jason in his world of pretend.

"Gran is tired now," she said placing both hands on the small of her back.

Jason sat at her feet, looking at her for a moment and then continued to play in his determined way. At two, his resemblance to her father was uncanny, with his pale skin, the questioning spark in his eyes and his dark hair that stuck up on the crown of his head. She sighed with love. Then she thought of Steve at court. He was missing out on this precious time with his grandson.

"Good boy," the child sang to himself.

"Come my darling," she said lifting him onto the couch and stroking his head. "Gran will read you a story."

He pointed to a book with animals on the cover. Halfway through the story, Jason's eyes closed and he was asleep. Gently she placed a cushion behind his head and covered him with a rug.

Deanne burst into the house carrying shopping bags.

Carla put her finger to her lips and pointed to the sleeping child. The two women moved to the dining room. Deanne placed her parcels on the table.

"Before you say anything about spending money, Mum, this is for the children – basics they ran out of."

"I'm glad you enjoyed some time out and we enjoyed ourselves playing too,"

"Thanks, Mum, it was great to have some free time and go out. Please come back to play with Jason again."

"Of course, I will, but I must go back to work now."

Deanne relaxed with a cup of coffee. Jason and David were playing and Brad was at a dinner meeting. Once the children had eaten she would have the evening to herself. With shopping in the morning and now Brad away, it was the longest spell of free time she'd had for months. She thought of her morning's shopping. It was fun to browse in the shops but she sighed as she thought of her need to curtail her spending. Shopping and then meeting up with friends for a coffee was a favourite activity. She moved the unopened parcels to her bedroom. She didn't tell her mother that she fell in love with a midnight blue evening dress and bought it. She told herself that it suited her colouring and looked great on her, and anyway, it was on sale and not expensive. There would be a function in two weeks and she would wear it then.She was certain that Brad would compliment her.

She thought about what her mother would say and shuddered. Her mother would probably say something about not needing to buy another dress, especially when money was tight. That was the trouble with her being a psychologist. She made comments about everyone's behaviour and thought she had the right to do so. Though her mother had praised her a lot as a child, it was her criticisms that hurt most and that she remembered. Her father was less judgemental or perhaps less concerned about her upbringing. Both her parents were busy and often late home, so she spent a great deal of time with her grandmother. She thought of her often and missed her. Her gran adored her with no comment or criticism.

Deanne was grateful that her mother was spending time with Jason, who seemed happy with her. She wondered how long it would take for her mother to comment about Jason and give her psychological tips about how to care for him.

Carla had enjoyed the time spent with Jason and promised herself to do so again. If only work wasn't so consuming and she had more energy.

Though she thought about her family background, she hadn't begun to search the Internet for clues. Later that week, after a less demanding day, she went to the study after dinner to discover more on the Internet about the places with connections to her family. She clicked onto images of the medieval city of Regensburg, her father's place of birth. No wonder UNESCO had earmarked it as a heritage city. It was a city with Roman historical remains. The Danube flowed through it, the Black Forest was near and it was renowned for its Gothic cathedrals and elaborate Romanesque buildings. Though the original Regensburg synagogue and everything connected with Jewish life was destroyed in 1519, a new synagogue stood there now.

I'd love to visit Regensburg and see it all - the streets Dad walked, enjoy the views and the mountains where he spent summer holidays and skied in winter.

She left the views of the old city and searched for family

names but without luck. She wasn't able to take her search into her family further. A professional genealogist was the answer.

The following evening, she searched for professionally qualified, genealogical researchers in the Regensburg area who spoke English. Two appeared to be suitable – Susanna Schmidt and Maria Ebert were both from Regensburg. After reading their biographies she decided on Maria Ebert and sent her an email.

She stood on the porch and sighed enjoying the cool air and pale flowers glowing in the moonlight, as sounds of night surrounded her. After thinking about her family for so long and then procrastinating about searching for them, she had started the process of discovery.

Two weeks later, she was home from work earlier than usual and it was light enough for a short walk. The brisk walk was energising and she promised herself that she would walk more often after work. The post box attached to the gate pillar was full. Steve must've forgotten to empty it. There were a handful of letters, some bills, those still sent by post, and an envelope with foreign stamps addressed to her in neat handwriting. Excitedly she carried the letter to her study. It was from Maria Ebert, written in perfect English. Maria wrote that she would like to assist with research into Carla's family in Regensburg, but she was unable to start work on it for two months as she had to complete her thesis. The warm and helpful tone of the letter gave Carla confidence in her choice of a researcher.

Steve wasn't home yet. While she waited for him, she relaxed on the living room couch. She thought of her older clients who like her sought answers about their ancestors. Who were they, was the question they often asked. Aging drew us to examine our lives and the lives of those who came before us. It was like the question her children asked. Who do I look like and take after? She looked at the faces of her grandparents in photos on the table near her. When they were young, they struggled to cope with feeding and clothing their large family and later, they battled to escape from persecution. Family survival overwhelmed them. Day to day life was enough to deal with. They didn't have time or energy to worry about philosophical issues. Her grandfather had stern eyes and a tight mouth and her grandmother, with brown eyes like her own, seemed to smile at her. The couple met in the small inn Helena's father owned. Her grandfather fell for Helena's looks and the innkeeper's money. The photographs of her grandparents together showed them as smiling, but she would never know if they were happy together.

As Carla waited for Maria to contact her when she was ready to go ahead with her genealogical search, she wondered whether she was wasting her time. Would Maria unearth more than dates and basic information? Carla longed to find out as much as possible about family members who had lived before her.

Chapter 36

Steve unwound the ribbon holding the thick folder together. He looked at the set of documents and rubbed his forehead. Defending Dennis Westley would stretch him to the limit. He anticipated a long gruelling week or more in court with this complex case. He recalled how previously he had discussed some of his cases with Carla, though strictly this was out of bounds. She had added to his insight of the person he was defending and gave him an edge. Now her tired, gaunt look and tired eyes prevented him from mentioning Dennis Westley.

While he waited to enter the courtroom, he thought about the change in their relationship since their children had left home. Admittedly, their careers demanded a great deal and their energy levels had decreased with advancing years. They were no longer close, hardly touching lovingly and they rarely discussed personal matters. When they occasionally made love she was less passionate than previously. However, his respect for her as a confident and longing for her as a lover had not waned. Only rarely she cooked for him with the love she once had. She prepared those special dishes he termed soul food like his mother made – chopped herring, potato pudding and cheese blintzes that could melt his heart. Though she asked after his health, it wasn't in the same caring way with her head to the side and a kiss on his cheek, that said I worry about you and I love you. He was unable to describe his feelings of isolation, and though he was dissatisfied with their relationship, he hadn't mentioned it to Carla. He thought of particular incidences when she came home late with a take-out dinner too tired to speak and rushed to bed immediately after eating. Then there were the weekend seminars she attended to catch up on new trends in therapy, that left him alone in the house. Possibly there was more to her remoteness. Perhaps she was bored with him or the routine of their marriage, but he was certain that she wasn't having an affair or even a fling, as her honesty would've forced her to reveal it. With a growing sense of helplessness, he wondered what he could do to remedy the situation. No matter how he had tried, he was stumped as to how to break through her barrier. Bringing her flowers, eating out, or taking her to the concerts she enjoyed, had not made the difference he had anticipated. He loved Carla. The idea of separation was unthinkable. He was prepared to accept what she was prepared to give him. The court was convening and he turned his attention to defending his client.

He fought a successful battle for his client but it exhausted him. He was home late, the house was quiet and she was already asleep with the cat cuddled next to her. He was not hungry and after coffee and biscuits, he went to bed.

Steve functioned best when he followed a routine. In the office, he kept a diary with detailed notes. His secretary, employed when he started his practice, was still with him. Her typing wasn't always up to scratch and she had days when she was forgetful. A difficult personal life with a sick child often impinged on her work, but he was used to her.

When he arrived home after work, he liked to see the house and garden tidy. He was grateful that Carla kept it that way. When he opened the front door after work, welcoming lights and the smell of dinner cooking relaxed him and made him think of his home as a child.

That night, the house was in darkness. The cat was meowing insistently for food. Stepping quickly through the house with the cat following, he turned on all the lights and drew the curtains.

"The place is like a barn," he muttered to himself. "Where is Carla?"

After feeding Zoe and filling her water bowl, he poured a large whiskey into a crystal glass. He inhaled the aroma before sipping it. Carrying the glass with him, he went into the kitchen and peered into the fridge. Nothing. Disgruntled, he sat in his favourite chair and waited. He acknowledged that he was becoming set in his ways, but he couldn't help longing for Carla to be at home waiting for him with dinner ready. This past week, she had been late home almost every night. The pressure on her to keep up with work and home was obvious to him.

He was upset. Though he would've liked to tell her how he felt, he knew that he would say little when she arrived. He had the reputation of arguing his cases brilliantly in court, scoring more wins than many other barristers, but when he faced Carla he was a tongue-tied adolescent. Fear that he might break into the dominant voice he used in court, that frightened her, silenced him. In any event, the thought of a long talk with Carla was unappealing. She would talk him into a corner and nothing would be achieved. He wondered if she was aware of his unhappiness or if she cared.

She was a psychologist, after all, a specialist in ailing emotions, so she should know.

He went to the window, parted the curtains and peered into the black. No sign of her and no phone call or message. With a packet of chips he found in the top cupboard in one hand, he topped up his whiskey with the other and returned to his chair.

The cat ran to the front door before he heard Carla's car rumbling up the driveway.

"Sorry I'm late, darling. A client held me up," she said with one of her engaging smiles. She dropped a flat package on the benchtop and rubbed her hands along her thighs. "It's pizza again. I'll keep it warm while I make a salad. And there's fresh fruit and ice cream afterwards."

Too tired to talk, she rushed to bed immediately after eating.

Two days before their wedding anniversary, Steve met Ralph for lunch at a café near his office. Ralph was one of his oldest friends. After they caught up and asked after each other's families, Ralph launched into an enthusiastic description of his trip to Europe with his wife, Julie. Steve found the places of interest to Ralph boring listening and gave his friend half his attention. Ralph was in advertising and tended to exaggerate. When his friend turned the conversation around to his marriage, Steve became more interested. He leaned forward not knowing what to expect. Ralph and Julie had one of those marriages that had survived drug experimentation in earlier days, and more recently, affairs.

"We decided on a trip to Europe at the last moment. Our marriage was in trouble and we were desperate. No more pretending things would just work out. A split was looming, but our kids read the signs and tried to keep us together. So, we decided to take the overseas holiday we'd promised ourselves for years. What could we lose?"

"How did things work out?" Steve asked.

"The trip was fantastic, a wow. And before you ask, yes, it worked. Romance blossomed and now we are like two lovebirds."

Steve laughed and placed an arm around Ralph's shoulder.

"Wonderful, my friend, I'm pleased for the two of you!"

He put his napkin on the table and stood.

"I'm sorry, I have to rush back to the office."

That night after dinner, though he knew he was drinking too much lately, he poured another whisky and sought solace in memories of his childhood. He had lived in Carlton, a suburb where many of the people in his street were Jews whose parents and grandparents fled Europe as refugees in the aftermath of World War Two. In those early days, they suffered financial hardship and like many were traumatised by their experiences during the Holocaust. They were relieved to live in a peaceful country with freedom of movement and association, even if the culture was alien.

Before the war, his father, Dov, had been a tailor trained in Europe by a master who made suits for wealthy businessmen. His apprenticeship lasted only two years when he was apprehended by the Gestapo and sent to a labour camp, and from there to a concentration camp. Steve knew little about his father's experiences during the Holocaust other than that he had survived. Like many parents then, his father wouldn't talk about it. His mother was equally silent about her suffering during this terrible time. In Melbourne, his father worked at the back of a tailor's shop doing alterations until he had saved enough to rent a shop and hang out his sign. His shop flourished and the family lived well. Well enough for his parents to move to the suburbs where they owned a house with a garden and backyard.

A biscuit tin held pictures of the narrow streets and old buildings of the European ghetto where they were forced to live once Hitler was in power. These were painful memories his parents couldn't forget. For Steve born in Melbourne and a modern Australian who had studied law at university, the archways over cobbled streets and old buildings resembled most other medieval towns in Europe. There seemed nothing special about his parents' hometown and he paid little attention to the details of people and places that they frequently discussed. Though his parents spoke English and tried to assimilate as best as they could, at home they lapsed into Yiddish and the ways of the past.

His mother, Miriam, was half a head taller and broader than her husband, and her thick hair scraped from her face into a small bun at the nape of her neck, added to her monumental appearance. When she went to synagogue or visited friends she dabbed 4711 cologne behind her ears and in the cleft of her breast. The cologne was her one extravagance, but a small bottle lasted her a year. She barely talked when her eyes were on bubbling oil frying their dinner. After Steve helped her wash the after-dinner dishes, she removed her apron, hung it on a nail behind the door and sat at the kitchen table. Her hand reached for his. *'Kum, my Stevie, talk with me.'*

He told her about his day at school and his adventures with his friends, and his mother nodded. Time was precious and when his father thought they'd talked for long enough he'd cough. She would withdraw her hand, kiss Steve's forehead and stand. Once she'd smoothed her clothing and pinned back any stray hairs, she gave her attention to his father who was usually reading in the sitting room. At first, he read books and articles written in Yiddish. When his English improved, he borrowed books from the library. Steve couldn't recall his parents arguing, but in those days couples didn't have long discussions. If his father didn't agree with a comment his mother made, he ignored it in a way that made it seem to join the smoke from his pipe wafting towards the window. He was a calm man who weighed up his decisions carefully. A serious change in routine or a demand for money gave him much to consider. Without pressuring Steve he encouraged him. Fortunately, Steve excelled academically with distinctions in most subjects. Though his father didn't verbally express his pride in his son, a warm hug and kiss on the cheek was all Steve needed.

Before he married, he was the youngest of three boys and the only one still living at home. He enjoyed sport, hanging out with his friends, and when school debating whetted his appetite, he developed an interest in a career in law. His pleasures combined with his studies made his life full and stimulating.

"I'm not marrying for a while. I'm not going to be tied down," he'd say to his married friends. That was until he met Carla.

A sudden shower with rain pattering on the roof brought him back into the living room. Their anniversary was due to fall in two days. They had stopped giving each other anniversary gifts, though they hadn't relinquished a celebratory dinner. This year he decided to try harder. He figured that finding a gift that expressed his love for her was his last chance of evoking a flicker of her interest. The idea of being doomed to live separate lives like many of their friends of a similar age, horrified him.

His late afternoon visit to a large department store in the city to find a gift for Carla proved fruitless. He wandered past the perfume counter and shook his head. At the jewellery stand, he became increasingly confused. He was lost. Carla wore little jewellery lately. What she did wear was expensive and small. It wasn't cost that bothered him, but he wanted to buy her something she would find precious. Perhaps, the children would have some ideas. He was about to phone his daughter when he recalled what Ralph had said about his trip. Four weeks overseas! They had saved for it and Steve was satisfied that they could afford it. Tickets for a flight to Europe would make a perfect gift. As Carla was interested in finding out more about her family origins in Europe, a trip that combined searching for her roots with sightseeing could provide an opportunity to grow closer.

He checked his watch. There was still time to visit a nearby travel agent. Once the tickets were paid for and the envelope sat in his breast pocket, he felt a pleasant warmth beneath his striped, suit jacket. If he was buying her love he didn't care. He was optimistic, as she often talked about finding out more about her family's origins. He could devote himself to her family search, as he had already delved into his background.

The hotel he chose for their anniversary, celebratory dinner was tastefully decorated in a Rococo style. As they walked up the long staircase with its plush carpet, carved banister and fountain, they glanced at each other appreciating the tasteful opulence. They were shown to their seats with a view of the trees swaying in the wind along the narrow strip of river.Steve wore a new suit for the occasion and complemented Carla in a black dress that hugged her trim figure. They both tried to be jolly.

"Let's drink a toast. *L'Chaim*, to Life and another happy, healthy year together," Steve said raising his glass to her.

They drank and stretched across the table to kiss, their lips brushing. The candlelit table was perfect. The buffet was tempting and they had worked their way through the fish, with complimentary remarks about the food, when Steve handed Carla an envelope.

"Surprise!"

She opened it quickly and took a deep breath.

"How exciting! Two tickets to Europe."

"We both need a change, a holiday...to improve things between us," he stumbled over the words. "We could go to France, your favourite, and I'm sure you'll want to go to Regensburg in Germany."

She took his hand and kissed it.

"Thank you...what a great idea! Wonderful!"

"I'm looking forward to it," he said.

"But what about your family history?" She said looking up at him.

"Do you remember that I made a special trip to Poland? I was in theCzech Republic for a client. I don't want to go back there."

"I'm going to love it. All those amazing old buildings and the paintings!" She smiled at him as she sipped her wine

Within a week, their holiday was planned. From the moment Carla opened the envelope containing the tickets, he sensed her enthusiasm. He was optimistic that the trip would bring them closer. But the effort involved in preparation was a dampener. Before they left, some of his work had to be handed over to other barristers and dates for court appearances changed. At the end of each day, he stayed back dictating letters and arrived home late. Both tired, they communicated little.

He discovered that Carla had been working longer hours

too, completing her reports and fitting in extra patients for consultations. A locum wasn't necessary. She intended to leave a phone message with the names of colleagues her patients could visit while she was away. There was the cat to place in a cattery and arrangements to be made for the mail to be cleared and the garden watered. She had started looking for new premises. Fortunately, her landlord gave her a few months to move. That was something to worry about when she returned.

While driving home in congested traffic, he anticipated the pleasure of a long holiday spent with Carla. Anticipation of the enjoyable event was part of the pleasure. From pictures in tour brochures, he conjured up images of old historic buildings, lakes, mountains and friendly coffee shops. It would be winter during their trip. They would be spending Christmas in Europe with its magnificent streets and window decorations, markets and pageants. Hopefully, there would be snow. Life in the warm climate of Melbourne provided no opportunity for revelling in snow. The snowfields were a long journey away and often sparsely covered. In Europe snow would surround them.

Chapter 38

Carla was late again. Mike lifted the top essay from the pile on his desk and began to read it. He looked up to check that the door was open for Carla and continued his work. So far, the assignments were uninspiring and predictable, not a single original idea. When he was a student his desire for individuality was important. Now students appeared to find comfort in being alike. There were a few bright sparks at the top – there always were. Most were mediocre. If only he could leave the marking, the tutorials and the same old lectures to travel or study further. Stimulation and change seemed like a dream.

Carla stood before him breathless and full of apologies. Her dark hair was windswept and her cheeks fiery from running. She looked radiant and desirable.

I wouldn't mind... no, don't even think of it! He chided himself.

He stood to greet her.

"You're looking well. Very well!"

"I'm feeling great," her words were garbled as she told him excitedly about the surprise trip to Europe.

"Wonderful! Let's work on your cases first and then we can talk about your trip."

She placed her iPad on the desk between them. They discussed each client she presented with barely any comments from Mike.

"As always, you're handling them so well that I have nothing to add."

Then they discussed her trip. She said that a visit to Germany, to Regensburg, might not deliver as much as she hoped. Not wanting to build up her expectations, she emphasised that a brief visit could only answer some of her questions about her family history.

"Don't be so negative. You might discover more than you imagine about your family and their way of life."

"You're right, Mike. Who knows what I'll discover."

She told him that they planned to visit *Dachau*, and about her concern about whether she would cope when confronted with the grisly reality of the Holocaust?

He listened and as usual, provided no answers. He never did. As she was about to leave, he wished her a stimulating and enjoyable trip.

The campus lights focused on a throng of part-time students gathered on the steps of the psychology building. As Mike took the familiar route to the car park, he thought of Carla's trip to Europe and hoped she would find the answers she was seeking. He hadn't told her that he was disappointed with his pilgrimage to Munich a few years earlier. The old synagogue and houses where his family once lived no longer existed and a museum was erected in their place. When he visited the *Dachau Concentration Camp* it seemed too neat, too sanitised for the horror that had occurred there. All the Holocaust sites he had visited were tourist destinations now and none were as raw and brutal as he felt they should have been.

It was Sunday, and he left home without his wife and family to visit his Aunt Janie, as he did every month. Of all his relatives, he was closest to her. She was fondly named *The Family Chronicle* because she stored and spread information about family members that others had forgotten. After her husband died she lived the life she had always wanted when he was alive, but couldn't due to his complaint of economic pressures. Despite his 'business problems' he left her with more than enough to buy a smallholding on the outskirts of the city. She was eccentric in her appearance with long grey hair she wore in a plait that almost reached her waist and she dressed in workers overalls and dungarees in winter. Apart from 6 dogs and countless cats, she kept sheep, four milking cows, two horses that she rode and grew more vegetables than she and her relatives and friends could eat. What was leftover went to her workers and needy people in her area. Farming on a small scale was her pleasure and her work.

Many people thought her strange living alone in the country, but Mike understood her and found her lifestyle refreshing and interesting. Away from the noise of the city and its pollution, he relaxed as soon as he took the pebble road that led to her house. He would've liked to spend a week away on the farm without his wife and family, but it wasn't possible. As it was, they complained of seeing too little of him with his work, academic and other commitments.

On this trip, he thought of more than a long chat over coffee with homemade scones and coffee. He was dissatisfied, craving for more in his life. He told himself that his feelings were common and that he was probably going through a male midlife crisis. His work as a lecturer and tutor at the University, once interesting, now bored him. He hoped that a day at the farm would help him to find some answers. After a chat with Janie, he did his usual round of visiting the animals. His favourites were the horses that he fed with apples he had brought for them. The fresh air, wild grasses, trees and animals relaxed him. As he thought of his stress, an image of Carla popped into his mind. Perhaps Janie wouldn't mind him inviting her, and her husband Steve, if he wanted to join them. He was certain from what he knew of Carla's interest in gardening and nature, that she would enjoy it and find a visit relaxing too.

Chapter 38

Josef's reduced working hours were not well received by the clerical staff at the office. They sniggered and gossiped that he was given special treatment. He overheard them whisper about him 'needing to pull himself together like everyone else who felt blue now and then.' He ignored them and threw himself into his work. He completed all of his tasks, in the expected time, but after work when he pulled up in his garage, his exhaustion was often so disabling that he went to bed without eating. On the days when his down moods peeked through, knowing that he was expected to perform as he once had, made him edgy. Luckily, his overall productivity was positive and his down days went unnoticed.

As his strength began to return, he had more free time after work. His grandfather and his background were still on his mind. One evening, he drove to the retirement home to see Kristian again. He hoped to squeeze more information about his grandfather out of Kristian. As previously, he found the old man in a small room off the main lounge, playing poker. The group of elderly men had just completed a round and judging by Kristian's wide grin, Josef assumed he had won.

"Ah, Josef, you're back to see me," Kristian said standing slowly. He shook Josef's outstretched hand and patted him on the shoulder.

"I hope you are well?" Josef said in a respectful tone he did not feel.

"As well as can be expected at my age," Kristian replied.

"The chocolates you asked for, the best Belgian ones," Josef said, placing a large box in Kristian's hands. "Enjoy them."

"And the Schnapps?"

"Sorry, no Schnapps. It's no good for you."

"Anyway, thank you for the chocolates. They'll help me to forget my miseries while I'm eating them," Kristian poutingly replied.

"I brought you an apple strudel too, from the German delicatessen."

He hoped that the gifts would encourage Kristian to relax with him and talk.

"Very thoughtful indeed, my boy. I'll put the strudel in my little fridge," he said, taking the narrow box from Josef. "Let's sit on the porch. It is enclosed and pleasant out there," the old man said, shuffling past a group of tea drinkers. Josef noticed how Kristian had aged, even in the short while since his last visit. His once darting eyes were glazed and his movements uncoordinated.

Kristian arranged his position in a wicker chair for comfort and looked hard at Josef.

"So, what can I do for you this time, my boy?"

"I was hoping that you might have remembered more about my grandfather's past."

"You're in luck. I was thinking about him just the other day. Such good memories." He pursed his lips.

"Last time I was here you said that my grandfather and his family came from Bavaria, somewhere near Munich. Have you remembered the name of the town?"

"Sorry, I only remember that it was a small town in the *Schwartzwald,* you know the Black Forest. The forest is stunning. Nothing can equal the magnificent pine and birch trees in summer and the snow like a white blanket wrapping the mountains in winter." He closed his eyes relishing his memory.

Josef nodded.

"Anything else you can tell me about my grandfather?" He added hopefully.

"I think I've told you all I know."

"Did you meet any of our relatives - my great grandfather, great grandmother or any of the other Martinsen family?"

"Martinsen?" His laugh was almost a cackle. 'Erik told me once that in Germany his name was Martin and that there were lots of families with the name Martin in the area – all related."

"Where does the name Martinsen come from, then?"

Kristian looked up and smiled.

"Your grandfather changed his name to Martinsen in Denmark. It was more Danish and helped him to fit in."

Josef's stomach lurched. It was as if every foundation that was once solid and known had shifted. Now it was their family name, his very identity that wasn't as he knew it.

"What next? I expect you'll tell me that I was adopted."

"Definitely not! I remember when you were born, chubby and pink and what's more, you're the image of Nils, that father of yours. Same colouring and the shape of your face, but you have your mother's eyes," he said with a chuckle.

"Well, I guess that's a relief, I suppose."

"And by the way, talking of Nils, what's he doing these days? I haven't seen or heard of him."

"I hardly see him either." Josef hesitated. "Is Nils my father's real name or was that altered to mask his German heritage?"

Kristian cut in. "I have no idea. You'll have to ask him about the name he was baptised with." He paused. "Well, that's all I can tell you." Kristian rubbed his wrinkled hands, his prominent veins giving them a blue tinge.

Josef sensed Kristian knew more but chose not to reveal it.

"Do you know anyone who knows more about my family?" Josef asked sharply.

"Let me see. There's Trudie Kranz. She might know something," Kristian said scratching his balding head. "My carer took me to a marvellous symphony concert last year. Wagner, you know. I was surprised when a woman came up to talk to me during the interval. I didn't recognise her at first, but her voice was unmistakable -Trudie, the last of Erik's lady friends before the war. She's probably still alive and could be worth a phone call. You never know. I have her phone number, somewhere." He searched in his wallet and found the number. Josef copied it and left. What more could he find out? Whatever it was, he was driven to uncover it.

It didn't take long for Greta to settle back into Josef's comfortable house with its minimal, tasteful decoration. They communicated more openly and were closer than before. Every evening over dinner they discussed their day and later they talked before bed.

Sunday morning was cold, but Josef and Greta were up early for a walk on the beach. Bjorn followed on a lead, his stubby legs having to work fast to keep up with them. Greta would've preferred to leave him at home. The small dog prevented her from breaking into a run, but Josef insisted that he join them. They must have walked for an hour when they rested on a sandbank with a view of the beach. Though the air was still cool and the sea icy, swimmers in wetsuits were already in the water. They had no intention of joining them. The morning sun was surprisingly warm, and they removed their outer layer of clothing. Josef carried a bag with towels and two bottles of water on his back. When he poured some of his water into a plastic bowl for Bjorn, Greta placed her hands on her hips and laughed.

"He's just a dog. You make too much fuss."

"Good boy, drink. It's hot and we have a long walk back," Josef said to Bjorn ignoring her comment.

Greta moved away and draped herself over a flat boulder in the sunlight. Josef's eyes travelled over her body in her tights and a clingy top. Aroused, he sighed and looked away. At midday, they trudged through the sand back to the car. On the journey home, Josef found the opportunity to tell Greta about his meeting with Kristian and to share the shock of his discoveries.

Her golden hair flicked as she turned from him. Her reply was swift.

"You're overreacting Joe. It's in the past and happened ages ago. Try to move on."

Her reaction was sobering. In her practical way, she attempted to put his information into perspective.

"He was your grandfather after all. He loved you and did so much for you when you were growing up. Everybody has skeletons in their cupboards."

"Do you have any?"

She shrugged. "My mother told me that my uncle was a Nazi at heart, but a serious injury in a road accident prevented him from enlisting or he'd certainly have fought for Hitler. He did his bit working for the Germans behind the scenes. My father was too young to enlist, but from his talk, I can assume that even as a youngster he was a Hitler follower."

"Doesn't it upset you?"

"No, the war was too long ago to worry about now."

Bjorn sat at Josef's feet. Since Greta had moved back he wasn't allowed on the couch and Josef missed the dog's warm body next to his. While Greta prepared a meal in the kitchen, Bjorn looked about and then jumped onto the couch. Josef stroked his head.

"Pity you two don't like each other."

"Bjorn licked his hand."

"We are different in our ideas and approach to life - in everything. She's a caring person but she hasn't owned a dog or cat and is not fond of animals. It's a pity that she thinks dogs are dirty and a nuisance."

The dog closed his eyes.

Josef realised that he knew little about Greta's background other than that her parents had migrated to Australia when she was seventeen, just after she completed her basic schooling. Soon after arriving in Melbourne, her father, a baker, took a job and then went on to buy a small bakery of his own. Both her parents worked in the bakery and it flourished. After school and on Saturdays Greta helped out. He didn't know much more about Greta's family. She appeared to be happy in Melbourne. In her perfectly matched clothing, the way she insisted on neatness in the house and her respectful way of addressing people, he saw a glimpse of the formality of her European background. Their backgrounds were similar in many ways but Josef had embraced the casual Australian lifestyle fully and had no intention of changing.

After work the next day, Josef phoned Trudie. Her soft, German accent made her sound younger than he expected. She said that she was thrilled by Josef's phone call and after a brief conversation invited him for coffee.

Her apartment was in an old building close to the city. The area was exclusive when the rich lived there. Now that they had moved on, the few remaining shops and buildings were shabby and needed renovation. He took the rickety lift up to her apartment not knowing what to expect. He was surprised by her tasteful combination of Persian carpets and rich furnishing sprinkled with ornaments from all over the world. She was dressed stylishly and her almost unlined heart-shaped face accentuated by red lipstick was framed by a silver bob. He gauged her to be in her late eighties. He remembered seeing her at his grandfather's funeral – an elegant stranger in a dark cape. They sat at a small, round table laid with porcelain cups and saucers, sparkling cutlery as well as a cake, tiny sandwiches, biscuits and chocolates. On the centre of the richly, embroidered tablecloth stood a figurine of a dancer holding coloured napkins.

When he began to tell her the reason for his visit, she put her fingers to her lips.

"Shush, shush! First, something to eat? Talking can wait," she insisted.

"Everything looks wonderful. You shouldn't have gone to so much trouble."

"*Bayerische* hospitality for Erich Martin's grandson," she said with a tilt of her head.

He noted that she pronounced her grandfather's name in the German way as Erich rather than Erik.

"Martin?"

"The family name I knew him by."

"We call ourselves Martinsen," he said emphatically.

"Changed for the Scandinavians, eh?"

So, Kristian was correct about the change of their family name.

She poured steaming coffee into gold-rimmed cups.

"This is real coffee and the best cake in the world, *Schwartzwalder Kirschtorte*", she said as he inhaled the aroma of the coffee. "Help yourself to *schlagsahne*." She pointed to a bowl of whipped cream to add to the already rich, black forest cake. She hovered, watching him eat. "Eat and enjoy," she said, opening her arms as if to embrace the food on the table.

It was just as well he hadn't eaten much for dinner, he thought, as he bit into a huge slice of cake.

"It's delicious."

"Have more, please."

He held his stomach and groaned softly.

"A sandwich or a small slice of cake, then?"

"Just a sandwich," he said. "They look so tasty that I can't resist them."

She smiled a satisfied smile and crossed her arms over her flat chest.

"I'm glad you are enjoying yourself."

With his mouth full he nodded.

"I knew dear Erich when we were children. We grew up together in the small town of *Zwiesel* and went to the same little school. There were only about thirty children at the school, one teacher and her assistant. Ah, what a childhood! The trees and

173

mountains, skiing in winter and when it was warm we climbed the mountains and swam in the streams." She stared out the window remembering.

He coughed to keep her on track. At least he had discovered the name of the town where his family once lived.

"I'm sorry, I get carried away when I think of the forests of my youth. You said on the phone you wanted to ask me about Erich." She put her hands together and tilted her head to the side.

"Please tell me about *Zwiesel* first," he asked.

"Well, it is a small town deep in the forest not far from the border of Czechoslovakia, close to the highest mountain, the *Grosser Arber,* and near two rivers. On a sunny day, it is *wunderbar* to look down from the mountain at the view."

"And?" He tried to mask his impatience."

"*Zwiesel* is famous in Bavaria. It's the centre of glass and crystal production. For hundreds of years, families have been making glass there."

"Oh! Were my family involved in making glass?"

"Ja! I remember your great-grandfather, Rudi, well. Such a tall man and fat too. He died while I was still at school. He was a master glassblower at the old glassworks and made beautiful bowls and ornaments. When I visited Erich, their house was filled with the many ornaments Rudi made."

Josef's thoughts flashed to the goblet in swirling cream and red, the minute, glass elephant and the glass candlestick that his grandfather had left him.

"That's fascinating. Do you know whether any of my other Martin ancestors who lived in *Zwiesel* worked at the glassworks?"

"Every family in *Zwiesel* had relatives at the glassworks. From what I've heard, glassmaking began in *Zwiesel* about six hundred years ago. At the turn of the seventeenth century, a wealthy family bought the existing glassworks and developed them into the large company it is today. The Martin family was well known in *Zwiesel* and in the towns in the area. Maybe someone can help you to find out about your great grandfather."

"Thank you very much for all you've told me today. It's a start, I knew nothing about my ancestors."

"I'm surprised at Erich and your father. They should've told you."

He shrugged.

"How is your father?"

"He's fine."

She looked at him quizzically before offering him another cup of coffee.

"Ah, ja, families!"

He couldn't resist tasting a biscuit with his coffee.

"One of Erich's favourites," she said with a sigh.

He listened attentively, afraid to miss a crumb of her story.

"In summer when I was fourteen and Erich a year older, we spent our summer holidays in the mountains. We hid in gullies, under the flower-lined shade of birches. Here our friendship developed into 'a deeper kind of loving'".

Josef winced at the pictures forming of Trudie and his grandfather's escapades in the forest.

She took a sip of coffee and continued. "Like most of the boys, he belonged to the *Wandervogel,* a back to nature movement for young boys and men. The aim was to build a *Jugendkulture* or youth culture. Occasionally we girlfriends were invited to join the boys over a weekend. We would all hike and cook on a campfire, free of our parents' stupid rules. It was so romantic singing and sleeping under the stars. There was sex too, but we called it free love then." She closed her eyes as her head swayed. "How manly Erich was in his shorts and hiking boots. No wonder I fell for him."

By now Josef was feeling nauseous. The images Trudie conjured up were too personal and detailed to stomach.

"Even then, we had the custom of saying *heil* when we greeted each other. You can see this being the early days of the Hitler youth movement."

As she continued talking, Josef wished he hadn't eaten so much cream and the rich biscuit.

"When I left school, my parents enrolled me in a secretarial course in a nearby town, and at the same time, Erich began an apprenticeship at the glassworks. By then, we had pledged our love for each other, walked hand in hand in the town and talked of early marriage."

She continued talking fast. "One afternoon when I returned from my classes, Erich was waiting for me outside our house. I knew immediately by his worried face that something was wrong." She gasped slightly as she relived the shock of many years earlier. With a gulp of coffee, to fortify herself, she went on with her story. "Erich shuffled his feet and with his head down, he blurted it out, 'Our family must pack our possessions and leave Zwiesel within three days. It's a secret and no one must know that I've told you.'"

"Why was the family leaving in such a hurry?" Josef asked.

"Many of the glass ornaments made in the factory were gold plated, a demanding task that only gifted and most experienced glassblowers would dare to tackle. As Rudi knew the technique and had decorated many ornaments with gold, he was given a key to the safe where the gold was kept. At night, the owner of the glassworks weighed the gold used that day and added to it if necessary. Only he, the manager, and Rudi had the keys to the safe. She thumped the carved table next to her. "When one morning the metal box where the gold was kept was empty, Rudi was suspected of stealing the gold." A sneer formed on her face. "The workers are always the thieves. Months later they found out that the manager had stolen the money, but it was too late then. We all knew that Rudi hadn't taken the gold, but he was branded a thief and the family's reputation in the area was ruined. Leaving was their only way out."

She sighed loudly.

"And where do you think they went?" Before he could speak, she added, "Of all places, to Copenhagen. Denmark is such an uninteresting place, almost as ugly as Holland. But his father convinced the family that Denmark was a good place to live."

She offered Josef more to eat and drink, but he shook his head. She poured another cup of coffee for herself and went on with her story. She explained that she wrote to Erich from the day after he left *Zwiesel*, but after a few months, he tired of writing letters back to her. When he visited her over the first Christmas after his departure, the spark that had bonded them was doused. It was their daily life, their shared involvement in the community and their love of the forest and its seasonal changes that had cemented their relationship. Trudie's childhood dream of marriage to her sweetheart was shattered. Her father was not going to allow his eldest daughter to mope and throw her chances away. He saw to it that she was married to Helmut within eighteen months. Helmut a forester, who lived two blocks from their home had shown an interest in Trudie for years.

She shrugged.

"The Christmas before the war was declared, I received a greeting card from Erich with a Danish postmark. He was a Danish citizen by then. But what did he hope to find in Denmark?"

Josef's father's explanation of the neighbours discovering his grandfather's Nazi sympathies and shunning him came to mind as he tried to interrupt her. He was determined to have an answer.

"But, Trudie, did my grandfather give a reason for leaving just as the war broke out?" He was tired by now, his hands were clammy and his head swimming with trying to keep up with her chatter. He wanted answers to his grandfather's past, but he wished she would hurry.

"My memory isn't as good as it was and I can't remember what he wrote about his move to Sweden except that he'd found work there."

She must've noticed Josef's distressed expression.

"I'm sorry, I don't mean to upset you with my memories. Don't forget I loved Erich, just like you did."

He nodded.

As she continued talking, now about her miserable marriage to Helmut, her two sons with him and later how hard she'd worked to save enough to leave him, her words floated with the mixed aromas around the table. He felt rooted to the chair but his mind drifted. All he heard were snippets of her story – a second marriage and her move to Melbourne. He managed to keep his eyes open and nod occasionally, but he missed the rest of her long story. Finally, she stopped talking, placed her hands together and looked at him waiting for his comment.

He took a deep breath before speaking.

"What an amazing life you've led, Trudie!" He held her old hands. "Thank you for the wonderful tea and cake, and your story."

He left after much handshaking, promises to stay in touch, and possibly meeting again. Exhausted and queasy from the rich food, he walked slowly to his car. Once inside, he sighed deeply and placed his head on the wheel. He fumbled on the seat beside him for bottled water and drank it all.

It wasn't until the next morning when he woke early still feeling full, that he thought about his meeting with Trudie. If he was honest with himself, he didn't like her. There was something he couldn't put his finger on that bothered him about her. It wasn't her love for his grandfather or her rather exotic appearance for an older woman. Then he hit on it. She was still a pro-Nazi – possibly a racist. He shuddered. Unless necessary, he would have nothing further to do with her.

Chapter 39

When Lars flicked on his answering machine, he heard Josef's unmistakably resonant voice complaining that he had not returned his phone calls. He dialled Josef's number.

"We must meet. I need to know what's been happening – what you've discovered so far," Josef said. "I have plenty to tell you too," Lars added.

"Tomorrow night at my place, then. We can have a long chat. I'll bring dinner," Josef replied.

Lars was a carpenter. He had worked on a site of a building Josef had designed only once. Lars joked to his fellow tradesmen about his brother the architect with his head in the clouds and no hands-on experience. He was reluctant to admit that he was proud of Josef and that secretly he wished that he had followed his mother's advice to study engineering. The long course and the fact that his father was an engineer who worked until late most evenings, made him take the easier path. But talented and skilled, his father had managed to create fine furniture as a hobby.

As Lars drove to work, he thought of the weekends in the early days in their new country, when their grandfather took them both on excursions to explore the city, its buildings and arcades. They learned about the suburbs by taking different buses and trams on long rides. They ventured further to the Dandenong Mountains which their grandfather joking called 'the small blue animal in the distance'. On their walks through the forests at the foot of the mountains, they were delighted by hopping Kangaroos with tiny joeys popping out of their mother's secure pouches, but the picture-postcard koalas were not as cuddly as they looked. Their desire to be away from the city whether in the forests, the bush, or the beach grew as the years passed. Lars' garden was simple with a lawn, flowerbeds and shrubs, while Josef attempted to recreate his piece of nature on the large slice of bushland in front of his house that he landscaped.

The brothers met often for a beer. They were comfortable with each other and their conversation flowed easily. As adults, their once boyish rivalry was replaced by friendship. There were two topics that the two brothers vehemently disagreed on - their grandfather and Greta. Lars disliked his grandfather but admitted that when he and Josef arrived in Australia his grandfather gave them a taste of the city and introduced them to their new homeland. Any further discussion of their grandfather led Lars to throw up his arms. As for Greta, Lars made it clear that she had left his brother in the lurch when he most needed her love and support.

A powerful wind swirled around the house Josef had built on tall boulders. Dressed in a parka, he came out to meet Lars. The brothers shook hands and gave each other a hug.

"Let's move inside out of the wind, bro," Josef said as they shivered.

With the wind roaring outdoors, they sat in the warmth eating chicken and chips washed down with beer. A bottle of red wine stood unopened.

"We have a lot of catching up to do. What did you want to tell me?' Josef asked.

Lars stretched for the bottle.

"I'll open the wine before getting on with my story. We'll need it. Remember how I've always said I didn't trust our grandfather?"

Josef crossed his arms and waited.

Lars looked down before speaking, "There's something important I should've told you."

"That's okay Bro, tell me now."

After sipping his wine, Lars described an incident that occurred on the 20th of April two years earlier.

"I was visiting a mate who lived near grandpa's place. I hadn't seen the old man for ages and I thought it a good opportunity to pop in. As I reached his house, the lights inside were blazing and there were sounds of men singing. I crept up to a window and peeped through a slit in a curtain. You won't believe what I saw."

Josef stared at his brother in anticipation.

Lars took a deep breath.

"It was scary. Five old blokes and some in their late teens and early twenties, all skinheads, were togged up in *SS* uniforms. As I said, you won't believe it. They were singing in German and prancing around giving the Hitler salute. Grandpa was too old to do that, but he sat in full uniform on his favourite chair. One of the old blokes seemed to be the leader. It took me some time but I recognised him – grandpa's old friend, Kristian. Then someone brought out a huge chocolate cake with masses of cream on it and they sang happy birthday - happy birthday to that bastard, Hitler! I was that sick that I threw up in the bushes." He kicked the side of the table. "I checked it out later. Hitler's birthday was on the 20th of April 1889."

Josef clenched his fists but said nothing.

Lars looked at his brother.

"You okay bro? You're not looking good."

"I need some brandy," Josef said.

"Now maybe you'll understand why I wouldn't attend his funeral?" Lars said with a sigh.

"Why did you keep this to yourself?" Josef asked.

"I should've told you earlier, but it was awful and you weren't well. I didn't want to upset you even more. You loved him so much."

Josef nodded and wiped his eyes.

"Unfortunately, this fits with what I've already discovered

about our grandfather. I'll fetch more brandy before I tell you about it. We're going to need it."

Josef told Lars how he had found the photograph of the four men wearing badges with Nazi insignias, and that their father had revealed that their grandfather was a Nazi sympathiser. He described his meetings with Kristian and Trudie who confirmed their grandfather's Nazi leanings. He then shared his discovery that their grandfather had left Denmark when war was declared.

Lars put up his hand to stop his brother and poured more brandy into his glass.

"Don't tell me there's more."

"Oh, yes, prepare yourself."

Slowly Josef told his brother about their origins in *Zwiesel*, Germany and not Denmark as they had once thought. Then he revealed that their real name was Martin, a German name. When Lars covered his head with his hands Josef stopped talking. He decided to tell his brother the finer details of his meeting with Trudie later.

"Right, more brandy," Josef said lifting the bottle.

"The brandy doesn't help. It's hard to take in all of this. Worse still is the thought that we might find out more if we keep digging," Lars said with a deep sigh.

"That's what's bugging me. Part of me wants to know it all but the rest is scared about what else could come out," Josef said, as he stroked Bjorn's head. "I wish we could let it go, but I don't think we can."

"How are you these days, Bro," Lars asked placing his hand on his brother's arm.

Josef shrugged.

"Better. I felt lousy for a few months but it seems to be settling down."

Depression?"

"Yeah."

Lars looked through the window at the moonless sky.

"I'm sorry you've had it so tough, Bro." Lars said.

When Lars began hunting for his car keys, Josef shook his head.

"We've had a lot of booze, better sleep here tonight," Josef said taking his brother's arm."

"Okay, you're right. I'll stay over."

Josef turned the couch into a bed and fetched sheets and blankets.

"You should be warm enough and comfortable."

"Thanks, bro," Lars said pumping up a pillow.

"Greta isn't home yet. I know she bugs you, but if you bump into her in the morning don't let it get to you. You're my brother and as entitled to be here as she is."

Lars nodded.

Josef heard Lars leave early. He drifted back into sleep until Greta woke him for breakfast.

Chapter 40

Lars drove fast in the dawn light. To be home with Susanna and the kids was all he wanted. He loved Josef, but he was intense, and too much time spent with him made him edgy.

As he opened the front door, Susanna was waiting for him.

"Glad you're home but it's just as well you slept over. You get drunk as a skunk when you're with your brother."

He fell into her arms and they hugged. Then he told her about his discussion with his brother and she lifted her arms in despair.

"When you told me you were going to talk to Josef about your grandfather, I knew you'd be back feeling miserable, so I made you a stack of your favourites - pancakes. You can add as much maple syrup as you like."

"You're amazing," he said as he eyed the pancakes. He finished the whole stack with hot coffee. "That hit the spot. Nothing like my favourite food to demolish the demons. Poor Joe, he takes all of this stuff about our grandfather too seriously – more seriously than I do, anyway."

"He was close to the old guy and you weren't," Susanna said.

"Joe couldn't see that he was phoney," Lars said.

"You two are brothers but nothing like each other...and just as well,"

"Everything okay with the kids?" he asked.

"All fine. They've taken the bus to school."

"I'm going for a walk to clear my head. Then I'll catch up an hour or two of sleep. Work can wait."

Lars took his favourite route, a sandy path in the bush. As he walked, he relaxed. Though he could put thoughts of his grandfather in a box in his mind and forget about him, he knew that Josef couldn't. Josef was the sensitive one and with his sensitivity came his fine intellect and artistic talent. He remembered how jealous he was of Josef's high grades at school. Only two years after arriving in Melbourne, Josef had picked up the language and was reading books in English, while he was still struggling. From the age of five, Josef drew his world and his talent was obvious. Sport and working with his hands were Lars' thing and carpentry was his talent. He admitted to himself that he hadn't complemented his brother enough on his designs of magnificent houses and buildings, while Josef was quick to appreciate his carpentry and woodworking skills. Despite his brother's abilities, Lars knew that he was his mother's favourite. She told him often that he was like her – easy-going and good-natured.

Josef was no softie. He recalled his brother at seven going on hikes with his grandfather during Denmark's summers. Once they were in Australia, his older brother had stood up for him against school bullies and even fought them off. Josef had learned how to fight from their grandfather while Lars wasn't interested.

Josef was made of tough stuff, he'd recover soon, but Greta wasn't the woman for him.

He walked back to the house, longing for sleep.

Chapter 41

The house was still. Greta was asleep and over a late coffee, Josef thought about the past few weeks. The talk with Lars about his grandfather and the disquieting information Lars had given him about Hitler's birthday party swirled in his head. It was disrupting his sleep and robbing him of the sharp concentration he required at work. He wrestled with his need to see Carla. He'd tried to discuss the new information with Greta, but she insisted that he was being ridiculous and once again suggested he put the past aside. At first, he brushed off her comments. When she became adamant that not all Germans were Nazis, and that the *SS* was an elite force that had to follow orders like any other soldiers, he knew that he had to talk to Carla.

Slashing rain accompanied him on the short walk from his car to Carla's office. Inside the waiting area, he removed his wet jacket and rubbed his hands for warmth. He was early for his appointment and her closed door told him that she was busy with a client. Restlessly he paced the small area. There was so much he had to tell her. Where would he start, he wondered.

The door opened and she ushered him into her room. The only change he noticed in the room was an arrangement of blossoms. It was spring again! Blossoms were in the vase when he'd first visited her. He sighed. A year had passed already.

She looked down, twisting her ring around her finger as she waited for him to speak.

Words, awful words about his grandfather were trapped in his throat.

"I er... made the appointment because..."

"Because you have something important to tell me?" Her voice was soothing.

"Yes, I've had a miserable few weeks since our last session. I found out more about my grandfather and my brother Lars told me some awful stuff he'd been keeping from me so as not to upset me." He closed his eyes and swallowed. "Some days I've just about boiled with rage".

He watched her expression of genuine interest as he talked.

"Upsetting things can be hard to talk about."

He nodded, cleared his throat and began to tell her what he had discovered about his grandfather.

"Lars and I carry his vile ancestry in our blood."

"You carry your family genes but that has nothing to do with your family's choices and actions," she said in a soft voice.

"I hadn't thought of it like that," he said as he changed his position in the chair.

"A different perspective on a nasty discovery," she said.

They continued to talk about what he learned from Lars as well as his last meeting with Kristian and his visit of discovery with Trudie. After they briefly discussed his work, he looked at the clock. The session was running over time, but she did not comment.

"I think there's more nasty stuff to come. My father knows more and my grandfather's old Nazi friend, Kristian does too, but they're not talking." He placed his head in his hands. "After finding out all this disgusting stuff about my grandfather, I'm not going to lapse into depression again, am I?"

"If you take your further investigations slowly and digest them bit by bit, you should be fine. I know it will be tough, but try to distance yourself from any new information you discover. I'm here for you if you need to talk."

He left feeling lighter after sharing all he had learned with Carla, but he had no answers. Perhaps there were none, he mused.

After another restless night, Josef was out of bed early. He dressed in shorts and runners and after a quick breakfast, he was outdoors ready for a long walk. In the early light, the air was a bouquet of spring fragrances. He passed an old house with a tall pine tree in the garden that reminded him of their garden in Copenhagen. His mother planted rows of flowers and in the centre of the patch of lawn, a single pine encircled by violets and forget-me-nots dominated. At the start of spring, his mother laced the pine boughs with blossoms and at Christmas, she decorated the tree with shiny tinsel and angels.

He recalled their Danish house, one of a strip linked to the next, like train carriages. Each was individually decorated. The outer walls of their house were vibrant mustard, the window frames white and tan. A framed attic window peeped onto the street through a shingled roof. The rooms were relatively spacious and during winter, a fire burning night and day spread its heat through the house. He remembered spring in the park at the bottom of their street, erupting into a kaleidoscope of colour – pink and white blossoms, lime birch buds and saffron crocuses nestling in emerald grass. At twilight, migrating starlings returning after a winter in a warmer climate swooped across the sky, their calls drowning children's shouts and yelps of laughter. He recalled his precious memories of spring in Copenhagen so often, that by now he embellished them. The pink blossoms became cerise and the grass a brighter green, while the shrieks of the starlings throbbed in the darkened sky. He thought of autumn in the park too. It was his next favourite season in Denmark when deciduous trees changed colour and overwhelmed the landscape with their rusts, ochres and oranges.

Young children on their way to school rushed past him. Their chatter and laughter reminded him that at their age he had been ripped away from his home to Australia, a country with a warm climate and a way of life that was bland in comparison to Copenhagen. When he arrived, Australians laughed easily at jokes he did not understand. He loathed the narrow double storey house his parents chose with its rusted trellis work and peeling white walls. He and Lars shared a room with "bunk beds". Lars had the top bed as he was the younger brother, while he had the luxury of the lower bed. In Denmark, he had his own small room with a larger bed and privacy.

Once his father had signed the papers for their migration to Australia, his mother insisted that the family speak only English. Though he could make himself understood at his new school, the boys laughed at his accent and he had trouble following their Aussie slang. It didn't take him long to learn to use slang and swear as well as they did. Gradually he found his place.

He was immersed in the past and walked further than he intended. The sun was up and he ran the rest of the way home.

Over the weekend, Josef and Greta were invited to a barbeque at Terry and Jean Davis' home. Initially, Greta refused to go, saying that she found Terry rough and rude and that she hardly knew Jean.

"They are *your* friends", she said. When she noticed that her refusal upset Josef, she reluctantly agreed to go to the barbeque.

Josef visited the Davis' simple house often. Greta looked at the brick, veneer ordinariness of the exterior of the house with runners lying outside the front door and shook her head in disdain.

They were greeted effusively at the front door. Terry thanked Josef for the wine he'd brought and held it up to the light.

"We'll enjoy this one," he said with a grin.

The children, Mia, Rachel and Jack ran to Josef. They were thrilled with Josef's gift of chocolates. Their mother's predictable warning of not too many were ignored. As they made their way through the house to the deck. The smell of meat cooking on the barbeque made Josef hungry.

"Bread and salads are on the table and cold beers in the

kitchen," Jean called. The two girls helped their mother with the salads while the eldest, Jack, hovered around the two men.

"Right Jeanie, we'll grab a beer and give the meat our expert attention," Terry said placing an arm on Josef's shoulder. While the two men turned the meat they talked.

"How are things going?" Terry asked.

"Good, so far. I'm back at work and enjoying it," Josef replied.

Terry nodded. "Well, you're looking like a new man." He stood back from the barbeque, rubbed his hands and put the skewer aside. "Jack can look after the cooking for a bit," he said nudging his son.

"Yeah, well, last time you saw me I was done in," Josef admitted with a wry smile.

"I wasn't the best then either, but I've got a new job now and things are humming along nicely," he added cautiously. He explained that he was working for a group of carpenters who paid well. "So far all is good."

While they drank their beers, Jack cooked the meat with their occasional instructions. They discussed the cricket teams for the season in detail. Apart from changes in the names of players and the dates of fixtures, it was the same discussion they'd had for years. Jack prodded his father when the meat was cooked. Together they carried the platters of meat to the table.

"Dinner's ready, everyone," Jean called.

Josef ate his charred sausage with beer, revelling in the ordinariness of the occasion. It was a gift, he thought, to enjoy simple pleasures again. He noticed that Greta nibbled her steak and pushed her sausage aside.

Mia and Rachel sat on the grass near Josef, Uncle Joe, as they called him. They were fond of him and he was the sitter they asked for if their parents were going out for the evening. When he cared for them they kicked the ball outdoors. If it was still light he joined them playing on the computer.

Jean and Greta were cold and moved indoors. While the two

women were engrossed in conversation, Josef watched Greta through the flywire door, the silhouette of her body swaying as she laughed. Though she was attractive, his desire for sex with her had waned. Since she was living with him again, their differences showed themselves. She changed his house by adding expensive furniture and rugs. Her need for all that was fine in crockery and cutlery was a surprise. Previously, he wasn't aware of how materialistic she was. He realised that she was more superficial than he imagined. Lately, they barely talked about books, films and art. Her request to tame the natural bush near the house upset him as it was a key feature of the property and he wondered how long their relationship could last.

Perhaps it was the pleasant evening spent with his friends that made Josef wonder what Terry and Jean would think if they discovered the awful facts about his grandfather. He didn't have to think for long. He knew the answer. They would try to hide their revulsion but tell Josef that he wasn't to blame for his grandfather's activities. Like Greta, they would suggest that he put his findings aside and get on with his life.

When Terry moved away to talk to his children, Joseph's thoughts turned to Carla.

She was right as usual. It was time to let his obsession with his grandfather go. She'd annoyed him when she'd said it, but she was talking sense. He was upsetting himself over each discovery and reacting emotionally. Sure, he'd thirsted for the truth and would continue his quest for it, but a new approach was needed – to review any discoveries in a reasonable, balanced manner. It meant attempting to stand back and observe.

Josef was surprised when his father called him. It was something he rarely did. They talked and Josef was intrigued when his father suggested that they ought to meet for lunch. They agreed on a café, a family favourite when his mother was alive. Josef did not find the café as easily as he'd expected. It was nothing like the shed of a place with whitewashed walls and a cement floor where they once enjoyed fish and chips served by the owner or one of his sons. The exterior in blue had a large, mosaic fish decorating the outer wall. Inside the floors were tiled. Fishnets and crayfish baskets hung from wooden beams. Now the café seated more than twice the number of customers, mostly in their late twenties and thirties. Large glass doors opened onto an outdoor dining area where several tables had already been taken.

Josef wondered if his father had booked a table. He didn't need to wait long to find out. A waitress met him at the door and asked if he had a reservation. Luckily, Nils had booked a table outdoors partly shaded by a colourful umbrella.

The café was upgraded to a bistro and served alcohol. He ordered a beer, sipped it and relaxed while he waited for his father to arrive. The sun peeked through the clouds as sailing boats moved sluggishly on flat waves. A feast of briefly clad women caught his attention, and he failed to notice the lanky man with grey speckled hair ambling towards him. Their last meeting at the cemetery was tense and both men wore dark suits. His father in a sky-blue shirt hanging out of his shorts looked far too casual to be the closed man he knew. Josef climbed out of his chair to greet his father.

"About time we got together again." Nils Martinsen's face was expressionless as he thrust out his dry hand. "How's life treating you?" he asked.

Josef hesitated. "Yeah, fine." He glanced at the tall man. He's lost weight and is looking pasty, he thought.

They consulted the menu for the day and ordered the special of snapper and chips. Over beers, their conversation that ranged from climate change to politics flowed freely.

"How's work?" Nils asked catching his son's eye for the first time.

Josef's voice was clipped "I was working at home on a design but now I'm back at the office."

Suddenly he's interested in my life.

"A design?" Nils asked again.

"Community housing for the underprivileged."

" I hope your houses aren't as flimsy as some I've seen - an engineer's nightmare."

"Believe me, they're pretty sound." Josef said as he glanced at his watch. As if offering a dog a bone, he threw out a question. "Are you still working for the local government?"

"Oh no, I gave that away last year. I'm a consultant now. Much more free time, less travel and less stress. It can be tough but I'm free of bosses."

Josef caught a fleeting image of a scowling tense man rarely at home. The relaxed version of his father didn't deceive him. The same person in looser clothing. Find out what you need to know, cut and run, he told himself.

"When I talked to you a while back, you said you weren't sure what my grandfather was doing in Sweden. Have you thought of any other reasons?" Josef asked.

"What do you mean, other reasons? We've been through this before?"

"I thought there may be something you forgot to tell me."

"As far as I know, soon after war was declared, he hid on a ferry that took him across the Straits to Sweden. He told me that he'd found a job there almost immediately." A familiar expression of disgust formed on his father's face. "At the *Brauhaus* in Malmo, a popular dive for German troops - beer and sex. They gave him a room upstairs. A hole of a place."

Nils looked out at the bay.

"I didn't want to tell you about all this unpleasant stuff about him."

"The bar and brothel doesn't bother me," Josef said. "It's consorting with the bloody Germans that bugs me."

Nils made a vague stabbing movement with his hand.

"Once I found out about this place in Malmo, I didn't want to know what he got up to next."

Josef cut in. "Lars and I went to see Kristian, his old mate. He's living at the retirement home where Grandpa spent his last days. Kristian told us a little about his Nazi involvement."

"I knew about the bar in Sweden..., but that's it." Nils straightened his knife and fork. "Kristian's a wily fox. He worked with Aussie Intelligence after the war. God knows you won't get much out of him."

"Is there anything more about the old man you haven't told me? Josef asked in a desperate tone.

Nils shrugged and shook his head. "I've told you all I know."

They sat drinking in uncomfortable silence. With nothing further to say to each other, they stood. Nils paid the bill and they left.

His father had provided Josef with nothing new. He tried to brush away his irritation and disappointment by concentrating on the waves. When that didn't work, he mumbled an obscenity about his father and kicked the sand. He took the shortcut across the beach to the nearest hotel. The lunchtime crowds had left but the bar was crowded. Perched on a stool, he sipped his whiskey slowly. He knew that he was drinking too much but he told himself that he needed it.Anger surged in his throat as he almost whipped a beer coaster across the bar. He was certain that his father was holding back some important information. Clenching his glass, he reminded himself to be a cool observer. Then he thought of Anders and the Viking story. Picturing himself as a traditional Viking made him smile and relax.

Chapter 42

As the weekend with her family neared, Greta looked forward to being with her parents. She thought of her mother's cooking, especially Sunday lunch with crispy roast pork, applesauce and roast potatoes, followed by a raspberry and cream tart. They were the foods she enjoyed as a child and her taste had not changed.

The road to the beach town of Rosebud was congested with traffic. An hour and a half later she arrived at her parent's home. The simple house and neat garden where she grew up hadn't changed. Her parents, Marie and Willem had worked hard and saved. They could have moved on, she thought, found a larger, more attractive house. She walked across the narrow strip of grass and past the single flowerbed to the front door.

As her father greeted her, she was assaulted by the familiar smell that impregnated the walls. Nothing had changed since her last visit apart from two new bright cushions that she thought her mother must've bought on the sales. Her mother was a thrifty woman and created an attractive sitting room from a bargain basement sofa and armchairs covered with throws. Some pieces of pewter were the only items of value. She followed her mother's voice to the kitchen. Her mother's head was almost in the oven as she bent over the roast. She closed the oven door, smiled at her daughter, and wiped her hot face with the side of her gloved hand. After a hasty kiss, Greta placed her handbag on the kitchen chair. Ignoring her mother's protest, she began to wash the pots and pans.

When her mother was satisfied that the meal was ready, she

summoned Willem and Greta to the formal dining table. Her insistence on a large table and chairs cramped the adjacent lounge area. She and Willem argued initially about the narrow lounge room when they first moved into the house, but Willem gave in to his wife. Formal dining was too important to her for him to disagree.

Greta enjoyed the meal. She had forgotten what excellent cooks her mother and her grandmother were. Once the serious business of eating was over, they moved to the sunny, wind-protected porch for coffee and her favourite – a slice of chocolate cake with hazelnuts. Greta complimented her mother on the meal and smiled. With no desire to communicate further with her parents, she lifted her head to the sun and closed her eyes. They were large people and their imposing presence still intimidated her even though she was in her thirties and had moved away from home.

Her father had been a baker in Vienna and though he was near retirement now, he continued to work in his bakery. The business had grown enormously since his early days in Australia. He rose every morning before dawn except on Sundays when they went to church. Going to sleep early every night restricted their lives. They did not entertain or go on holiday. Contact with their community was through their shop and regular church attendance. As a child, Greta's friends were not welcome, mainly because the house needed to be quiet as her father needed to catch up on sleep during the afternoon while his wife minded the shop.

Marie put down her coffee cup after scrutinising her daughter. She coughed to gain Greta's attention. She had never been subtle in her approach and asked Greta why she was looking thin and had dark circles under her eyes. Her father put out a restraining hand but her mother continued talking.

Greta looked away without answering.

"Are you and Josef getting along okay?" her mother asked.

Reluctantly Greta admitted that they were having some minor difficulties. When her mother nagged for more information, Greta replied, "I love Josef, but our relationship isn't as good as I'd hoped, but things will improve, I'm sure."

Her father's gentler questioning was drowned by her mother's insistence that she leave Josef before a baby arrived and she was trapped into marriage. Greta stopped listening to her mother's loud voice. Switching off was the way she had learned to survive as a child.

Her parents were good people, she thought, even if they were boring and narrow-minded. They attended church, gave their day-old bread and cakes to the poor and lived simple lives. During the hour and a half that politeness dictated, she sat with her parents after their meal. She nodded her head often pretending interest in their chatter, while her thoughts were about Josef.

After the hour and a half passed, Greta fabricated a pressing engagement and drove home. She was relieved to find Josef out. In the quiet house, she lay on the couch and unwound her coiled hair until it hung past her shoulders. In the silence, she attempted to unravel her thoughts. Her mother meant well but overwhelmed and unsettled her. She drank a glass of white wine and rested her head.

She thought about her relationship with Josef. They were merely jogging along as a couple. She was convinced that none of it was her fault. He was almost well now but they kept an emotional distance from each other that bothered her. Her desire for a passionate relationship made her consider leaving him. But leaving would entail another upheaval for her just when she had settled into the house and made it her own with fine china rimmed with gold, new pots and pans, as well as pure cotton bed linen. He appeared to like the alterations in the house despite the cost.

She battled to pinpoint what was bothering her about Josef. He was no longer the man she loved a year ago. He was critical and more demanding with his food and was finicky. Sex, once central to their relationship, had petered out. Now that he was well, he could no longer blame his wilting libido on depression. She smiled as she remembered how sweet and tender he was before, with those blue-grey eyes of his - a handsome man/boy trying to please. He was still considerate, but he liked to please himself. She was certain that the woman he saw for counselling had played a major role in changing him.

She sighed. She had spent hours helping him return to work, fed and encouraged him and now the bond between them had eroded. Their goals were different. His work was a primary goal. Though he was born in Denmark, by now he was more Australian than Danish. Her mother was probably right. She would be better off leaving while she was young enough to find someone else. It was just as well she had held onto her apartment. She wiped a few tears from her eyes and waited for Josef to return.

Chapter 43

Greta and friends from her office were enjoying dinner at a Chinese restaurant. They shared dishes with wine as they chatted and laughed. Greta was relaxed and drank more than usual. While she was eating a delicious dessert, she noticed an attractive man from the table opposite looking at her. Flattered, she smiled at him. While drinking her cup of jasmine tea, the man brushed past her. He stopped for a moment.

"Hi there, I'm Paul. I've been watching you all evening," he whispered.

She looked up at him and smiled. He was handsome and she was immediately attracted to him.

"I'm Greta," she answered softly trying not to draw the attention of her friends to her conversation.

"Perhaps we could meet – go for coffee or drinks?"

"I'd like that," she replied.

He slipped a card into her hand.

"Give me a ring and we'll do that," he said as he left.

"Who's the tall, dark stranger?" her friend Val asked.

"His name is Paul. We've been eying each other through the meal and he cam over."

"You're a quiet one. I'd never have taken you for a flirt especially when you have that gorgeous guy Josef crazy about you."

"Not so crazy these days," Greta said.

"Okay. I'll not be nosey and ask too many questions," her friend said.

Josef was asleep on the couch when she came home. She covered him with a blanket and went to the bedroom. Before undressing, she took the business card Paul had given her out of her purse. His name was Paul Roydon and he was an investment consultant.

Thoughts about the way she had flirted with Paul kept her awake. She was too conservative to be a flirt – not the type of woman who did that sort of thing. Her parents would be horrified. It must've been the alcohol that affected her judgement.

The following day a bouquet of roses arrived for her. It was more embarrassing than pleasing.

She didn't want Joseph to find out that Paul had sent her flowers. She needed time to sort out her feelings about him soon.

She handed the flowers to her friend who sat opposite and asked her to pretend the flowers were hers. Concentrating on her work was difficult. She was indecisive about phoning Paul to thank him, as she knew that a phone call could set an affair with him rolling. By the end of the day, she made her decision and phoned Paul.

They met after work at a bar far from the office. Paul was waiting for her and smiled when she arrived. Though their conversation began hesitantly, soon they were chatting about shared interests. Unlike Josef, he enjoyed his wealth and found pleasure in an elaborate lifestyle. The most striking difference between the two men was his energy. Paul glowed with health and was sexy. Though he had to leave immediately after they had eaten, he invited her for dinner later that week. His parting kiss on her cheek lingered. Greta's breaths were fast as she drove home to Josef. She didn't know Paul, but she was attracted to him, and she was no longer happy with Josef.

Chapter 44

Josef was spending more time at the office and enjoying his work, but the signs of pressure - headaches, a buzzing mind and trouble falling asleep hit him suddenly. He thought of phoning Carla but dismissed the idea. She would tell him to pace himself. Gradually, he began to have more down days, but he considered his stress too minor to seek help. Two weeks later, when had almost no appetite and he had to force himself out of bed to go to work, he phoned her. She was able to see him later that week.

As her door opened, he sighed a sigh of relief, a sigh of coming home.

She noticed his down mood after his first sentence, and her questions that followed about his hours at work, appetite and sleep continued.

"I'm sure you don't need me to tell you that you've been pushing yourself too hard," she said.

"Everything went well and I felt fine until suddenly this down feeling hit me."

She looked away before speaking again.

"Has work been the trigger, or have there been other issues that set it off?"

He threw his hands in the air. "I don't know where to start."

She nodded and waited for him to continue

"My relationship with Greta isn't working out, and I've had enough prying into my grandfather's past and our family background. With each person I talk to about him, something unpleasant comes out – more awful Nazi material and it can only get worse."

"All of this plus trying to cope with your job must've been extremely stressful. And stress is no friend of depression."

When he'd finished talking about the stressors in his life, he looked up at her and blurted out a question, "You're Jewish, aren't you?"

"Yes."

"It can't be pleasant hearing all this Nazi stuff."

She raised her eyebrows before speaking, "I'm sorry that you've had to find out about this awful stuff, but it's nothing new to me. We have lived with Nazi sympathisers since the war, and anti-Semitism has been always present in some form or another."

Immediately he regretted asking her such a personal and insensitive question.

She tapped her toe before continuing.

"You don't have the full story yet. So far, you know that you have a German bloodline, that your family lived in the Black Forest in Bavaria, that your grandfather went to Sweden at the start of the war and that he was a Nazi sympathiser who joined pro-Nazi clubs. You talk of your German bloodline. Many Danes have German ancestry. You should be proud to be born in Denmark, and never forget the wonderfully brave actions of many Danes who saved Jews during the Holocaust by ferrying them to safety. Their actions were heroic. Many Jewish families today still thank them."

"True, but what about all the lies my grandfather told me?"

"Maybe he told himself lies too. There was a gentle, caring side of him that you knew and loved. I know that there is a lot you have to come to terms with and none of this is easy, but try not to forget how much he cared for you."

"You're right, of course. I have to try to keep things in proportion, strike a balance."

When she asked about Greta, his face felt suddenly warm.

"At first, I couldn't get enough of her sexually and I wanted to be with her constantly. Now the passion is drying up."

"Tiredness isn't passion's best friend," she said.

"It's more than that. We're at one another, arguing over little things. It wasn't like that before."

"What things?"

"She's taken over and I don't like it – changed the house to her taste. She makes arrangements without asking me and I've realised that we have little in common. There's a void between us, that wasn't there before, or I didn't notice it," he said placing his head in his hands.

She waited for him to speak again.

He rubbed his brow and looked away. "It's not working out. We'll split up again. I can see it."

"Don't be too hasty. Talk it through."

Suriptiously she glanced at the clock. He wasn't listening to her suggestions about slowing down at work, creating a sleep routine or easing up on his investigation of his grandfather's past.

1"I'll try," he said as he stood.

He walked to his car slowly. He struggled to concentrate on the road as he drove into the late afternoon traffic. When he reached a favourite strip of grassland, he parked the car and sat there until the first stars were out.

When he arrived home he found Greta waiting for him.

"I'm tired of waiting up for you. I cook meals for you, but you don't eat them," she said angrily.

After a muttered apology, he showered and went to bed. To make a point of her annoyance, she slept in the spare bedroom. Bjorn made his choice by following Josef and slept next to him in the large bed.

The next evening he stayed back at work to finish a project and was late for dinner again. When in a blast of anger, she threw his spoilt dinner on the kitchen floor, he wasn't surprised.

Chapter 45

Six Months Later

A breeze swept through the living room ballooning the curtains. Josef closed the window and turned on the television. Restlessly, he switched from one channel to another.

Greta had moved back to her apartment for two months of separation rather than make final decisions on their future as a couple. He was not accustomed to the stillness of the house and the rooms seemed larger and colder without her. He was missing the company of a person in the house, but not her. Their relationship had worked on a superficial level but sadly failed on a deeper one. For him, there would be no going back.

Bored with reruns of sport and cop shows, he consulted the television guide. Perhaps it was luck or fate, that a documentary about the Scandinavian countries during World War Two was about to start. He knew only what his grandfather had told him about the topic and what he had learned at school. It was an opportunity to discover more about the war. He clicked onto the programme as the credits merged into a scene of Copenhagen harbour at dawn on April 9, 1940. In the early light, through heavy clouds, the advancing German, naval fleet was barely visible on the horizon. When the ships reached the docks, troops poured out. While the Danish Royal Guards attempted to resist the invaders, German planes flew overhead. Simultaneously, a German infantry battalion moved towards the Amalienborg Palace, the home of the Danish Royal Family. The Royal Guard put up a strong fight but were overcome and within two hours King Christian and the government ceded to the Germans.

Old films of the attack showed the Danish population shocked by the invasion and the occupation of their country. An announcer explained that Germany's attack on the harbour and the airfields aimed to subjugate the country as fast as possible and that it was part of a plan to invade Norway as well. The German's strategy for the invasion of Norway was to seize the port of *Narvik* and secure the raw materials needed to produce steel. Gaining Norway's wide coastline would have been an important means of controlling the North Sea and securing the passage of German warships and submarines in the Atlantic.

Josef scratched his head. The history of the war was more complicated than he expected. He sat up and tried to concentrate as the announcer described how initially, the Danish authorities accepted their German occupation to prevent attacks and maintain their usual way of living. He backed this up by showing Danish archival material.

Josef was interested when the narrator explained that an active Danish Resistance developed plans against the Germans. The Resistance printed an illegal newspaper and carried out sabotage by destroying German railway lines to prevent their transport through Sweden and on to the Eastern Front. Josef turned up the sound. He was keen to learn more about the Resistance Movement in Denmark during the war.

"Sabotage activities continued and strikes in large Danish workplaces began," the announcer said. "As unrest grew, there were street demonstrations. To maintain control, the Germans responded with attempts to clamp down on the demonstrations by declaring martial law, which led to arrests and executions."

Then the narrator told his audience that the Germans aimed to subjugate and ultimately deport the Danish Jews. In most European countries Jews had been forced into ghettos and wore yellow stars. However, the Jewish citizens of Denmark had always been regarded as legitimate members of the population and were well accepted. The small number of Jews in Denmark had the support of the Danish population, so at first, the Germans decided not to interfere with them. But by 1943, Germany's tone changed. In September of that year, they planned to round up Jewish citizens during *Rosh Hashanah,* the Jewish New Year, when Jews would be at home celebrating, and send them to concentration camps. An old film snippet showed the Gestapo listing names of Jewish homes.

Josef gasped. He knew a little about the Nazi's treatment of the Danish Jews, but not these details.

The announcer said that most Danish Jews lived in Copenhagen. When the Chief Rabbi of Denmark was tipped off about the Nazi raids expected to occur during the Jewish holidays, he cancelled all religious services. The citizens of Denmark heard of the German's plan and actively resisted the Nazis attempts at deporting their Jewish citizens. Most Danes were opposed to any harm occurring to their Jewish population. Bishops of the Danish Church did something unusual as they were not political. They sent letters to the Danish population to denounce the German action and to all political parties apart from the National Socialist Party, the largest Nazi Party in Denmark before and during the Second World War.

Once Jewish Danes were warned of the German's plans to act against them, some began to leave. With the help of Danes, some Jews were offered hiding places in homes, hospitals and churches. Escape routes were pointed out and false papers and money provided. Then the Resistance organised a daring escape operation of Jewish citizens by sea to Sweden, a neutral country. Fishermen in seaside villages along the rugged, Danish coast acted together to ferry about 7,200 Jews across the narrow body of water from Denmark to Sweden. The operation was successful apart from some 580, who unfortunately failed to escape to Sweden. Other Jews remained hidden in Denmark until the end of the war. A few Jews died of accidents or committed suicide. It was estimated that 464 of the 580 who failed to escape, were captured and sent to the *Theresienstadt Concentration Camp*.

Josef was glued to the screen, watching camera footage of the escape at night as boats avoided the German searchlights. He was amazed as he learned of the daring details of the escape of fellow Jewish Danes during the war that he knew nothing about.

An older, stout man appeared. He was introduced as the son of one of the members of the Resistance. He talked proudly about the members of the Danish Resistance Movement who were honoured collectively by *Yad Vashem,* the World Holocaust Remembrance Centre, in Israel. He described how *Yad Vashem* documents, researches and commemorates the six million Jews murdered by the Nazis and their collaborators, and thanked the *Righteous Among the Nations* who risked their lives to rescue Jews during the Holocaust.

"The rescue of the Danish Jews is represented at *Yad Vashem* by a tree planted for the King of Denmark and the Danish Resistance Movement, and a fishing boat from the Danish village of Gilleleje," the man said.

As the scene on the television changed, Josef hurried to the fridge to replenish his supply of beer. As he sipped his beer he shook his head in confusion. His grandfather liked to tell stories about how proud he was that the Danes helped the Jews to escape when all the while he was pro-Nazi and anti-Jewish.

Then the announcer talked about how Germany sought additional recruits for its army from Scandinavian and European countries. The camera panned on old posters seeking recruits for *Freikorps Danmark.* He knew that the *Freikorps* were originally German volunteer units that were active in the nineteenth and early twentieth centuries but he hadn't heard of *Freikorps* in Denmark during World War Two. A poster of the *Freikorps* brigade grinned at him from the screen. He noticed that the soldiers in the posters were wearing German army uniforms with

Danish colours and an SS emblem was superimposed on the edges of their left sleeves. Josef sat up in shock.

He turned up the television sound to listen to the information about the *Freikorps*.

"Shortly after Germany invaded Russia in June 1941, to bolster their forces, they formed a voluntary infantry division or *Freikorps* comprising Danish men aged seventeen to twenty-three. The men signed up for two years and were given joint German citizenship. There were approximately 1,000 Danish recruits," the man said. As he talked, photos were shown of recruits from Norway, Finland and a few from Sweden who joined the Danish volunteers. Together the recruits formed the *SS Waffen Norland Division*. News reels and a scene depicting the *Norland Division* engaged in a vicious battle in *Demjansk*, a small town near Leningrad, flashed on the screen.

Josef gripped the side of the couch. War films were commonplace, but not with Danish soldiers fighting alongside the Germans. The documentary was disturbing and he flicked off the television. Questions about his grandfather's whereabouts during the war nagged him.

Had his grandfather worn the *Nordland Division's* uniform? It seemed possible.

With a sense of dread, Josef collected his empty beer cans and threw them in the bin. While he waited for the kettle to boil for coffee, he thumped the benchtop. He had to get answers!

No one knew his grandfather well enough to provide definitive answers except his father.

Since their last meeting at the fish café, he hadn't talked to his father. He was certain that his father was hiding the truth from him. He dialled his father's number. Nils answered the phone, and after uncomfortable enquiries about each other's health, he surprised Josef.

"I was going to phone you to let you know that I am not well."

"Oh, what's happening?" Josef replied.

Nils hesitated before speaking, "I have cancer and it is terminal. I'd just finished a course of chemo last time we met."

Shocked, Josef mumbled his response. "I'm sorry...that's awful. Why didn't you tell me?"

"I'm having treatment and tablets are easing the pain. I'm not one to make a fuss."

Josef knew that he ought to feel concerned about his father's poor health but he felt nothing. What he wanted was answers from his father, but he continued going through the motions of discussing his father's condition.

"I'll be okay, I have excellent doctors," Nils said.

"That's good."

After an awkward pause, Josef explained the reason for his call.

Nils was silent as if gathering his thoughts.

"It would be better if we talked about this face to face. Anyway, as I won't be around for much longer, we'll need to discuss a few things. Come to the house tomorrow after work and I'll tell you all I know."

Chapter 46

The dying sun was barely visible in the sky when Josef drove to his father's house. His anger rose during the drive. Why had his father taken so long, and waited for a health crisis to tell him the truth? It was dark when he arrived at the house. Though he knew his father was ill, when the door opened he was unprepared for the gaunt man standing before him. His clothes hung on him and his head was almost bare apart from a few tufts of hair. Since their last meeting, his father had changed dramatically and looked nothing like the man he knew.

"I know I look like the walking dead," Nils responded to Josef's shocked expression.

Josef nodded and smiled stiffly. They sat in the sitting room and talked stiltedly about Nils' illness and the dark prognosis from his doctor.

"My oncologist told me that I have up to nine months if I'm lucky," Nils said wryly. "I've made a list of what we need to discuss about practical matters and things I must tell you about your grandfather."

"Surely you didn't have to wait until now to tell me the truth about him" Josef's voice was sharp.

"What more do you want to know about him?" his father said tersely.

"I decided to phone you after watching a documentary about Danish volunteers who joined the *German Freikorps* during the war. Dirty traitors!"

"You can imagine that they weren't exactly popular when they came home on leave, so the government tried to put a blanket over their activities," Nils said.

Josef swallowed and looked away.

Nils grimaced. "I expect you want to know if your grandfather was one of the volunteers in the *Noordland* division of the *Waffen*. Well, the answer is yes. I'm not proud of it. He joined up with other volunteer units to fight with the Germans. When they returned to Denmark like rats, some served jail sentences. The old man was lucky not to be branded a traitor. Don't ask me what lies he told the authorities to manage that."

Josef 's head spun and his feet no longer felt the floor.

Nils dragged himself from his seat and walked slowly to the kitchen. He placed a glass of water in front of his son.

"You've known he was a Nazi sympathiser, and this was the next step. After he and the family left Germany, he had no faith in the weak Danish government. He carried a dual passport – a Danish and German passport." Nils swallowed and looked up at Josef. "I don't think I've told you about the family's German background. I grew up in Zwiesel in the Black Forest – a wonderful place."

Josef cut in. "Kristian told me about it, but it would've been better coming from you."

Nils nodded.

"I know I've been a lousy father. Too busy with my own stuff. I should've told you and Lars long ago."

Josef looked at the floor.

"I've made a casserole," Nils said. "Let's eat, then I'll answer any of your questions."

The casserole was surprisingly tasty. Nils talked of his shame and his desire to protect his children from the knowledge of his father's unsavoury past. No Dane wanted to have a family member associated with the Nazis. Nils explained that his father had enlisted in the Freikorps in 1941. That he was known as

Martinsen in Denmark but to join the corps, it was a simple step to revert to their original German family name, Martin.

Josef nodded. "Kristian told me that our name is Martin though he left out the details."

"With Kristian, there is always more," Nils said with a nod.

"Just checking," Josef said. "Where was the old man involved in fighting?" Josef asked with a cynical expression,

"On the Eastern Front."

"But where exactly is that?

"A large area, stretching from the Baltic Sea in the North to the Black Sea in the South, involving most of Eastern Europe, and stretching as far as Central Europe. That's all I know and all I wanted to know," Nils replied.

Josef thumped the table. "You may not be interested in details but I want to know it all."

"Sure, I understand."

"Kristian started in the same regiment as my father but he soon moved up in rank, so he may not know everything." Nils adjusted his glasses uncertainly. "There's Hans Weber, an old friend of your grandfather's who was in his unit. Possibly he'd be able to give you more information. That's if he's still alive."

"Where can I find Hans Weber?"

"He lived with his son in the hills," Nils said, pointing in the direction of the Dandenong Mountains, just visible from the window.

Josef felt for his briefcase under the table and opened it. After fumbling, he withdrew a photograph and slapped it on the table. It was the photograph of the four men wearing Nazi insignias he found earlier.

He pointed to the one man he did not recognise in the photograph.

"Could this be Hans Weber?"

Nils scrutinised the photograph and nodded. "Yes, that's him."

"I'll try to find him," Josef said emphatically.

As Josef stood to leave, Nils pointed to a wood and glass cabinet.

"Before you go, take whatever you want. You might as well." He rose slowly, wincing with pain as he slid the glass panel of the cabinet open. Shimmering colours blinked at them. "Zwiesel glass. Some made by your great grandfather and uncles. Isn't it something?" he said, his smile tender as he held a goblet. "All handmade. It will be yours and your brother's soon enough."

Embarrassed by his father's unusual generosity, he refused the offer at first, but finally chose a sparkling blue bowl and a white one for Lars. He wrapped both in newspaper and walked to the door.

"Bring that brother of yours along one night if you can," his father said as they parted.

Once he was home, Josef placed his glass treasure on a side table and admired the colours and fine workmanship. Lars' bowl he put in a cupboard to give to him later. He thought of the talent of his great grandfather and uncles. He wondered about them and about the forests of Bavaria where they once lived. When he searched the directory listings on the internet for Webers living in the Dandenong Mountains, he found nothing. Then he phoned Lars to share the information he had gleaned from their father. Lars listened to Joseph's account of their father's illness and their grandfather's war history.

Lars was quiet at first, unable to respond. Finally, he spluttered angrily, "It's disgusting – makes me want to puke! He had choices – we all do. He didn't need to join the enemy"

"He even hung onto his German passport," Josef said. "Dad reckons he had a mate, Hans Weber, the fourth man in that photo I found. I've tried to locate him, but no luck so far."

"Give me the details and I'll have go," Lars added.

As Josef relaxed on his couch, he was determined not to overreact to the latest bit of information. He selected some

Beethoven, one of his favourite classical composers, lay on the couch and closed his eyes.

Chapter 47

A week later, Lars phoned Josef with the address of the caravan park where Weber lived. The two brothers knew the area well. They had walked along the mountain's paths, climbed to the peaks and swum in the streams. The Belle Vue Caravan Park situated on the lower slopes of the Dandenongs with the view of the forest and undulating landscape did justice to its name. They found the door of the caravan, number 6B, open. A wiry, bronzed man who looked too young to be in his late eighties was planting flowers in one of the ceramic pots that served as his garden.

"Hans Weber?" Lars called.

The man dropped his garden fork and glanced about cautiously.

"Yes, who wants to know?"

Josef did not have to consult his photograph to confirm that the man before him was his grandfather's old friend.

Once Josef mentioned their grandfather, Weber beamed.

"Good God! Two grown-up grandsons!" he said sizing up the two men. "I heard about your grandfather's passing and I'm sorry I couldn't be at the funeral. I was away, in Estonia, with my family."

"Not to worry," Lars replied with a shrug.

"Such a surprise to see you both that I've lost my manners." Weber wiped his hands on his shorts. "Come in."

The caravan decorated in muted tones was unexpectedly comfortable and spacious. While Weber boiled water for coffee, the brothers glanced at the books and knick-knacks, all carefully placed.

Weber returned with coffee and biscuits.

"So?" He looked at them questioningly.

Josef coughed before speaking, "My father told me that you were in the same unit as our grandfather during the war. He opened his briefcase and placed the photograph of the four men on the small table next to the coffee mugs.

"There's our grandfather, his friend Willie, dead I believe, and then Kristian. You're the fourth man in the picture, Josef said pointing to Weber's young face. It's from you that we're hoping to learn more about our grandfather's fight on the side of the *Third Reich*."

Weber put his hand to his brow for a few seconds and looked uncomfortable.

"That photo is a shock. It was taken long ago."

Josef ignored Weber's discomfort and explained that they knew that their grandfather had served on the Eastern Front. What they were seeking was more information about their grandfather's involvement on the Front and his return to Denmark.

At first, Weber claimed to know almost nothing and did his best to block their enquiries, but Lars and Josef kept hurling questions at him.

"Enough! This is like an interrogation after the war. I will tell you what I remember. First, I will fetch my pictures and then we'll pour *schnapps* into the coffee. If a man talks about war he must have *schnapps* inside him."

"Just a drop," Josef said. Lars, the athlete, placed his hand over his cup.

"Before I start with my story, let me ask if the two of you know that your Grandfather received the German medal of honour, the Iron Cross? His action saved the day during a forty-eight-hour attack by the Reds when we struggled to defend the *Tannenberg Line*. All I got was a handful of brass."

Josef looked at his brother and shrugged.

"*The Tannenberg Line* -never heard of it."

"Never heard of it!" Webber said with a frown and waggled a finger at them. "Ignorant youngsters! It was a defence line in Estonia close to the Baltic Sea and strategically important to Herr Hitler."

"Tell us more about the Iron Cross," Lars said with a snigger.

"Your grandfather was a brave man, a great leader and fighter. If anyone deserved it, he did."

"A pity it wasn't the Victoria Cross," Lars muttered.

"A leader, eh?" Joseph said.

Josef scanned his memories of Copenhagen. There had been a charity drive for a footballer in their street who was injured in a game and became paraplegic. The community in the area wanted to help the footballer and his family. His grandfather took over the organization with vigour and sent out leaflets to residents. Money was collected from the nearby streets amounting to a large sum which was presented to the injured man. The only other illustrations of his grandfather's leadership were to do with the baseball games he and his schoolmates played in the park. With his grandfather as their coach, their side, the scruffy bunch they called the *Terriers*, won just about every game. By the end of the season, they were third in the junior league. His grandfather insisted on training before the matches and used smart strategies in the game. His voice was not raised but he was firm and decisive. Flaring nostrils and flashing eyes were the only signs of temper if team members didn't follow orders.

Josef turned his attention back to Weber, restlessly tapping the floor.

"Back then, I must've been crazy to throw my lot in with the Germans," Weber said. "I volunteered after the Russians took over my country, Estonia. After invading Russia in 1941 Germany was hungry for more land and occupied Estonia. At first, we Estonians thought Germany would free us from Russian repression. It didn't take long for us to realise they wanted to occupy our country. They murdered thousands of Estonians, Jews, gypsies and prisoners of war."

"I was trying to place your accent. You speak good English, but you must be Estonian," Lars said slipping lower into his chair.

Weber nodded.

"And proudly!"

"Out of interest what was your occupation before the war?" Josef asked.

"In Estonia, I was a high school teacher but here I don't have acceptable qualifications. Now I teach migrants English, but let's get on with it. You want to know more about Erik's role in the war."

Josef nodded.

"Well, I was a junior officer in the same regiment as your grandfather, but he held the higher rank of *Obersturmfuehrer,* a SS rank of platoon commander of fifty to a hundred men. We became friends after we met at the local bar during our training. It didn't worry me that Erik held a higher rank."

Josef watched Weber's face sharpen and his eyes glint as he turned the pages in his photograph album, pointing and smiling at Erik and himself and others in the tailored regimental SS uniform.

"We looked smart, didn't we?"

Josef sneered and Lars muttered an obscenity. He moved closer to Lars and spoke to him in just above a whisper, "Shut up, Lars! You want to get some answers, don't you?"

Weber watched the brothers and shrugged.

"So, do you want me to continue?"

"Of course," Josef said.

Weber closed the album and stroked its leather cover before speaking again.

"And how much do you two know about the battles on the Eastern Front?" Weber asked.

"I covered the subject at school, but I don't know much more," Josef said looking at his brother for confirmation.

"Same goes for me," Lars added.

Weber looked agitated and took a few gulps of *schnapps*.

"Get it straight! The conflict on the Eastern Front during World War Two was between Germany, Italy and Japan against the Soviet Union, Poland, France, Great Britain, the United States, the Soviet Union and other Allies."

"Forget the unimportant details. Tell us where Our Grandfather earned his iron cross," Josef said tapping the table restlessly.

"I'll try to explain simply what I can remember about your grandfather's finest hour."

"Okay," Lars said impatiently.

"Erik saved us by single-handedly destroying ten Russian tanks in one night. It was for this action that he received his Iron Cross. It allowed us breathing space. We were undermanned but our troops fought brilliantly," he said as he rubbed his forehead.

After more *schnapps*, Weber began to stare out of the caravan window muttering to himself in German. His face was shiny and red and his voice angry when he spoke again.

"Erik is dead, and I'm putting myself through some terrible memories that I want to forget. When I think of all the killings it makes me crazy."

Lars' loud cough distracted Weber.

"We're sorry that remembering the war has upset you. We would like to compensate you for all the pain that your memories have caused you," Josef said.

"Would three hundred dollars be enough?" Lars suggested.

"It will do. Go now and leave me in peace," Weber answered tersely.

With a nod, Lars drew money from his wallet and placed the notes on the table.

"We'll be back in a few weeks."

As they walked away, Josef said, "he received an Iron Cross! The idea of it makes me feel sick."

"I don't think I've absorbed what a horrible discovery this is – the top award from the enemy!" Lars said.

The brothers were quiet as Josef drove home.

When they reached Lars' home the brothers hugged. They hadn't been as close since their childhood.

"What's next Joe?" Lars asked as he opened the car door.

"I guess we'll have to do some background reading if we want to gain anything from talking to Weber. He's not great at explanations," Josef said.

"I haven't the spare time and anyway I hate study," Lars added.

After feeding Bjorn, Josef threw off his clothes, headed for the shower and scrubbed his body.

Chapter 49

Josef was up early after a troubled night. As he sipped a strong cup of coffee, he thought of his friend Anders. They had arranged to meet later at the Viking restaurant. He was the one person who Josef thought was knowledgeable and objective enough to help him to understand more about the war.

Anders was seated when Josef arrived. As Josef rushed to greet his friend, he was surprised. Anders wore a woven tunic with a heavy, leather belt and brown boots. A woollen cape was tied over his left shoulder.

"My everyday Viking clothing, or the closest I can get to it according to records," he said opening his arms to show off his outfit. "I've left my warrior gear at home."

At first, Josef was stunned and then he laughed.

"We need beer and plenty of it to drink to you and the Vikings."

When Josef looked around the packed black-walled restaurant, he noticed strange symbols on the walls and Viking warrior decorations.

"Wow, is all I can say! This Viking blood thing is serious for you!"

"My dad started it all by checking our background and he's convinced we have direct Viking ancestry. I'm not as sure, but it's fun. We join in with Viking war re-enactments once a month and they are great fun. You must come along, you'll enjoy yourself."

"Thanks...a great idea, but I haven't a clue about my Viking history.

"I'm trying to deal with other stuff right now."

Joan Zawatzky

Anders lifted his glass of beer, "*Skol*, here's to you Joe, whatever you discover!"

After their toast, Anders bent to retrieve something from the floor.

"A gift for you, Joe...a Viking shield," he said placing it on the table.

"Wow, what a beauty! Thanks, Anders. This should give me all the protection I need for anything to come," he joked.

"Last time we met we talked about World War Two. I had to leave early and you said you had more questions for me. What's going on?"

"I've found out some awful things about my grandfather's activities during the war and I want to talk to you about it."

Anders nodded sympathetically. "Elena is home with the children today, so I have the time to answer your questions. I can tell that we are going to need a few more beers to get through this."

"I'm ashamed to tell you that my grandfather was a member of the Danish *Freikorps* during the war. It's so difficult to understand."

"You're not alone. I have an uncle who joined up with the *Freikorps* too, but he didn't survive, " Anders said.

We were a country occupied by the Germans and the people hated them. How come volunteers fought alongside the enemy?" Josef asked.

"The Danish *Freikorps* was a volunteer force of Danes with Nazi leanings formed in 1941, just days after the German Invasion of the Soviet Union. Dutch, Norwegian, Flemish and other groups joined the *Freikorps* to form battalions that were integrated into the *Waffen SS*, German forces."

Josef remembered the documentary he had watched and Anders explanation made the information clearer.

"A stupid question, but why did Germany invade the Soviets?" Josef asked.

"The invasion of the Soviet Union was given the code name

of *Operation Barbarossa*. It was an attempt to put into action Hitler's ideological goal for expansion and gain more living space or *lebensraum* for Germans. He had his eye on Russian resources for his people – Russian minerals, food and oil. Huge forces were committed to the Eastern Front in intense battles where all sides suffered enormous casualties. Worse still, were the terrible atrocities committed, and the Holocaust."

Josef looked down. "To think that my grandfather was part of that is beyond comprehension."

Anders nodded sympathetically.

"I didn't tell you that he received an Iron Cross for his action on the Eastern Front. Knowing that, plus the lies he told me is too much to stomach," Josef said.

They drank more beer and talked on about the war.

"I want to find out more about the battles the bastard fought in," Josef said.

"Maybe you'll find some of the information you're looking for at the State Library. Take your time over it. None of it is pleasant reading," Anders said giving Josef a man hug.

"Not pleasant, but I need to know the details ...and then I think I'll be able to let it go."

"Think rather of Vikings! You have your shield now!" Anders said with a laugh.

Josef thanked his friend for his help and the shield, and they parted.

The following day, Josef went to the State Library in the city. His task was enormous, and rather than scour the shelves, he asked one of the librarians for help. She listened patiently, noted numbers and led him to the shelves. There were rows of books about the Eastern Front. She narrowed down the sources and produced a full trolley. She must've taken pity on him when she saw his appalled expression.

"Start with these two, they're reliable references," she said. "If they don't give you what you're looking for try the others. And don't forget there are more on the shelves."

The account of the war in the first two books was too detailed to follow. Then, an encyclopaedia gave him what he was looking for with the movements of the war outlined simply and a clear account of the involvement of foreign forces fighting with the Germans. He hoped for more information and turned the pages of some of the other books on the trolley. Honours were listed for German soldiers who were awarded for bravery or exceptional service. He found what he was looking for in a book about the German army. His grandfather, *Obersturmfuehrer* Erik Martin of the Danish division of the *Waffen - SS*, sixth panzer regiment was listed as having received a Knights Cross for his defensive action.

Josef turned to books that described the atrocities committed during the war and the horrific action taken towards people who were considered *Lebensunwertes Leben*, or unworthy of life, and should therefore be killed - Jews, the mentally and physically impaired, the sexually deviant, and all those considered racially inferior such as gypsies, and members of the Communist Party. He read that from early in the war, Nazi policy was to murder large groups of civilians, especially Jews. Horrified, he read about the Jewish populations of villages wiped out - Riga, Koval, Grodna, Vilna, Smolensk and many more. He was appalled that Germans with the aid of their volunteer forces formed killing teams called *Einsatzgruppen* that followed the German army as it advanced deep into Soviet territory to carry out mass-murder operations. They rounded up the Jews from their towns and villages to killing centres and marched their victims to execution sites, where trenches were prepared. In some cases, the captive victims – men, women and children, were forced to hand over their valuables and then dig their graves. They were undressed and then shot by machine guns either standing before the open trench or lying face down in their prepared pit.

Could my grandfather and Weber have been involved in those massacres? It was too awful to even consider.

He knew about the concentration camps, but little about Hitler's *Final Solution*, the systematic murder of millions of people during the Holocaust. In 1945, when Allied troops liberated the concentration camps they found thousands of sick and dying prisoners and dead bodies. There was evidence of gas chambers and mass graves as well as medical equipment and documentation of experimentation on prisoners.

He left the library feeling ill. Once home, he ignored his usual refuge, the couch, and went to bed. He lay there devastated. He was unable to weep, sleep or eat. A week later he was still unable to concentrate on work and lay in bed trying to forget what he had read.

Lars tried to contact his brother but Josef didn't pick up his phone. Eventually, Lars went to Josef's house where he found a hungry dog and his brother in bed. After giving Bjorn food and clean water, he dragged Josef out of bed and forced him into the shower. He prepared a light meal for his brother and spoon-fed him like a child. When Josef drank coffee and ate a slice of toast Lars was relieved. He helped his brother to dress and they sat on the couch with Bjorn between them. Tears streamed down Josef's face as he told Lars what he had read. Lars attempted to remain calm but soon he was weeping too.

Was their grandfather a monster, involved in these terrible acts? How vile was the blood pumping through his veins?, they asked each other.

Two days later, Josef managed to regain some distance from their awful discoveries and managed to go to work, but his sleep was interrupted by nightmares. Though he knew that he ought to phone Carla he didn't. This was something he felt he needed to cope with alone so that he could look at his face in a mirror again.

Chapter 50

"I've had enough of our grandfather and Nazis," Josef said to Lars over a chicken and chips.

But Lars insisted that Weber had more to tell them before they drew a line under the story of their grandfather's past. As reluctant as Josef was to visit Weber, they waited a month and set out for the Dandenongs.

After Weber ushered them into his caravan, they placed the money they had promised him on the table. He scooped it up immediately with a smile.

"I told you the truth before and I will do my best now, but understand that my memory isn't as good as it was."

The brothers nodded.

"First, some *schnapps*," Weber said filling his glass. Both Josef and Lars declined his offer.

"What do you want me to tell you today?" Weber said.

Josef was firm as he asked his questions.

"Tell us how you and our grandfather escaped near the end of the war and about the massacres of the Jews. Were you and my Grandfather involved in that?"

Weber sipped his drinlk slowly before answering.

"About our escape. Well, the Reds were making mincemeat of us and with what was left of our unit we planned to move on towards Berlin. We could tell how badly things were going. There was no doubt we would lose the war. Our armies did well at the beginning of the war and made huge inroads into Russia. Hitler and his generals assumed that the Red Army was inferior and would collapse, but they had a huge well-trained army to call on, while our generals seemed to have lost the plot and our supplies were insufficient. It was tough for us, starving on the front line with no winter uniforms to face the cold."

Lars nodded.

"It was Erik's idea to escape. Our battalion was camped near a river. We planned to move along the river's edge that opened into the sea. When we reached the port we intended to hide on a supply boat to take us to Denmark. We waited until the heavy fighting eased and one night we crept away from the camp, passed the dozy sentries and moved as fast as we could. Near dawn, we reached the river's edge and stepping carefully, we picked our way through reeds and tall grasses. Dead soldiers lay amongst the rushes." Weber closed his eyes and lowered his head before continuing. "Fumbling in the dark, we searched the bodies for coins or mementoes in gold or silver." The expression on his face was one of revulsion. "It was vile work among the stench of death. We filled our pockets with gold chains, crosses, rings, coins, a lucky, gold elephant and a silver rabbit's paw. We had little money left after spending most of it on beer and cigarettes. We hoped that our loot would help to buy a night's rest in a farmer's barn or some bread as we travelled to the port."

Lars sniggered, "Back to Denmark was it?"

"It was our best option," Weber said. "During the day we hid in the swampy grasses and at night we worked our way along the riverfront. By then our bread was eaten and our water flasks were dry." He sighed and rubbed his head. "If we had known how much we would struggle we wouldn't have considered trying to escape. We were starving and exhausted when we approached a small farm. When the farmer saw our dishevelled state he reached for his gun. We still had the riches we had stolen from the dead in our pockets and offered him a selection. Of course, the farmer grabbed them. We made sure he fed us, gave us a warm place to sleep and clean clothing. After resting, we continued our journey towards the port. Close to our destination, we passed another farm, and the farmer was willing to let us work for food and a place to sleep. I can't say how long we stayed. The farmer was satisfied with our work and the food was good. While we worked at the farm, we watched planes flying overhead on their way towards Berlin. The news came that the war was over. People were drunk, shouting and dancing in the streets. With all the craziness nobody was guarding the boats. That's when we took our final steps to escape and hid in a boat headed for Copenhagen."

"A long story," Lars said with a yawn.

"It was a long and tiring journey," Weber replied.

"What happened when you arrived in Copenhagen?" Josef asked.

"Erik knew some old people in the country where we could hide for a few days. I'd picked up a bit of Danish by then and we blended into the population. We found work or stole food. Later, I returned to Estonia and Erik remained in Copenhagen. I guess Erik was lucky. He could revert to his Danish name, Martinsen. No one knew about his exploits in the war and so he pretended he'd spent the period in Sweden. In this way, he avoided prosecution as a traitor. I was a little fish. They didn't worry about me."

"The sly bastard!" Lars muttered.

"Any other questions?" Weber said ignoring Lars' comment.

"Yes, we want to know about the massacres. You haven't answered that question. Was my grandfather involved in the massacres?" Josef demanded staring at Weber.

"That's not something I can talk about. We were instructed not to discuss that subject. Any other questions?" Weber said clenching the sides of his chair.

"Instructed? Instructed by whom?" Josef replied angrily. "It happened years ago and now you're afraid to admit the truth."

Weber swallowed more *schnapps* and stared at the caravan floor.

"You're wasting your time, Bro. Let it go," Lars said. "

"Erik started as an ordinary soldier like me. Later he went into special operations and intelligence. Secrets behind the scenes. I don't know much about what he did," Weber said.

"We also want to know about Kristian. How did he fit into all of this?" Josef asked.

"Kristian was in intelligence but in a different section to Erik."Reminiscing did not appear to bother Weber this time. Perhaps it was the offer of money that made him want to talk about details of the war. He finished the bottle of *schnapps* and didn't notice the two men leaving his caravan.

"What was so secret that he couldn't tell us?" Lars asked his brother as they drove through the gates of the caravan park. "And all that about not being able to discuss the massacres."

"Who knows!" Josef said with a shrug. "I hate this war stuff. Right now, I'm starving. Let's find a bistro with a view of the mountains and the magnificent scenery."

They ate and drank silently, absorbing their discussion with Weber. They were close as brothers now, but as Josef bit into his steak, he recalled early jealousies that had divided them. Lars was his mother's favourite. She smiled sweetly whenever Lars' name was mentioned. Josef was certain that she pretended to love her sons equally. Though she had taken him on outings without Lars hanging on as he did then, it was clear that he came second. It wasn't Lars' fault that he was the more handsome boy, easier to talk to and more charming. Lars was athletic too with fast, fluid movements, while Josef was artistic, contemplative, and not particularly sporty. However, Josef was his grandfather's favourite. His grandfather often muttered that Lars was muscle and no brain. Over the years, Lars blamed Josef for monopolising their grandfather and turning the old man against him. It was just as well that neither brother longed for their father's attention, Josef thought cynically. Their father was rarely home and didn't appear to be fond of either of them.

"Quite a pickle all of this," he said stroking his brother's arm.

"In some ways, I wish we'd never looked into it. There are some things I'd rather not know."

"It's too late now," Josef answered.

"Yeah bro, but at least we can get something out of this – see each other more often... don't you think?"

"Agreed. We've kept apart for too long," Josef added.

Beer cans clinked as the brothers toasted to the change.

After their drive home, they parted with tired goodbyes.

Chapter 51

Josef was well now and working full-time. He had almost forgotten the depression he'd suffered only months earlier. His reputation as an innovative architect producing unusual but structurally safe and functional buildings was growing rapidly. Now he could pick the projects that most interested him. He enjoyed his work and his enthusiasm filtered through to his team.

The retirement village Josef had designed was built. He was satisfied with the result and the residents appeared to be comfortable in their homes. He had just completed work on another project when a new client asked him to design a hotel on the peninsula. The client had secured a site with a breathtaking view of the waves caressing the rocks in gentle tides, but bashing against them when the weather was wild. He couldn't resist the scope this project offered. Soon after the client left he began scribbling ideas for a hotel that would blend into the environment. After months of drawing, he designed a building that melded with the cliffs and each of the rooms had a magnificent vista. The hotel would be nothing like some of the pink or orange eyesores that were presently overlooking the beach.

"Great to see you in top gear again, Joe," Tim said as they passed in the corridor. "The hotel will be something special!"

"Thanks, Tim. Yep, things are looking good." Josef replied rushing away.

Josef's enthusiasm and enjoyment of his work consumed him. He stayed back at the office when others in his team had left hours ago. Instead of relaxing, most weekends he worked instead of meeting his friends. He missed having Greta around but tried to push her out of his thoughts.

One summer's night, instead of joining his colleagues for drinks after work, he went home. He turned on the air-conditioning and lay on the couch exhausted. It was too hot for Bjon to sit close to him Alone and with no desire for music or television, he stretched out on the couch. He recognised the creeping flatness of his mood. Sleep was failing him and he hoped a beer might be relaxing. When it didn't have that effect, he turned to whisky. He emptied the bottle and his decline followed. He fooled himself into believing he could manage a trip to the liquor store for a new supply of whisky. Fortunately for him, a policeman cruising past in the lane next to him was too absorbed in other areas of crime to notice Josef's erratic driving. With the weekend to recover, he pulled himself out of his down mood sufficiently to return to work on Monday.

He knew had to see Carla.

When he phoned he was relieved when she answered.

"I hope you have a free appointment for me," he pleaded.

"I'm due to go away at the end of the week but I'll fit you in tomorrow," she said.

When her door opened, she smiled warmly. They sat and she opened her arms to encourage him to talk. He ran his hand through his hair and looked down.

"I've been feeling so flat for the last week. It feels like the depression is back."

"Are you eating and sleeping?" she asked.

"Not much as far as either go, and I'm so tired."

"It's a low patch. Let's try to nip it in the bud," she said.

"I hope so," he said uncertainly.

"I haven't seen you for a while. What's been happening in your life?"

"I'm working full time and some overtime now, trying to

finish off one project and get another even bigger one going. I've been enjoying it and it's been full on," he said.

"All of that sounds very stressful."

"Yes, it's taken all my concentration and energy to handle it, but I was doing well."

"Anything else happening?" she asked.

"Well, Greta left. I'm not sorry, but I am lonely and I'm too tired to go out – not interested either. And then there've been discussions with my father about my background. Lars and I visited Kristian and Hans Weber again and learned more nasty stuff about my grandfather. He lied so much."

"So much to deal with! I'm not surprised you've been stressed. It could've triggered this down mood."

"Finding out the worst about my grandfather is still eating away at me. I've been trying to put it aside and get on with my life, but I can't."

"It must be extremely tough for you, but remember that he loved you and wanted you to think well of him," she said gently.

"I feel tainted. Surely it bothered him. It must have since he kept it secret all these years."

"You are not responsible for your grandfather's actions, and actions do not flow from one generation to another. You will come to terms with it," she said emphatically.

He placed his hand on his forehead and sighed.

"It will take ages."

"Try to hold onto the positive moments spent with your grandfather and the important things you learned from him. These are the precious memories to remember."

"Maybe the precious moments will come later, I hope, but for now, I think I've done enough digging and I should put it aside. I know that," he replied.

"Indeed. Now that you know the facts, continually seeking more information about your grandfather doesn't seem to be helping you. It's a cliché, but time does help to put things into perspective. It will do that for you too."

He stared out of the window at the banking clouds.

Trite messages today! I hope to find some help from this session.

"The thought of being depressed again and not being able to work is scary," he said looking up at her. "And you'll be away?"

"Yes, we are going overseas, but you'll be fine without me."

"How do you know that? I'm not so sure," he said.

"You've learned a lot about yourself by now and how to cope. More than you think."

He shrugged and looked unconvinced.

"The way to avoid a recurrence is to be much more aware of any stress feelings you might have, especially from pushing yourself too hard at work. As we've discussed before, constant stress can trigger a depressive episode. You know those symptoms by now and you're are aware of stress building up inside yourself, so don't ignore it. You can't escape stress by working harder, drinking or pretending it's not happening. You'll need to take it seriously and slow down. It will be difficult, I know, as you're involved in many projects. Perhaps there is someone at work who you can chat with about it and change things to make it easier for you. We've talked about exercise helping too. "

He shook his head and sighed.

"It will be tough as I've been so productive at work during the past month or two and they'll expect more...but I will have to slow down. I can't risk falling in a heap again."

"You'll come through this, but in case you want to talk to someone while I'm away, I will leave a number to call on my answering machine. You won't be left without support."

He nodded as a rush of emotion surged in his chest.

He was quiet, absorbing her comment before speaking again. "Can I ask where you are going?"

"We are taking a holiday and then I will be tracing my roots in Germany," she said

"Germany?"

"Yes, my father and his family came from Regensburg."

He stared at her for a few moments unable to speak.

"How weird! I found out recently that my family are from a small town called Zwiesel. It's in Bavaria, near Regensburg.

He watched her twist her ring.

He didn't wait for her to comment and stood quickly.

"Enjoy your holiday," he said rushing out of the room.

Later he sank into the couch with Bjorn beside him. He patted the dog's head.

"We'll be fine, Sausage!"

Chapter 53

Steve and Carla boarded the plane. Steve had qualms about the trip they were about to begin. Carla was thrilled, but she did not show him a scrap more affection. Their lives had been virtually separate lately, connecting only for meals and public or family occasions, and now they were to spend all this time alone together.

He ran his hand through his newly, cut hair that he hoped made him look younger. The casual clothing he wore was expensive. When Carla commented on his modern image and said it suited him, he hoped she would find him more attractive. Perhaps the trip would bring them closer.

Once their seatbelts were buckled, Steve watched Carla settle into her seat and close her eyes. Her head on the small pillow moved when she was uncomfortable and her eyes opened briefly when food was served. He ate the unappetising meal of rubbery chicken. She pushed her meal aside and nibbled at the fruit and chocolate before her eyes snapped shut again. With her dark hair ruffled and a stray curl on her cheek, she looked almost child-like. The flight attendant who collected Carla's uneaten food asked Steve about Carla's health. Steve smiled and whispered back that she was fine, and that all she needed was rest.

During the long flight, Steve drifted in and out of troubled sleep. The anticipation of a long break from work and holiday in Europe had sustained him over the last days of madness at his office before leaving, but their plan to leave in autumn did not work out as hoped. It was now winter in Europe. Perhaps the trip could have been postponed until summer, but they needed a holiday and Carla was growing increasingly interested in her family background. A winter holiday was out of the tourist season. An incentive was lower costs and no crowds. They were to visit Paris, stopover in Frankfurt and then fly to Munich. From Munich on to Regensburg, the focus of their visit to Germany. The holiday would start for him once they left Germany with two weeks in Crete, with its warmer climate. Germany was the one place he would've preferred to avoid. He associated Germany with the Holocaust and had no desire to go there. If not for Carla's hankering to visit her father's and grandfather's birthplace, and graves, nothing could've induced him to visit the country. If she returned home satisfied that she had unravelled some of her family history, he was prepared to swallow his biases.

About ten years earlier, a genealogical researcher traced four generations of Steve's Lithuanian family back to a *shtetl* in the *Vilna* area. The following year, he stole a few days from a business trip overseas to visit Vilna, or Vilnius, as it is now known. He wandered through the old streets that bore traces of the community once renowned for a love of learning and Torah study, that had been destroyed in the war. A Holocaust survivor who had returned to the city was his tour guide. Her account of earlier Jewish life in the city and his visit to the only remaining synagogue still in use, corresponded with his parent's numerous stories. He recalled how he fell to the ground and sobbed in the *Ponary Woods* outside Vilna where in 1944 members of his family were rounded up by the Germans, forced into the woods and shot at the edge of a pit.

Nightmares plagued him for months after the trip and he was concerned that Carla could suffer as he had when confronting her family history. When he warned her, she spurned his warnings and answered that a brief period of discomfort was a small price to pay for tracing one's family.

It was not the best part of the year to visit Paris but the travel agent assured Steve that they would enjoy the intellectual

Paris that visitors rarely saw in the crowded, summer season. He provided Steve with a detailed list of museums, famous bookstores for browsing and historical landmarks to visit.

After the long journey, they arrived in Paris on a night when cold bit into their lined gloves and coats. Layers of clothing beneath their coats would've helped. The fairy-tale view along the Avenue Champs-Elysees glittering for Christmas with endless garlands of light was compensation for the cold. During grey days, it was the ideal place to unwind, and they ambled down the long boulevards dotted with leafless trees and spent hours in pavement café's warmed by braziers. The people they met appeared to be uncharacteristically patient and indulgent as Carla practised her schoolgirl French. In the busy Christmas markets, Steve noticed the dull tiredness on Carla's face change to rosy alertness. But they had no desire for intimacy in Paris, one of the most romantic of cities.

The morning they arrived in Frankfurt it was even colder than Paris. They planned to sleep over in Frankfurt, fly on to Munich for a few days, and then drive the short distance to Regensburg.

As they searched for a restaurant near their hotel, they wound their scarves tightly into their coats. They intended to take a city tour during the few hours they had in the city before their connecting flight to Munich, but once they had eaten and returned to the room for a warm shower, they slept until morning. Both were awake before dawn. As Steve flicked on the television searching for news in English, they moved closer to each other under the feather quilt. They held hands briefly and kissed.

As they returned to the airport, they drove past Frankfurt's new steel and glass buildings overlooking the river. The dark-suited, briefcase-carrying population and their black limousines were reminiscent of Wall Street. The magnificent older parts of the city bombed during the war had been rebuilt and there was almost nothing left of the once prosperous, Frankfurt Jewish community.

Neither talked during the brief flight to Munich. Steve looked at Carla and realised that she was no longer aware of him or her surroundings. She was in the past with her dead relatives, hoping to discover more about them and to be reunited in spirit with them. He shrank into his seat and waited for the plane to land.

At their hotel, they unpacked quickly. They had three days in Munich to see as much of the city as possible. Carla looked forward to discovering Munich's blend of the old and new. both in terms of architecture and lifestyle.

They left their hotel dressed warmly and walked the short distance to the city centre. At the *Marienplatz,* they shivered in the icy wind as they watched the famous *glockenspiel* chime the hour and life-sized statues re-enact sixteenth-century legends. Walking briskly, they explored the old city with its markets and feast of Gothic architecture. Among the throng of people were those in modern dress as well local men dressed in traditional *lederhosen,* as knee-length leather breeches.

The following day, they decided to take 'The Third Reich Tour.'

"After all, we are in the Nazi's birthplace and in the streets and squares where Hitler and his Brown Shirts walked. This was where Hitler gave his most persuasive speeches and grew his power base," Steve said.

They followed their guide to parts of the city that had been partially rebuilt after extensive air raids. Then in the famous drinking hall, the *Hofbrauhaus,* Steve imagined he heard the songs of Hitler's fanatic followers. At the *Platz der Opfer,* they stood before the eternal flame burning in memory of concentration camp victims. Overwhelmed by emotion, Carla's hand felt for Steve's. They agreed to leave the tour for a break and a hot drink.

After coffee, they visited the new Jewish Centre, a museum, synagogue and kindergarten, which opened in 2006. It was erected on the spot where the Nazis had demolished the city's original synagogue. The museum was packed with tourists and groups of schoolchildren showing interest in the exhibits.

"The people of Munich are trying hard to welcome back its Jewish community and to make amends," Carla said as they admired the new synagogue. There was a lot to see as they walked through the new buildings.

"Perhaps we can come back here if there's time. We're both tired and footsore," Carla said.

Steve nodded and swung his teary eyes from her vision.

"It's all magnificent with attention to detail, but the Germans can never make amends. This bears testimony to their guilt and it's a symbol of our survival. You're more tolerant than I am, Carla," Steve said brusquely as he tried to mask his raw hatred of Germans.

"Come on Steve, they are trying hard to right a terrible wrong."

She saw the stubbornness in his eyes as he tried to look away. That night after dinner, they lay on the bed in their hotel and discussed the day's touring. Neither told the other how deeply they were affected by being present at the foundation stones of evil perpetrated by Hitler's *Third Reich*. They talked broadly about places and people rather than about their feelings.

They woke early, hugged briefly and lay close. That next morning, they decided to split up for the day, before their pilgrimage to the *Dachau* Concentration Camp.

When Carla left, Steve was in bed catching up on sleep. She had the day to herself to marvel at the city's magnificent architecture. She intended to visit the *Npmhenburg Palace,* the summer residence of the last German Emperor, Wilhelm the Second. From her reading, she knew she was in for a treat. The train journey to the baroque palace was briefer than she anticipated. Its opulence, range of exquisite paintings, frescoes, porcelain and furniture was lovelier than any photograph she had seen in books. After viewing most of the palace with its exotic richness, she found a seat where she could enjoy the magnificent garden modelled on the Palace of Versailles.

Steve spent most of the day in the hotel room reading. He had no desire to see the city, though he hadn't admitted it to Carla. He was relaxed and pleased to see her when she returned for dinner. They ate in the hotel, and after watching American television they slept.

Chapter 54

When Steve woke it was morning and Carla was still asleep. Instead of waking her, he lay back against the pillows. They were due to visit *Dachau* Concentration Camp later that morning. The visit to the camp was their main reason for visiting Munich. He shuddered. The tour of Dachau would be unnerving. He would have to concentrate on Carla instead of himself during the tour. It was likely to upset her as several members of her extended family had died there. With that pain to carry, he thought her brave to visit the camp at all. He envied those of his friends who shook off the serious side of life.

After a small breakfast, they left the hotel and were caught up among the rush of city workers pouring from trains in their heavy overcoats. Groups gathered around vendors selling hot sausages, pretzels and coffee. The smell was tempting but they didn't stop. They followed the station's signs to *Dachau*. The train was packed with a variety of anxious-looking tourists. At the back of the carriage, a group of school children and their teachers huddled.

Carla's face was pale and drawn. Steve worried that she may buckle under the stress of visiting the camp. He noticed her watching him. He felt his tight jaw and presumed that she was aware of how anxious he was too. Her hand grasped his as the train chugged hypnotically.

"A concentration camp like *Dachau* only about ten miles outside the centre of Munich. Don't tell me that the German citizens didn't know what was happening under their noses?" Steve said as they passed through the medieval town.

"Look how well they have maintained the place for tourists," Carla said huskily, her voice full of emotion,

Steve shook his head. "I don't know how people can live here."

Neither mentioned the cattle trucks that had carried their victims to the camp or the walk for prisoners from the train to their fate at the camp.

After the bus ride from the station to the camp, Carla took Steve's hand again as they passed through iron gates that boldly proclaimed *Arbeid Macht Frei,* or work brings freedom. They joined the long queue at the starting point of the tour. Steve squeezed her shoulder to reassure her. After a wait, they were allotted to a group with a leader. They followed him over a pitted cement path and then entered the prison barracks.

"Heidrich Himmler built the camp in 1933 to house all those considered a danger or liability to the *Third Reich*," the guide said to the large group. He took a deep breath. "The camp was intended to be a model for the other German concentration camps that followed. Jews, gypsies, homosexuals, political radicals, the work-shy and repeat criminal offenders were incarcerated here as a source of slave labour." He hesitated, "They were also used as subjects for medical experimentation." He took another breath. "Most German communities had citizens placed in camps like this."

Steve tried to mask his horror as the guide continued describing how prisoners lived in fear of brutal treatment and death.

The guide pointed to the rusted barbed wire fences and watchtowers.

"If prisoners walked past this area they were shot on sight."

The group trudged on to inspect the areas associated with murder, from the gallows, crematorium to the so-called 'bathhouse' with gas pipes in the ceiling. The guide's words drifted past Steve as he attempted to steel himself against the rush of gruesome details and statistics. He was aware that he was among thousands of ghosts. One look at Carla and he could tell she was seeing them too.

"They are still here. All the skeletons," she whispered battling not to cry.

Behind them was a young German couple. Steve had noticed them in the train. The woman fumbled in her handbag for a tissue, wiped her eyes and felt for the man's hand. A group of school children were silent, the blush in their faces drained. One of the boys rushed from the group to vomit in a garbage can. Witnessing the boy's reaction to the horror resonated within him. At least others and the new generation were sickened as well.

Two Jewish bearded men dressed in black wearing large hats and their wives in sombre clothing stood near them. The women were in each other's arms weeping. The men tried to calm them. Steve caught the attention of one of the men. They were religious Jews from London, whose families had been prisoners in the camp. After a discussion, Steve and other Jewish men in the crowd made up the ten required for a *minion or* quorum. With their heads covered, the men stood before the crematorium and recited the *kaddish,* the ancient prayer for the dead.

They moved on to the museum where they looked at the display of ghastly photographs of suffering. Women grovelling for their lives, a young girl of four or five, her wispy curls caught in a top-notch, looked at them with eyes of dread. Young boys' faces were caught in screams. Steve turned away knowing that the faces would haunt his sleep.

When the sun peeked from the clouds, it sharpened the awfulness of the place. At the memorial erected for those who had died during their incarceration, they were confronted with a bizarre scene of guards attempting to remove two young women. The women had been lazing against the memorial wall with their heads back and shirts unbuttoned to catch the winter sunlight. Men and women spat and called them whores in different languages. The distressed guide apologised and then explained that during the year, swastikas were found scribbled on the wall. He maintained in upset tones that some visitors didn't understand the background of the camp and shouldn't be there. Once the women left yelling obscenities, a buzz of discussion followed. Carla and Steve stood silently before the wall, imprinted with the words 'Never again'.

"The murder of innocents on this earth is never going to end," Carla said wiping away her tears with her sleeve.

As they left the camp, Carla thought of her murdered relatives, and of Hannah, Anna Lisa and others from the aged home she visited, who had been in various concentration camps. No wonder they had nightmares, she thought.

Once their tour was over they left the camp as fast as possible and took a taxi from the station to their hotel. They had no desire to eat or do further sightseeing. Carla removed her warm clothing, kicked off her shoes lay on the bed. Steve joined her.

"That was one of Life's starkest lessons about evil and hatred," Steve said with a sigh.

"And it is about the importance of love and caring for those close to us," Carla added taking Steve's hand. "It is also about living each moment of every day to the fullest."

He nodded and put his arms around her. They hugged and kissed.

"I'm sorry, I've been self-absorbed lately and so exhausted from work that I withdrew from you. I should've told you how I was feeling," Carla said.

"I noticed, but didn't know how to push past your barrier. I tried everything except tell you how I felt. Crazy isn't it?"

"We have time to make up for it now," Carla said.

"Enough talk," he said putting his arms around her.

Chapter 55

With Carla away, Josef was anxious. When she was there and he could talk to her if he needed her, he was more relaxed. He paced in front of the television with the news blaring but he didn't hear it. He was locked into a worried place as he scratched his head agitatedly.

I have to get out of the house or I'll drink myself into a stupor and won't be able to work, he muttered to himself.

It was a warm Saturday morning. He grabbed his car keys. He drove past a local shopping centre, busy with customers stocking up for the weekend and then towards the inner city. With no aim or place in mind, he took the busy Freeway, crossed the Yarra River that divided the city and drove on. He realised that he was near the suburb of Caulfield, where many Jewish people lived. He knew some Jews from his work – partners in his firm and clients. They were pleasant people and he couldn't think of one he disliked. He wanted to know more about the suburb and drove towards the main shopping strip. It was the Sabbath, and almost all the shops were closed for trading. Jewish, shop owners compensated for any losses by opening on Sunday, a busy shopping day in the suburb. The traffic was so heavy that he turned off the main road. Driving slowly, he noticed throngs of men dressed in black suits and wearing black hats. The women wore modern but modest clothing. Families walked together proudly and young friends laughed and giggled. He wondered where they were all going. He didn't have to wait long for his answer. He noticed an old synagogue with people entering. Some of the crowd walked around the corner to enter a large, more modern synagogue in the next street. He thought about the many families and wondered where their ancestry lay – Poland, Lithuania, France, Germany or elsewhere. Was it possible that his grandfather had killed some of the grandparents, uncles, aunts and cousins of these people? The thought sickened him and tears rolled down his face.

Josef's withdrew from his colleagues. He found excuses for discussions and avoided meeting with them or relaxing after work with drinks. His previous high energy levels slipped and his mood was despondent. Most mornings he struggled to get out of bed, found his concentration deteriorating and he was drinking too much. He realised that he was teetering on the edge of depression. Though Carla was away, he heard her voice in his head asking him if he was eating well and able to sleep. The truth was he was sleeping little and barely bothering to eat. He didn't want to phone any of the psychologists who were mentioned on Carla's answering phone. He told himself that Carla had taught him how to pull himself out of his down mood and that he would use the tools she had given him to help himself.

He struggled as he forced himself to eat nutritious food and exercise. With Carla's voice in his head, he lowered his work pace and took short breaks when he could. With Tim's approval, he began to delegate tasks to a group of young architects he called his team. As a result, he was calmer. Work was completed on time and Tim and the other partners had no complaints about the team he had amassed to assist him. He smiled when he thought of how he had changed his approach for the better.

After work, he and Anders met regularly at the Viking restaurant. His friend usually had a tale to share about the new people he was meeting at Viking reenactments. Josef hadn't been to one of the Viking reenactments and had no desire to attend them.

"My life has changed now that I believe I have a Viking

connection. I feel stronger inside and I'm handling work far better," Anders said. "You should look into your background on your mother's side. With her name and family background, your Viking ancestry is possible."

"It is fascinating but not at the moment. I'd rather hear you talk about your findings."

"I'm sure you'll eventually change your mind," Anders replied.

"I have enough to deal with now, but your Viking talk has given me ideas for redecorating my house. It is too boring and characterless," Josef said with a smile.

"Great, I can't wait to see the changes."

Chapter 56

The visit to Regensburg was the focus of the overseas trip for Carla. Before they left for the trip, she managed to do only basic genealogical research. She tried to lower her expectations of finding out about her family. Steve warned her kindly that the visit might not provide the answers she hoped for in tracing her family records.

When Steve employed a genealogical researcher, he was only able to trace four generations of his family until the nineteenth century, when Jews were required to have surnames for government record keeping. Tax records established that Steve's great, great grandfather, Yehuda Rosenzweig and his family were originally from Germany and left for Vilnius (Vilna) in Lithuania. Jews in this region during the eighteenth century and into the nineteenth, experienced years of intellectual growth, learning and a thriving culture. There were periods of persecution in Vilna, but his family survived until the Holocaust when most of his extended family were killed. He gave up his search when he could find no further information about his family.

The bus trip from Munich to Regensburg took about an hour. It was an opportunity to unwind after the morning's rush to pack and leave the hotel. Carla watched Steve's eyes close. Like her, since the visit to Dachau, he was emotionally spent. She understood that his presence on the tour had been for her.

Sitting opposite them in the bus was an old blue-eyed man with sprouts of silvery hair. He put down his newspaper and smiled at Carla. She returned the smile but less enthusiastically, and gave her attention to the cover of a brochure about Regensburg.

Josef's description of his Nazi grandfather wafted back to her. How could she blame him for being distressed? After what she had seen and read of the Holocaust, having a Nazi in one's family would be appalling. Fleetingly, she thought of her sessions with Josef and wondered if he was well and coping with his work. It was uncanny that their families came from the same region in Germany.

As the bus neared Regensburg, Steve sat up insistent that he was relaxing with his eyes closed. From the bus depot, they took a cab to their hotel.

"Isn't it a magnificent city? Dad told me that it was one of the oldest, medieval cities in Germany. I can understand now where his appreciation of art and architecture came from," Carla said excitedly.

The cab driver proudly pointed out the gothic spires of churches, both Catholic and Protestant. In the hotel room after unpacking, Carla stared out of the window at the view of old rooftops and the gothic spire of the cathedral, the *Regensburger Dom.*

The following morning, they met Carla's genealogical researcher, Frau Maria Ebert, at a coffee shop opposite their hotel. From the tone of Maria's letters, Carla expected an older, plump, bespectacled woman, but Maria was a slim, leggy blonde of about thirty, a student in Jewish history at the Regensburg University. In surprisingly good English she explained that she had made progress in tracing Carla's grandfather, Abraham Langermann. His birth was recorded in Regensburg as well as his attendance at a technical school in Munich. She even had a copy of the high grades he received.

"I'm glad to tell you that your grandfather's tombstone is intact in the Jewish Cemetery. Some tombstones have crumbled over the years or were vandalised. Unfortunately, your grandmother's stone is rubble now. What a pity that there's so little about her. I do have some details - a marriage certificate between your grandfather and Helana Horvath and the registration of the births of four sons. The youngest son, Gershom, is of course your father. There are records too of taxes that your grandfather paid to the state of Bavaria."

"That's great!" Carla said excitedly.

Maria pulled a folder from her large bag and opened it. She placed photocopied pages on the table. The relevant names and dates had ticks beside them.

While they were reading, Maria waved to the waiter.

"*Kaffee und apfelstrudel*," she called.

Carla put up her hand to stop Maria, but her protest was ignored.

"These records are amazing," Carla said as she ran her finger over the Langermann name on the documents.

"A great feeling, darling?" Steve said and placed his hand on her arm.

"It's probably too much to hope for, but is there any information about my great, great grandfather, Yehudah?" Carla said and pursed her lips uncertainly.

"There's evidence that he lived here. His date of birth was 1788 and his death in 1848 is registered. I found out something interesting," Maria said, "Since your father and his older brother studied art at the Polytechnic in Munich before they left Germany in 1934, I thought that artistic ability might have run in the family. So I checked the lists of artist's guilds and though I found nothing for your grandfather, your great grandfather, Isaac Langermann was listed in 1805 as a silversmith."

Carla smiled broadly. "That's an amazing find!"

Maria tapped the table gently.

"I searched, but unfortunately I couldn't find any earlier records of Langermanns in Regensburg or in the area around here before that. Perhaps your family lived elsewhere before they came to Bavaria, possibly Eastern Europe. I'm sorry to disappoint you."

"No, not at all. You've done well, so thank you," Carla said with a pleased smile.

"I'll leave copies of the documents with you to study later," Maria said as she edged out of her chair. "Come! You must see something of Regensburg. I'll leave my car here and we'll walk. It's walking only in the old city."

Steve stood quickly and stretched.

"Let's get going," he said.

The streets were packed with tourists and locals out to enjoy the Christmas atmosphere with the carol singers, markets and tinsel. As Maria walked she talked fast and often. It was hard to hear her above the human throb in the streets as she provided detailed historical, religious and artistic information. They joined a crowd gathered around the dominant twin towers of the ancient, gothic Regensburg Cathedral. Carla gasped at the richly ornamented arches and canopies. When they moved on, Steve pointed to small gold plaques on houses and footpaths.

"We saw something similar in Munich," he said.

"They are in remembrance of Jewish people who lived in those houses and lost their lives in the Holocaust," Maria explained.

"It's an excellent way of remembering and I hope that all the tourists notice them," Steve said.

"The German government is trying to do the right thing," Carla insisted.

"They are, but unfortunately it isn't stopping anti-Semitism springing up in Germany and Europe," Maria added.

"How bad is it?" Steve asked.

Maria shook her head worriedly. "It's awful. From reports in recent years, criminal offences, including acts of violence against Jews and Jewish institutions in Germany have increased significantly."

They followed Maria through the crowds as she led them down an alley to a house with a white wall.

"This was Oskar Schindler's house," she said. "I thought you'd be interested in seeing it."

They looked at the red plaque commemorating the man who had risked his life to save more than a thousand Jews in his factories in Poland. He returned to Germany and lived in this house between 1935 and 1950. They stood discussing Oskar Schindler for a while and moved on towards the stone bridge that spanned the Danube, built in the twelfth century.

At the medieval bridge, Maria explained," This bridge opened the way for new trading routes to Europe. The city flourished and the city's golden age as a residence of wealthy merchant families began. Regensburg was celebrated as the cultural centre of Southern Germany."

"Were there many Jewish traders then?" Steve asked.

"Oh, yes, there were Jews who settled here at the beginning of the Eleventh Century and many travelled across Europe buying and selling their wares. Jewish traders were important to the city's commercial development."

Maria steered Carla away from the market stalls selling everything from food to handmade gifts and trinkets.

"There'll be time for the markets later. Let's walk to the centre of the old city, the *Neupfarrplaz*. We'll have something to eat and drink and I'll tell you about the Jewish history of Regensburg."

Steve grumbled about the crowds but stopped complaining when they reached a corner stall rich in exotic aromas – a mix of coffee, wine, spices and sausages.

"Steve, find a table if you can, while I stand in the food queue," Maria suggested. They found a table and waved to Maria. She joined them laden with sausages, small pastries and coffee.

"You must try the *Gluhwein* or mulled wine," she said. "It will warm you up."

"Later, right now we need strong coffee." Steve said. "

They began to taste the delicacies Maria had bought.

"Delicious, a marvellous idea!" Carla said with her mouth full of pastry.

"I have a long story to tell you but I'll try to stick to the main points," Maria said, pushing her plate aside. "One of the first documented Jewish communities was here in Regensburg. Jews lived peacefully with their Christian neighbours until the start of the Crusades changed their lives. They became subjects of the Holy Roman Empire. Their movements were restricted and they were prevented from pursuing their former occupations. Viewed as non-believers, Jews were isolated from the rest of the community in locked ghettos"

Steve held up his hand to stop the history lesson.

"Enough for now. I'm starving," he said as he tucked into the rest of his food.

After they had eaten, they walked over the crowded cobbled streets while Maria attempted to continue her story.

"By the twelfth and thirteenth centuries, Jewish learning reached a peak. Synagogues, a Talmudic School, hospital, cemetery and ritual bath existed. But From the mid 13th Century life deteriorated for Jews again with limitations on their movement and trade."

"Didn't they flee from persecution following the Black Death in the late thirteenth century?" Steve asked.

"Indeed, and when Emperor Maximillian who had protected Jews died in 1519, they were blamed for the country's economic woes, and hounded out of the city and from Germany.

"The blame has been going on for so long and seems to never end," Carla said looking at Steve.

Steve took Carla's hand.

"That's why they were always on the move. Many fled to Lithuania and Poland due to the attacks on Jews or *pogroms*," Steve said.

"It's possible, Carla, that is the reason there is no trace of your family before your great-grandfather Yehudah Langermann. Your family may have been fleeing pogroms."

"Yes, it is possible," Carla replied.

"I'll contact my friend Eugenia who researches Eastern European families and ask her to look into it for us. Perhaps she can tell us more about your family links elsewhere in Europe. It's too early to give up the search." She touched the side of her glasses and looked up at the sun edging from behind dark clouds. "It looks like we'll have more snow before Christmas and a lot of carol singers."

They continued walking over the cobblestones until Maria stopped again and pointed. "Right here the garrison of the Roman army was housed and later the Jewish ghetto was built over the Roman ruins," she said pointing downwards on the grey slabs. "It's what is left of Jewish Regensburg after it was destroyed in 1519. We should return tomorrow so that you can have a look at the excavation of the Jewish quarter."

Carla was tired. She wanted to return to the hotel, but Maria insisted on completing her story.

"I'm exhausted," Carla protested.

"Just a bit more before you go back to your hotel. You need to know as much as possible."

Carla smiled. "Okay."

"Well, by the seventeenth century, the status of Jews in Germany changed. Their value was recognised and after the French Revolution, they were given citizenship and a new urban professional class developed." She coughed and looked down. "But once again anti-Semitism reared its head. The poor economic situation in the country was perfect for Hitler to look for a scapegoat and to blame the Jews for Germany's troubles and persecute them once more."

Maria stopped walking and lifted her hand. "This is *Neupharrplaz*," she announced, as they entered the square shimmering with lights and buzzing with tourists buying last-minute Christmas gifts. Snow was falling as they passed a group of children singing Christmas carols and they stopped to listen. The temperature had dropped and they shivered.

"It's dark now and we've covered so much. I'll send you an email outlining the main points I have talked about today and you can read it at leisure," Maria said.

"Thank you, an excellent idea," Carla agreed and started to walk away. Maria gave them a recommendation for a restaurant for dinner and left with instructions on where to meet the following day. As they made their way to the restaurant, Steve took Carla's hand and squeezed it.

"I'll admit that I was wrong being negative about coming here. Maria has been amazingly knowledgeable, and the people are friendly."

They found the recommended bistro and dinner was pleasantly relaxing. The restaurant owner spoke English amongst other languages and ensured that they chose well from the menu.

"I've been thinking of our children and grandkids. Deanne sent me a gorgeous photo of the children. All must be fine." Carla delved into her bag for her phone. "Look," she said to Steve.

"A great picture, but I'm enjoying the quiet without them," Steve said.

They took a brief walk before returning to the hotel. Steve slept immediately, but Carla's mind was too alert for sleep. She left her bed and pulled back the curtains to stare at the blanketed city. The streetlights and moonlight combined to cast a sheen over the rooftops of distant houses.

Chapter 57

Carla and Steve trudged through the fresh snow to the café on the square where they arranged to meet Maria. It was early and they had not eaten breakfast. Carla was biting into a fluffy croissant with jam when Maria arrived.

"We haven't much time and more to do," Maria's voice had a serious tone. "I hope you're finding our brief tour is giving you the background to your family that you wanted and answering some of your questions."

"I didn't have high expectations," Carla replied.

"I wish I could tell you more about your grandmother and her side of the family." She flicked her fringe from her forehead. "It's not knowing that leaves one uneasy."

"It sounds as if you speak from experience," Steve said.

Maria examined her pink, polished nails that shone in the light.

"My Jewish grandfather married my Omi, my grandmother, a non-Jew, just before the war. He's been dead for ages, but my Omi is still alive, thank God."

"Oh, that couldn't have been easy for them,' Carla said surprised by Maria's revelation.

"In 1943 they were living in Berlin when German police rounded up a large group of Jewish males married to non-Jewish partners and the male children of these so-called mixed marriages and held them in a community centre in Rossenstrasse. There was talk that the Germans would send their loved ones to Auschwitz. The wives and mothers of the men were furious. My grandma says that the women were so angry that they demonstrated outside the building for days in the icy cold until their family members were released."

"That's very brave," Carla said.

"If they were anything like my Omi they must've been a frightening bunch waving their fists at the Gestapo."

They laughed at the image of angry women.

"It is different when one knows how it feels." She looked down, removed her glasses and ran her hand past her eyes. "There's hardly anyone left from the Jewish side of my family. Most of them perished in the camps."

"I'm so sorry." Carla paused before continuing. "Doing this work must rub the wounds."

"In a way it helps," Maria said managing half a smile. Her professional face was back. She felt for her coat on the back of her chair, buttoned it up to her chin and wrapped her scarf around her neck.

"When you're both ready, we'll go back to *Neupfarrplaz* to see the archaeological finds of the old Jewish quarter and the museum."

"It should be interesting," Carla said.

The streets were teeming with sightseers and people buying gifts from market stalls, but Maria knew shortcuts to avoid the crowds.

"Hold on to me," Steve said as he took Carla's hand. "We don't want to be separated in this crowd."

At the north side of the square, they followed others through a doorway and down a staircase that led to the excavations. Then they joined a group with a leader who continued the tour.

"Extensive archaeological excavations were carried out here in Regensburg between 1995 and 1998," the tour leader said. "Layers documenting stages in the history of this place were uncovered, revealing the site of ruins of Roman officers' lodgings and the medieval Jewish quarter." He pointed to the foundations of two Jewish Synagogues and houses. Then they entered the remains of a Jewish merchant's family basement where spices, necessary food and valuables were once stored.

After the tour, they stood in line to watch a computer-generated video developed by archaeologists, that gave an impression of the ghetto and main synagogue all those years ago.

"It's all too fast for me and too much to absorb. I would've like to stay down here for longer, see it all again and explore," Carla whispered to Steve.

"Me too, but we can't stay with such a crowd queuing to come in," Steve said putting his hand on her arm.

"It's interesting. I'm glad you brought us here, Maria," Steve said. "It makes medieval Jewish life come alive."

Maria glanced at her watch.

"We'll have to move on if we want to go to the Jewish cemetery."

The cemetery was a short drive from the centre of Regensburg. In the open, the cold was unrelenting but at least snow wasn't falling.

"The original Medieval Jewish cemetery built around 1210 was destroyed in 1519 along with the ghetto. Many tombstones were stolen to build houses, but a few remained. This part of the cemetery was rebuilt in 1822. Carla, it is here that your grandfather was buried. Usually, it is closed but the warden opened it for us."

Skeletal trees shaded the tombstones that remained. Some families must have replaced the headstones with new marble. Maria found Carla's grandfather's grave. The tall headstone was covered in ivy and dirt. His name in Hebrew and German was barely legible. Carla wiped away tears before she and Steve cleared away the ivy and some of the dirt. Steve put his arm around Carla's shoulders and then walked away leaving her alone before her grandfather's grave. She followed the custom of placing pebbles on the grave, then brushed away more tears and whispered to him. Too cold for a walk around the cemetery, they hurried back to Maria's heated car.

After a brief tour of newer parts of the city, Maria parked near their hotel. In the warm hotel lobby, they sat in a row on the stiff sofa to recap their days of discovery. Carla had grown fond of the kind-hearted woman who had shown her something of her family's past.

"I feel sad when I say goodbye to people who have come here expecting to recover something of their family out of the rubble of destruction,"Maria said as she flicked a stray hair from her face and adjusted her glasses. "Sometimes there is little to give them. At least you found something about your family here and you will have memories to take home from Regensburg."

Before Maria left, she gave them the address of the new Regensburg Synagogue. It was Friday afternoon and the wintry sun coaxed in the Sabbath. They took a taxi to the synagogue through streets decked for Christmas. Early for the service, they stood to the side of the entrance watching the congregation arrive. It was a small community but a close one, greeting each other with handshakes, kisses and good wishes for the Sabbath. Soon Carla and Steve were noticed by the locals and after an initial attempt to communicate with them in German, a man who spoke English approached them. Laboriously he provided excessive information about the community and the synagogue. He helped Steve to a seat near the ark and his wife showed Carla to a seat upstairs with the women. If not for the words in German, the ancient Hebrew chants and melodies were similar to those they were accustomed to at home.

At the end of the service, they were introduced to the Rabbi, a young American, who had German parents and regarded his placement as an honour. They had several invitations for dinner that night, but they accepted the invitation from the most insistent couple - Gerhard and Thea Goodman who had three children at school. Both Gerhard and Thea spoke English. Their children who learned English at school filled in any misunderstandings where necessary. Once the Sabbath rituals were over, they ate a meal so well prepared and delicious that they both ate far too much. Watching and listening to the Goodman's young children made Carla think of their grandchildren, Jason and David. When the children went to bed, the adults sat in the formal lounge for cake and coffee. Gerhard put his cup down and faced the couple.

"I guess you'll want to know why we returned to Germany after all that has happened to us Jews here?"

"I find it difficult to understand," Steve admitted.

"It is not easy to answer, but I will try. We are Jews but culturally we are Germans and our identity is here. We are comfortable speaking German, we like the style of food, the way of life and the old buildings we grew up with. We were in America for three years and Thea was unhappy so we returned. No matter what the Nazis did to our people they couldn't take our feeling of belonging here away."

"It must be difficult. You are reminded of the terrible things that occurred, even here in Regensburg. It's all around you."

"Over the centuries, there has been anti-Semitism and persecution of Jews in almost every country of the world and it is still going on. We have plenty neo-Nazi's here and gentiles who resent us, but we ignore them."

"But...," Carla tried to interrupt.

"Many members of the new generation of Germans feel guilty about their past and have been accepting and positive towards us. They show interest in us as people, in our religion and are respectful and friendly. They have helped many Russian Jews and others to find a home here. The government has spent a fortune trying to make amends, but no matter how many synagogues they build or plaques they erect in remembrance of events of horror they cannot rub it out," Thea said.

"I know I am repeating myself, but I would have difficulty coming to terms with living here," Steve said.

"Steve, remember we weren't born here and this has not

been the culture we grew up with. It makes a huge difference," Carla added.

"You are lucky to have a Jewish identity in Australia," Thea said.

"Yes, we are lucky," Carla replied, as she smoothed wrinkles on her skirt.

"For us, we have the satisfaction that we can live here knowing that we are a reminder of the horrors of the past and a sign that we cannot be eradicated," Gerhard said emphatically.

They talked for a while, thanked the Goodman's for their hospitality and left early pleading tiredness. In the taxi back to their hotel they chatted briefly about the evening spent.

"You looked amazing tonight," Steve said as he squeezed Carla's hand. I couldn't take my eyes off you and neither could Gerhard."

They moved closer and hugged.

One more day in Regensburg. Steve went to the museum and left Carla to wander through the cobbled streets. She followed a path along the ancient bridge where she heard childish laughter and older children urging little ones along. She touched the stones smoothed by hands through the years and placed her fingers in the same cracks others had touched before her. She walked through the labyrinth of the old streets decorated with Christmas green and red wreaths and past historically important buildings. The smell of the damp, mossy stones, the aroma of chestnuts roasting, and bratwurst sold on corners filled the air. She followed the children's laughter with each step, sensing them in front, to the side and behind her, as she explored the old city. She stopped at market stalls admiring the wares. Deanne would love the market with their craft products and trinkets, she thought. One stall sold unusual candlesticks and a *menorah* as well as embroidered tablecloths and doilies. She had bought few souvenirs during the trip and considered buying some of the attractive items for herself and gifts for her children and grandchildren. She talked to the stall owner who turned out to be half Jewish with generations of her family who had lived in the city. She chose carefully from the array displayed and the woman packed each item carefully so that it would not be damaged during travel. As she walked on enjoying discovering the city, it was only when her aching feet halted her, that she knew she was forced to rest.

After a coffee at a busy café, she followed a different path back to the hotel. As she walked, she noticed an intersection with road signs displaying directions to nearby towns. One of the towns was *Zwiesel*. Immediately she thought of Josef and the town where his family had lived for generations. She was thinking how uncanny their connection was when she found herself outside her hotel.

Steve had arrived at the hotel earlier. He was relaxing on the bed in a white towelling gown the hotel provided.

"You look exhausted, and I see you've been shopping," he said with a grin.

Carla kicked off her shoes and put her parcels in the corner of the small room. I'll have a shower and then join you. The shower was soothing and relaxing. She wrapped her body in a towelling gown and with a sigh almost fell on the bed.

"Tired but happy," Steve said and kissed her.

"I had a great time wandering around the city. And you? Did you enjoy yourself?"

"You know how much I like history. I must've spent three hours at the historical museum – wonderful exhibits of Regensburg's Roman and Medieval history. It was a treat for me. I doubt you would've enjoyed it."

"This is a fascinating city," she said.

"Enough about the city for now," he said, pulling at her gown's cord. "Let's slip under the covers."

All her tiredness was gone as they embraced.

Chapter 58

Early the following morning, they left Regensburg and travelled back to Munich by train. After a sleepover in Munich, they flew on to Athens. They intended to spend two days in Athens before their holiday in Crete. During the flight, they talked little and slept. After landing, a wild cabbie drove them to their hotel.

Steve watched Carla's delight when they entered the luxurious, heritage hotel he had chosen. It was old-fashioned with a lobby in marble and wood and a view of the Acropolis from their balcony. In the milder climate of Athens, they discarded their heavy coats for jackets. They behaved like tourists, visited the Acropolis and strolled through the festively decorated streets eating ice cream to the sounds of carols. They stopped to gaze into shops packed with last-minute Christmas shoppers. Carla couldn't resist the street markets and bought more trinkets.

Though the hotel was costly, it did not concern Steve. He wanted the best for Carla, and for her to relish the luxury. She was looking happy and relaxed, he thought. The visit to Regensburg had answered most of her questions and he hoped that the trip to Germany would leave her with valuable memories.

They relaxed and Carla cuddled closer.

"Hello, there, you're with me again," he whispered.

They looked at each other and then without a word hugged so tightly that Carla began to cough. He touched her face outlining her cheekbones with his forefinger, her mouth and then her eyebrows. Taking her chin in his hand he pulled her towards him and kissed her.

The ferry for Crete departed from the harbour at Piraeus at sunset. They chose Crete from all the islands for its warmer climate and interesting scenery. Winter was off-season for tourists and that suited them. From the deck of the ferry, they watched brilliantly coloured ribbons streak the sky, the sea turn purple and then become black. They ate the meal offered onboard and holding hands, hurried back to their cabin-like teenagers.

"This is romantic, like a second honeymoon," Carla said as she planted a kiss on Steve's forehead.

"It certainly is," he replied with a smile.

As the ferry neared the ancient port of Chania the next morning, they viewed rows of ancient buildings and a castle against a backdrop of mountains peaked with snow. After disembarking, a taxi drove them to their hillside villa. Steve had chosen the privacy of a villa instead of a hotel. The white-walled building was set on the slope of a hill with an uninterrupted view of the sea. The days were sunny and they lived like the locals, eating simply. On cooler evenings, they ate at one of the many tavernas and then hurried home. They lit fires and like children watched the flames change colour.

Most mornings, when the weather was pleasant they walked along the nearest beach, with its warm shallow water and broken shells. They held hands stopping for an occasional kiss. In the afternoons they drove a hired car to other parts of the island. They stepped back in time when they visited the old harbour and its rows of double-storey Venetian houses. In the old town, they wandered through narrow alleys and pedestrian streets. They stopped for coffee at a café along the harbour's wall. The café was becoming a favourite.

Steve took Carla's hand and kissed it.

"I'm sorry that I've taken you to yet another place with a dark, Jewish history. We don't seem to be able to escape it."

"The Germans have left their mark in Greece and on the islands as well," Carla said sadly.

"They invaded Crete in 1941 in a massive airborne operation but were received with stiff resistance. The Cretans paid with brutal murders and the destruction of their villages," Steve said with a sigh. "There was a flourishing Jewish population here in Cania when the Nazis invaded Crete. Jews were rounded up together with local dissidents and imprisoned. Then all were herded onto a ship headed for Auschwitz. But the ship was torpedoed and sank killing them all."

"How sad," Carla said. "An awful way to die."

"It's sad to think that once there were two synagogues here that were destroyed by the locals. But on the positive side, *The Etz Hayim Synagogue* has been recently restored," Steve said.

"Let's have a look at it," Carla suggested.

After a short walk through the remains of the old Jewish Quarter, they reached a white-walled, Greco Roman synagogue. After passing through a gate with Hebrew lettering, they toured the building with a guide. He mentioned that the synagogue was now active and held weekly services. Most holidays were celebrated and there were concerts and cultural programs as well.

"It's great to see the restoration of Jewish sites is taking place here and in Europe, so many years after they've been destroyed. The generation before us couldn't face it. Now it's the work of our generation and the next," Steve said taking Carla's hand.

The rest of the holiday slipped by quickly as they talked and laughed more than they had for the five years since their children had left the house to marry. They had so much to catch up on. They reverted to the friendly intimacy of years past. They made love often and unhurriedly, remembering how frantic it once was.

Steve lay back in an easy chair pretending to be asleep. He was relaxed and happy – happier than he could remember being for years. The break had been enjoyable, but even more important, it had helped to mend their broken connection. Their eyes met when they touched and they listened to each other with interest.

Carla's love for Steve had returned. It was noticeable in the way she smiled at him, but it was in their lovemaking that he noticed the biggest changes. He smiled to himself, thinking that the trip had been a great idea.

Carla sat on the balcony of the villa sipping a glass of wine as she looked dreamily at the shadows forming over the sea. While the trip to Germany was harrowing in parts, discovering all she could about her family's roots gave substance to her view of herself. She had a stronger sense of who she was now. The holiday in Crete was a magical time spent together. The days passed quickly and she was happier than she had been for months. It was Steve who recognised her need for the trip to Germany followed by a romantic holiday. She smiled. She was the psychologist and Steve was more practical. Their relationship needed mending and he went about restoring it in his methodical style. In her counselling, she helped her clients to find their way, but in her life, she knew she could be trapped by her feelings blocking her from taking action.

She thought about how much they had both changed since they married. This was an ideal opportunity to discover each other again. The passion that seemed to have died during their long and stressful work hours was back. She smiled as she thought of how often they touched, kissed and make love. After months without sex, they were making up for it.

If she wanted her newfound joy to continue when they were home, she would have to make changes. She would cut her work hours to ensure she had more freedom for herself and Steve, and more time for her grandchildren. If only she could provide her grandchildren with the loving support that her grandmother had given her.

The air was suddenly cooler as the sun seemed to slip into the ocean when Steve called, "It's almost dinner time, aren't you coming inside?"

"In a few moments. I'm enjoying the sunset."

"Do you want to eat at the taverna or stay in tonight?" he asked.

"Light the fire and let's stay home," she replied. "I'll rustle up some dinner."

She found Steve rubbing his hands before the roaring fire.

"It's so warm in here. Where did you learn to light such great fires?" she asked.

"We had a fireplace in our house when I was a child. Lighting it was my job."

She put her arms around him and they hugged.

"Love you," she said as she kissed him. Within minutes they moved to the couch.

Chapter 59

Josef was tired of thinking about his grandfather. Not knowing secrets about him that Hans Weber refused to divulge, was a constant irritation. Every step of the unravelling of his grandfather's past had been thorny. He decided on a final attempt to discover the truth from Kristian. This time Lars joined him but he couldn't bring himself to take the old man any gifts. Kristian was not in the sitting room or seated around the poker table when they arrived.

"He's ill and in bed," a nurse said brusquely. "I don't want you upsetting him, but I suppose he might enjoy visitors. Knock on his door but please don't stay long."

When Josef knocked on Kristian's door, he gave their names.

"Come in," Kristian called in a raspy voice. "You've come to see an old man on his deathbed?"

Josef could not hide his shock. Kristian's face was puce and mottled.

"I'm recovering from pneumonia. At least they tell me I'm recovering. I refused to stay in the hospital a moment longer."He coughed and spat into a tissue.

Josef turned away. Lars screwed up his face in disgust.

"Not pretty, eh?" He pulled himself up on his pillows. "You're lucky to find me here, I almost didn't make it."

Josef looked down unable to make an empathic comment.

"We want to hear the truth from you - all the truth!" Josef said raising his voice.

"What more do you two want to know? I haven't the energy to mess about." He coughed as if to empathise his point.

"I'll get straight to it," Josef said. "We met with Hans Weber, your mate in the mountains. He told me about our grandfather's role as a soldier for the Third Reich. He mentioned the iron cross he won for bravery and hinted that my grandfather had carried out another act of courage. He claimed that the information was secret, and he couldn't divulge it."

Kristian sneered cynically.

Josef made a fist and thumped the bedside table.

"Weber gave us the story that he was forbidden to talk about it. I'm tired of all this closet stuff. Now I'm asking you to finally tell us the truth."

"Calm down! I don't need such excitability in my fragile condition."

"Well, get on with the truth and you won't see us again."

"First bring me water and extra pillows from the cupboard."

Josef handed Kristian the glass of water and the pillows. They put their chairs next to the bed.

The old man wheezed as he began to speak, "Early in the winter of 1945, it was so cold that the ground froze and the rivers became solid. The German army was *kaputt*, overpowered by the Russians. I was posted out to assist them, but it was too late for intelligence connections to help. We were in such bad shape that some men gave up and were talking about deserting." He sipped more water. "I hope you two realise that you are killing me with your questions."

"You are doing okay so far," Lars said with a sneer.

"One night the temperature dropped further. Our platoon captain thought that another freezing night was too much for the troops to endure. He gave Erik and me an order to drive a few miles down the road where he'd seen a small farm with a barn that he hoped would provide cover for the night and that there might be chickens or pigs to slaughter." Kristian's rasping voice was so soft that the two bent forward to hear him. "The major ordered me to join Erik. "Wipe out the peasants, check out the farm and come back immediately, were his orders."

Kristian coughed again and paused for another sip of water before speaking again, "It was almost dark when we reached the farm. There were about fifteen adults and their children cooking over a fire. I was starving and the smell of their food nearly drove me crazy. We noticed that the barn was large and had straw for warmth. Erik said, 'I refuse to kill them. There has been too much killing. They haven't done us any harm.' He told me to keep my trap shut if I didn't agree, and called out to the peasants warning them that the army would be moving in. 'Get out! Run!' he yelled, as he fired several rounds into the air. Then we drove back to camp. 'The peasants are dead, lying in the fields and the barn will be big enough for us, Erik told the Major.'"

He sipped more water before he continued, "I would've killed them all without a thought, but not Erik."

Josef nodded thoughtfully as Kristen's head dropped onto his pillow.

"You're making out that my grandfather was a saint," Josef said, his voice rising. "We need to know the truth about him. Weber refused to tell us if he was involved in the dreadful massacres of the Jews in Eastern Europe."

Kristian put his hands to his ears.

"Don't yell at me, I'll tell you," he said with a sigh. "Many German soldiers were involved in killing the Jews and others in villages. Sometimes it seemed as if the countryside was an abattoir."

Josef shuddered.

Kristian was breathing heavily now.

"Out with it, Kristian, you're dodging the question. What about our grandfather," Lars snapped.

"You asked for it." He paused and then coughed. "Erik and Hans Weber belonged to the *Einsatzgruppen* or task forces of the sixth panzer regiment. Himmler's Executioners." He swallowed more water. "In 1942 Erik was a member of the *Einsatzgruppen* that murdered many Jews and others in the capital of Estonia, *Tallinn,* and parts of the Soviet Union. After about two years Erik rejoined his original regiment. He must've had enough of the killings. Perhaps that's why he wouldn't kill the peasants on that farm." Kristian patted his chest. "He refused to talk about his experiences with the sixth regiment, and I didn't want to know."

"Did he choose to be part of the murder squad?" Lars asked.

Kristian shrugged. "He wasn't forced into it?"

Lars stared at Kristian incredulously.

Josef felt a shudder from his throat to his stomach as he demanded an answer, "So, you're telling us the truth now? Our grandfather wanted to be part of that horrific murder squad. This is not a bunch of lies?"

Kristian's rasping voice was even more difficult to hear now.

"Haven't you heard about just following orders?" he said starting to cough again.

Josef put his hands to his ears and muffled a shriek.

Killing hundreds of innocent people for whatever ideology or reason is too unbearable to think about.

"My hands aren't clean either. I haven't got long until I'm judged," Kristian said in his hoarse whisper. "Finding the towns and villages where the Jews and other undesirables lived was one of my jobs. I investigated and supervised rounding them up." He was struggling to talk now. "Hitler was determined to annihilate them all – wipe them off the face of the earth if he could and others organised his dirty work."

Josef looked at Kristen with disgust burning in his eyes.

"Now I understand all the secrecy. To have a member of one's family part of it is unthinkable."

"Now you know now why you were shielded from it." Kristian's voice was a tired whisper.

"So, we're told how my grandfather saved the lives of peasants on a farm in the hope we'd never find out about the massacres."

"You've got what you wanted, so get out!" Kristian closed his eyes and turned to the wall.

During the drive home, neither brother talked.

As soon as he returned to his home, Josef rushed indoors to the shower. Later he sat in his favourite chair and reviewed the awful day. Films and photographs of atrocities against the Jews and other groups during the war years flicked through his mind. Ken and Nina Levy had been their neighbours in Copenhagen. Nina was his mother's closest friend then and he had met most of their family and shared holidays with their friends. His mother had invited Ken, Nina and their children for Christmas lunch and all his family celebrated the Jewish New Year with the Levys. He scratched the stubble on his chin. He couldn't recall his grandfather ever joining them at the Levy's house. He behaved civilly if he met them in the street or if he couldn't avoid them over the fence adjoining the properties. It made sense now.

He thought of his visits to Copenhagen as an adult. He had been to the Jewish museum and the ancient tree-lined Jewish cemetery. How could his grandfather turn against people who were part of every aspect of Danish life and culture? He would never understand.

The following morning, the thought of work was impossible. He lay on the couch with Bjorn next to him, sensing his misery. Later, he felt stronger and hungry. He was eating a slice of toast with coffee when he looked up at the poster of the mermaid.

"You knew the truth about him, didn't you?" he muttered.

During the next three days, he felt strange and unreal. It was as if he was watching himself. Without realising it, he had slipped into a state where he no longer ate, slept little and did nothing but pace the length and width of his house. He thought of Carla. She would know how to help him. When he dialled her number, the answering machine's message told him that she was unavailable and gave him two numbers to phone in a crisis.

He no longer thought about the awful discovery about his grandfather and distracted himself by picturing Carla in her room, her smile and the decorative pictures on her wall. He imagined he was sitting in the comfortable chair next to her and she was talking to him in her softest voice, her eyes brimming with empathy. He imagined his head moving onto her lap as she stroked his hair with her tapered fingers and placed a kiss on his brow. Don't be ridiculous, he chided himself. Carla is your therapist. Nevertheless, he continued fantasising about her. Did she have children and even grandchildren? If she had a husband, would she listen to him with her head slightly tilted as she listened to him during their sessions? And that gentle voice of hers, did she speak to him like that? Did they have sex often? Quickly he obliterated that thought. He couldn't imagine Carla locked in a carnal embrace.

His strange mood continued as did his desire to find out more about Carla. He fought against it, but eventually succumbed, and searched for her address online under psychologist listings. The suburb was one he had driven through often, a mixture of older houses and new apartments. He could not imagine her living in an apartment. She would have an unusual house with a garden. He was sure of that. He continued to mentally stalk her. Anything to fill his mind with thoughts other than the reality he had discovered about his grandfather.

Still in his odd mood, not knowing about Carla festered until he felt forced to satisfy his curiosity. It was mid-morning when he left home. Her tree-lined street was easy to find. When he stopped outside her house he was surprised that she lived in an Edwardian, red brick heritage home with a typically symmetrical garden, resplendent with flowers and shrubs. The garage was closed and the street quiet. He pictured her driving up late every afternoon, as the outdoor sensor lights flared, guiding her into the garage.

He sat in his car gathering his nerve. Playing sleuth was a role he was familiar with from movies. After checking that the street was empty, he donned a coat, cap and sunglasses to disguise himself. He approached the wrought iron gate that was slightly open and headed down the tiled driveway. The recessed porch was tiled and had a wood-panelled door. A tiny case that he knew to be a *mezuza* was placed on the doorpost. He had seen one before when he built a house for Jewish people. They explained that the case contained a sacred Hebrew text. Nervously, looked around the empty house. Keen to see the inside, he trod softly, as he attempted to peer into the sitting room and then the rest of the house, but drapes prevented him from seeing any details other than muted tones. Disappointed, he returned to his car and stripped off his disguise. During the drive home, the realisation of his prying act hit him. He scolded himself.

What had possessed him? His actions were disgusting. He was stalking her. His obsession with Carla had driven him too far and had to stop.

He asked himself what had driven him to go to her house and snoop around. To try to deaden his shame, he drank whiskey followed by beer. Still aware of his shame, he lay sprawled on the couch and distracted himself with memories of spring in Copenhagen when wild crocuses poked out their heads, trees had budding leaves, and almond blossoms were everywhere. Then he was in the park with his grandfather. Almost as tall as the bushes, he could see into the distance. He had thought of these scenes so often that by now he embellished them. Blossoms grew larger and more plentiful, the grass greener, the shriek of returning starlings louder.

After a day of recovery, restlessness urged him out of the house, to the car and onto the road. He drove fast, well beyond the city limits into the countryside. A blinking dashboard indicated that he had lost track of the distance he'd travelled. His petrol tank was dangerously low. When he stopped at a service station, he found that he had forgotten his bank card and the money in his wallet just covered the cost. He wasn't accustomed to worrying about money. As a teenager, a paper round in the morning, fruit picking over his school holidays and some gardening were ways he ensured that there was money in his pocket for treats like the cinema or a new shirt. He lived and spent frugally and had more money at the end of the month than his friends. Once he secured a job as a junior architect, he spent freely, enjoying holidays and drinking imported wines. In his present predicament without the certainty of his job he cursed his recklessness. All his leave pay was used and the sick pay he was receiving would soon run out. Work was the answer. He had to return to work as soon as possible. After passing farms and small towns he turned around and drove home.

He tried to put thoughts about his grandfather aside, but his gut niggled. Something was still missing in the stories he had been told. Perhaps there were snippets of family information that his father had failed to tell him, but Nils was involved with his pain and illness and ignored Josef's questions.

At work one morning a phone call from his father surprised him. In a frail voice, Nils told Josef that he needed to see both his sons urgently. "I won't be around for much longer and I have something important to tell you both," he said.

"If it's that urgent I'll come tonight. I can't speak for Lars, but I'll tell him that you want to see us."

"I've had enough of our father's secrets," Lars snapped when Josef told him about the phone call. "You talk to him. For my part, the sooner he passes on the better."

"Okay, I'll go and try to find out what he wants," Josef replied.

The porch lights shone and the front door was open when Josef arrived at his father's house.

"I'm in the front bedroom," a whispery voice called.

Josef looked down on the man in bed who was more like a cadaver than his father.

He pulled up a chair. "So, what's so urgent you had to tell us?"

Nils ignored his son's question. "Where's Lars?"

"He had another arrangement that he couldn't break," Josef lied.

The old man is looking dreadful. He won't be around for long. It would've been easier not to see him like this.

Josef glared at his father. "So, what is it you want to tell us that's so important?"

"I should've told you about your mother's family. I haven't seen them for years, but they aren't our kind of people and I didn't think you'd want to know about them."

Nils' speech was slow and Josef leaned forward to hear his father.

"I haven't met them and know almost nothing about them, but you're going to tell me about them now," Josef said thumping the top of the chair with his fist.

"Well, your mother's father, Holger was a brute of a man. As I said, I hardly knew him. He was certain that he descended from Vikings. It's possible but he had no proof." As Nils stretched for his glass of water, a sneer caught his lips. "He was one of the fishermen who saved the lives of many Jews during the Second World War by ferrying them across the Strait to the safety of neutral Sweden. In Israel, he is regarded as a hero."

"Amazing! It's news to me." Josef said lifting his arms in surprise. "So, we had one grandfather, Holger, a hero, who saved many people's lives and might've been a Viking. He makes me proud. Then there's our other grandfather who was a disgrace."

Nils' eyes closed and slipped into their deep sockets. "One more thing, I guess I should tell you. Your mother's mother ... your maternal grandmother, Esther, was Jewish."

"What! You've known this and not told us something that important!"

Nils shrugged.

"That makes us one-quarter Jewish."

"I didn't think you'd want to know something like that."

Josef's face was red with fury. "I can't believe that you think like him. You hid a vital part of our background from us. I'm disgusted."

He stood quickly, turned from his father and raced out of the house. When he reached his car he sat with his head on the steering wheel and wept.

Chapter 60

Carla and Steve returned to Australia when the sun was unrelenting and the sky a faded blue. After unpacking and then cleaning the house, Carla attacked the mound of washing accumulated from the trip. She was about to call Deanne when her daughter rang.

"Welcome home! I missed you and dad."

"I missed you too. How are Brad and the children?".

"We're all well? How are you both? Did you have a good time?"

"Slow down. We'll have lots to tell you," Carla replied.

"What about Shabbat dinner with us? It's only two days away, so I guess I'll have to wait to hear all about your trip all until then."

"That'll be great. Can I bring anything?" Carla asked.

"Not a thing. Looking forward to catching up."

It was the first Sabbath meal they were to have at Deanne and Brad's home – something to look forward to.

Carla changed into the oldest clothes she wore for gardening. She imagined returning to a welcoming garden filled with an array of summer flowers, but she was greeted by straggly flowers and dying vegetables. The automatic drip system was a failure. It watered the flowers and small shrubs unevenly and the intricately designed garden was a mess. She called out to Steve for help in the vegetable garden and energetically they yanked out dying lettuces and pulpy tomatoes, making space for healthy vegetables. They were content as they worked to resurrect their garden, their trip momentarily forgotten. Working together in the warmth was enjoyable. By lunch, they were satisfied that the garden would thrive with their care.

She was taking an extra week off work and Steve decided to join her, though he knew he would pay for the time spent away from the office with piles of work to greet him. It was worth it, he thought. They needed to be together to process all they had seen and experienced, and more importantly to cement the gains in their relationship.

Though Carla would've preferred to relax at home, she had an appointment with Mike that was made before she went away. After lunch, she left for the University. It was holiday time and apart from administrators and a few keen academic staff members, the university was deserted. Carla's steps echoed down the corridor as she approached Mike's room.

"That you Carla? Come right in."

He was sprawled in his chair. The term-end had given him a relaxed air.

"My students have feted me with Christmas cheer and loads of cards. Christmas is not our holiday but I enjoy the caring, fun and all the glitter. They've gone now and await their results, poor sods. I have loads of exam papers to mark."

He rubbed his hands together and sat upright.

"You're looking marvellous, years younger. The trip must've agreed with you."

"I'm taking some extra time off, so no cases to discuss, but I thought I'd come for a chat."

"I bet there's a lot to tell about your trip."

"The visit to Germany was tougher than I expected, confronting history and ancestry but the rest, another honeymoon."

"Come on, details!" He made a clapping motion with his hands.

She began coolly with a summary of the places they had visited in Paris and then Germany, and gradually her feelings crept in. She praised Maria's competence and told Mike how fond they had grown of her. With a tight throat, she described the old Regensburg. Talking about the ancient cemetery and her grandfather's crumbling tombstone, brought the tears she promised herself would not fall. She left *Dachau* for last, knowing that she would cry again.

"After visiting *Auschwitz*, I was upset for weeks. I can't imagine it not distressing us. There'd be something essentially wrong with our psyches if it didn't," he said.

" A thorn that keeps pricking me asks *why us.* There are lots of theories but no real answers."

He sighed and threw his hands in the air.

"I've stopped trying to find the answer. None of us will."

She saw a glint of moisture in his eyes.

"We won't allow ourselves to forget. We need to hold on to it, to keep it alive and to pass it on to the generations to come," he said in a raspy voice.

"I no longer despise the new generation of Germans. Most are horrified by the past and feel guilty. They have attempted to make amends with plaques, memorials, new synagogues and museums built where ghettos were razed and Jews slaughtered," she said.

They were both immersed in their thoughts.

"Mike tapped the arms of his chair before speaking, "I have something to tell you."

"You sound serious," she replied.

"I have resigned after twenty years of working at this university. The challenge has gone. I'm taking a six-month sabbatical. After that, I've been offered a position at Cambridge. It's an exciting position with some teaching and research in comparing the behaviour of children with young animals. It's a topic that has always interested me and I have written several papers on the subject. I'm delighted, but it will mean a huge dislocation for Anna. My children are adults, but Anna has a job and roots here."

"Congratulations and well deserved! I hope Anna finds something to suit her."

"I've submitted my resignation and will leave in January, after finishing bits and pieces here."

Carla's joy for Mike was replaced by a moment of panic.

"I can tell by your expression that you're worried. You've become too used to me. You will be fine. All we've done lately is chat."

"You're right of course, and I am happy for you."

"I believe there's a party for me planned and naturally you're invited. I'll send you the details by email."

"Lovely, I'll be there." She took his hand and kissed his cheek. "Thanks for everything and lots of luck."

She rushed away with tears stinging her cheeks.

Carla was pleased that she could mull over their trip before returning to work. She thought of Maria often, the cobbled street of Regensburg, the ghetto under the city square and the icy cemetery with the few ancient tombstones still intact. Now she knew more about her grandfather and had an idea of how family members lived before them, but she knew nothing of them as people.

She was pleased that they had been to vibrant Munich and seen the sobering comparison of the horrific camp just outside the city at Dachau, an experience that would be with her forever. The special romantic period with Steve had brought them back together. Overall, the trip was a positive experience. Once the house was tidy and she had done all she could to save the garden, she was keen to return to work.

When she unlocked the door to her office it smelled musty. She opened the windows and looked out. The trees were starting to lose their leaves and swaying to the tune of the wind. She took a deep breath and allowed the breeze to kiss her face and hair. After her absence, her fresh eyes viewed each item in the room sharply. It was comforting that the clock, the old leather armchairs, too large for the room, pieces of delft and her porcelain cats were all in place. Her first client was due any minute. She wiped away a line of dust on her desk and logged on to her computer.

After a busy morning, she glanced at her emails. A message from Maria was new.

My dear Carla

I hope that you, Steve and the family are well and that you enjoyed your holiday in Crete. I think you must've needed it after all you saw and discovered in Germany.

I promised to ask my friend Eugenia to search for your grandmother's family in Eastern Europe. So far, she has not been able to locate your family but she promised to keep searching for further information.

I will check Eugenia's progress and write to you if anything new is discovered.

Kindest regards

Maria

Carla was pleased that Maria had written to her and was still searching for her family members.

Chapter 61

The doorbell woke Josef. It was Saturday morning and he planned to sleep late.

Tim stood on the doorstep looking uncomfortable

"Sorry, mate, did I wake you?"

"Yep," Josef answered grumpily.

"I have some bad news."

Josef rubbed his eyes. "What's up, Tim?"

"I'm so sorry, mate...it's your dad," Tim said hesitantly.

"My dad?"

"He...has passed way. A neighbour found him this morning. I was at the office this morning catching up and took the message. The neighbour must've noticed your work number on your desk and phoned the office."

There was silence while Josef tried to grasp what Tim had told him.

"Thanks for letting me know, Tim."

"Are you okay? Do you want me to stay a while?"

"I'm fine, thanks, Tim. I'll let my brother know."

He showered and dressed quickly. Apart from his initial shock, his only emotion was regret that he and his father had waited until the past few months for their first decent conversation.

Lars and Susanna were eating breakfast when Josef arrived. He delivered the news as gently as he could. Lars accepted it with an expressionless face.

"So, our dad's gone," was all he said and finished his breakfast.

An hour later, the brothers drove to their father's house.

"He was terminally ill and lived a while longer than he expected," Josef said."

"Every day counts," Lars said.

Henry Mulgrave, their father's neighbour, must've heard Josef's car pull up. He was waiting for them at the front door of their father's house as their car stopped.

"My condolences to you both! I've had the keys of your father's house for years. He asked me to check if all was okay when he went away. I'm retired and at home a lot. He told me that he wasn't feeling well lately, but he continued going to work. I admired the way he fought his cancer. When his lights didn't go on in the house last night and I didn't hear his car leave for work, I wondered if something was wrong. There was no sign of him and I thought it was strange. I went into the house and found him in his bed."

"Thank you, Henry. You've been his friend for years," Josef said.

"Right then, I'll leave you boys to it."

Lars hesitated as they entered the house.

"We don't have to go into the bedroom and see him, do we?"

"You don't have to go in, Lars, leave it to me. I'll have a quick look and then phone the funeral directors," Josef said taking the role of the older brother. He was surprised how cold and practical he was and that he felt no grief.

The funeral directors were efficient. All the brothers had to do was choose a coffin from a catalogue and agree on the date and time for the funeral. Lars left the arrangements to Josef, who chose a middle of the range coffin, one less expensive than his grandfathers. He asked the minister of the Lutheran church he had attended as a child to officiate at the ceremony and agreed to a service at the church before the burial.

About a dozen people, his father's workmates and neighbours arrived at the church. Greta didn't bother to attend. There were no eulogies other than the one the priest made. It was clear to everyone there that this father would not be missed by his children.

The internment was quick and simple and the brothers left after the priest's prayer.

"We've done our duty for our father," Josef said as he drove to Lars' house.

"Well, I'm glad it's over," Lars said with a heavy sigh and pulled off his tie. I'm pretty sure Susanna will have made something to eat, I'm starving."

"It's not over yet, Lars. We'll have to clean up his place and dispose of his stuff according to his will," Josef said.

"His will? Money for stray cats," Lars said throwing his arms in the air.

"Anyway, who cares!" Josef muttered.

"You're the eldest, have a look around the house. Later if you need me for moving heavy stuff I'll help out."

His father's house was just as tidy as it had been when Josef had visited. Apart from some *Zwiesel* glass ornaments, nothing of his father's interested him. He would share the ornaments with Lars and the rest would go to charity.

When he visited his father's house, he went directly to the book-lined study and his father's desk. All the drawers except the bottom one were filled with papers and office equipment. When he opened the last drawer, he found two envelopes secured with elastic bands - one brown envelope and one white, as well as a box that once held chocolates. He opened the brown envelope first and emptied its contents onto the bed. Pages in German were clipped together. Josef did not speak German, but from the underlined captions, he gathered that he was looking at his grandfather's military record. He recognised the rank: *Obersturmfuhrer* or First Lieutenant, and the areas where his grandfather had fought were listed. His face puckered in disgust. The envelope contained his grandfather's Waffen SS collar bands, a badge and his service medals bearing Nazi emblems. Quickly, he replaced the contents of the envelope and put it aside.

He grimaced as he fingered the white envelope. When he opened it he found a stiff sheet of cream paper with a gold border and black writing. Attached to it was a map and a red ribbon that held a gold-plated medal bearing his grandfather's name. A translation attached to the paper stated that the medal was from the community of *Munchenberg* in recognition of saving the lives of twenty-six farmers on the night of 12th January 1945. He recalled Kristian's description of this event.

He turned to the box. When he removed the string, the cover sprung back revealing photographs of soldiers, letters and paper cuttings. He leafed through the yellowed newspaper articles about the worldwide hunt for Nazis who had committed atrocities during the war. At the bottom of the box was something heavy. He gathered all the papers, the medal, emblems and the cross and placed them in the box. The box, he left on the desk for Lars to look at when ready.

Chapter 62

Josef was relieved that the final step in his search for the truth about his grandfather was over. He intended to concentrate on his work and push all thoughts of his grandfather aside. He had forgotten about his father's will until Damian de Vries, their father's solicitor, phoned him. De Vries explained that he had been appointed as the executor of their father's estate, that probate had been granted and that now their father's estate could be distributed. The will was simple with their father's money and investments divided equally between his two sons. The brothers were surprised that their father had amassed a great deal of money during his life and left them large amounts. Josef and Lars agreed to meet over dinner to discuss their windfall. Josef suggested the Viking restaurant and Lars agreed immediately.

Josef was first to arrive. As Lars entered the restaurant, he watched his brother look around the black walls decorated with Viking relics. Lars' initial expression of incredulity turned to laughter.

"They take this Viking stuff very seriously," he said.

"People who think they have Viking ancestors meet here, according to Anders. He invited me to re-enactments of Viking wars, but I haven't been yet."

"Far out!" Lars said shaking his head. "You'll have to tell me more. Could we have Viking ancestors?"

"I'll fill you in with all the details. Anders thinks it is possible but he's not an expert."

"I like the idea," Lars said with a grin.

Josef ordered beers and they studied the menu.

"Mainly stews of different types with a side serve of vegetables, flatbread and buttermilk. Mead is available too," Lars said looking uncertain.

"All very tasty. Try the lamb stew, I enjoyed it last time," Josef suggested.

After their meal, they discussed their father.

"He was a lousy father, but in his way he has made up for it with our inheritance," Lars said.

"I would've preferred a loving father. For me, money doesn't make up for his lack of interest in us other than to punish us," Josef replied.

"Anyway, Susanna is thrilled with the money. She wants to buy a new house and maybe travel. I'm not so sure, I'd like to take my time before spending wildly."

"Good idea to take it slowly!" Josef said. "I'm going to give most of my inheritance away. It will go to friends who need it and to a Jewish charity. I am considering donating a large amount to the Holocaust Centre in Melbourne so that they can keep educating people about the evils of the Holocaust."

"Does it help with feelings of guilt?" Lars asked.

"I'm over that, but I have enough and giving it away feels like the right thing for me to do. Unlike you, I am not married with a family."

Chapter 63

Tim and the senior partners of the firm decided to hold a party for their staff and clients after work on the following Friday. For the large number of guests, the office was perfect with a large open room and a wide balcony that wrapped around the building. The magnificent views of the city and the sea were expected to draw many onto the balcony. Previously, Josef avoided social occasions, but this time he wanted to attend. He wore a new suit and tie. Before leaving home, he glanced at his image in the mirror and smiled. He was looking forward to the evening.

The packed room didn't bother him. He greeted his colleagues and talked to his old clients, prospective new ones and their partners. He was enjoying himself when he noticed Jaques, an old client who was chatting to an attractive woman. Jaques beckoned to him and introduced him to Grace,a striking woman with shoulder-length, blonde hair and green eyes. Immediately he compared her to Greta. But Grace was taller and more curvaceous in her sapphire dress. He joined them and they chatted. They were sipping champagne when Jaques left to take an important phone call. Spontaneously, Josef and Grace moved towards each other. Their mutual attraction seemed almost instantaneous. When Jaques returned he couldn't find them. After searching, he noticed them settled away from the crowds in one of the offices. Aware of their interest in each other, Jaques didn't interfere.

Conversation continued to flow between the couple. When they had eaten snack food and emptied a bottle of wine, Josef stood and stretched.

"Let's get out of here and have dinner, I'm starving. I don't know about you, Grace."

"Me too," she replied as she gathered her bag and shawl. "But I don't feel like a formal dinner and anyway we're overdressed. Maybe something simple or a take out. McDonald's is my favourite," she said with a laugh. "We could eat on a bench overlooking the sea."

He laughed with her.

"I'm glad you're making the suggestion and not me. I've never taken a beautiful woman I hardly know for fast food. McDonald's it is then. There's a drive-thru a few blocks away."

They continued to see each other after work and over weekends. Soon they discussed her move into Josef's house.

When Carla answered her phone, Josef was relieved. She was back and she had an appointment for him later that week. There was so much he wanted to tell her.

She looked different, he thought. More relaxed. He hesitated before asking, "Did you enjoy your trip?"

"It was really interesting, I traced some of my family in Europe, and after that a holiday."

"I have a lot to tell you."

"I'm listening," she said shifting back into the chair.

"Some awful stuff and something new and great."

Once he had told her all he had discovered about his grandfather since she had been away, he looked at her waiting for her comment.

"Where to start. You've been persistent, I'll hand it to you. At least you have answers now, even though they aren't the ones you wanted."

He looked down and nodded.

"It became obvious to you from early on that your grandfather was a pro-Nazi. When you discovered that he was involved with the SS and responsible for some awful deeds, you were reluctant to accept it. Now unfortunately you've been through the painful process of being faced with the irrefutable truth."

"I know now that he was a Nazi who chose to fight with Hitler, joined the SS and took part in the killing of innocents. Perhaps it's his lies and attempts to cover up his past that have disgusted me most."

"I can understand that. Perhaps he wanted to protect you and your brother from finding out – being hurt by his actions."

"More likely to protect himself from our disapproval."

"Possibly."

"I'm trying to move on now." Josef bit his lip hard in an attempt to control his rising emotion.

"You said earlier that you had some great news," she said trying to help him to recover.

He swallowed and then smiled.

"Yep, I do. I have a new girlfriend, Grace, and she's moved in with me."

"That's fast. Tell me about her."

After explaining how they met, he sighed with pleasure.

"I haven't been interested in women since I broke up with Greta. She left our firm to work for another group of architects and we don't see each other now." He looked past the flowers on her desk and smiled. "When I met Grace, I was immediately attracted to her and she seemed to like me too. We want to be together and so far it is working out well."

"I'm so pleased for you!" she said with a smile.

"She's made all the difference to my life. I'm back concentrating at work and I'm happy. I'd forgotten I could feel like this. We have so much in common in our enjoyment of the arts, music, the outdoors and more. I've told her about my grandfather and she's supportive. She has a few ghosts in her family too."

Carla nodded. "It sounds good."

He couldn't stop telling Carla about Grace.

"Her connection with our firm is through interior decoration of our buildings, and she has magnificent taste. She says she can't wait to get her hands on redecorating my house."

He watched her glance at the clock. It had been a long session and she had given him extra time. There was nothing more either of them could say. He knew that this would be their last session. She had helped him all she could. After thanking her quietly, he did not discuss a date for another appointment. Overcoming the stain his grandfather had left would take time to fade, but Grace was there now and it made a difference. He would move on, acting decently and caringly to others. It was the only way he could uplift himself in his own eyes. He decided not to tell her about his Jewish background.

Carla stood at the doorway watching Josef leave. She doubted she would see him again. She saw him walk slowly towards his parked car, then pick up his pace and straighten his shoulders. He could cope without her now. She closed the door and returned to her room. Her next client was waiting for her.

🦑

Since her return to work, she hadn't done more than collect names and addresses to view new premises. The letter from her landlord lay on her desk bothering her. A late cancellation gave her the time she needed to view a room to rent only two blocks away. The room was part of a doctor's consulting suite. After viewing it she decided that it would fulfil her needs.

Chapter 64

Five Years Later

The Sabbath, the period of rest and reflection was almost over. A working week was on its way, and there was still a ritual for Steve and Carla to complete as they did at the end of every Sabbath. Steve's mother's silver tray holding a carafe of wine, a silver spice box containing cinnamon, bay leaves and cloves and a special *Havdalah* candle, lay before them on the table. The candle made from interwoven strands of different coloured wax, represented the past, present and future generations. Carla watched Steve perform the end of the Sabbath ritual by pouring wine into a silver beaker, making a blessing and lighting the stranded candle. She smiled as they moved closer, their fingers touching. As he opened the spice box, fragrant aromas filled the room, enriching and sharpening her focus on the new week about to begin.

Carla looked up at the sky, speckled with stars and thought of her family. Deanne and Brad appeared to be settled and their grandchildren were well and happy. She had much to be grateful for and cherish.

Though she anticipated eventually retiring from her counselling practice, she was reluctant to give up her work yet. Her skills had sharpened over time and her level of experience was at its peak. Clients who stayed the course with her benefited. Now she worked two and a half days a week in the room she rented from the group of doctors. It was an excellent arrangement with the use of the practice's receptionist. The room was small but comfortable and airconditioned. Her parents' large chairs and wooden tables had gone and the antique clock graced her lounge now. As before, her father's painting hung on the wall behind her desk for her clients to enjoy.

Her grandchildren were at school, so she had the time to devote to her interests. As a child, she painted, but later there was always something in the way preventing her from taking her skills more seriously. It was study, then work and her family. She once thought of herself as lesser than her father in many ways with his artistic talent, huge intellect and business acumen. But now she enjoyed painting too much to concern herself with comparisons. She was able to devote time to a weekly art class and work on her painting at home. Drawing and painting delighted her and with practice, she created work admired by her friends and family. Steve was her greatest fan, encouraging her to experiment with unusual colours and designs. In the art group, she made new friends with wide interests and she could move away from her world of therapy. At the Home, Hannah and Bertha had passed away, but when Sabine phoned for help, she continued to visit some of the residents.

Steve cut down his working hours to four days a week and returned to woodwork, a hobby as a younger man. The garage was large enough to set up a workbench and his equipment. Initially, he made tables and chairs. Later, with Carla's support, he gravitated to creating abstract, wooden sculptures, mainly depicting women and children. Carla was so enthusiastic about his work that she suggested they have a joint exhibition the following year. With their creative interests and hobbies, Carla and Steve had much to share. They no longer bickered or worried much about their grown children, and though they longed to see their grandchildren, they visited only occasionally. The family Sabbath dinner remained an institution and a way for the family to keep together. It was just as enjoyable but less formal and Carla made a simpler meal.

One afternoon, Carla was attending an art exhibition in the city by a well-regarded artist. As she entered the modern building, she was struck by its unusual design, the use of light and natural wood, and the patterned concrete on the walls. The building's foundation stone displayed the name of the building's architect, Josef Martinsen. She hadn't thought of Josef for ages. Once her clients were well and had left her care she tended to forget them unless something triggered a memory. A sense of pleasure rippled through her as she walked through the entrance and then on towards the exhibition.

Josef and Grace had been married for two years. She was in the early stages of pregnancy and both were excited, anticipating the baby to come. They walked hand in hand and were affectionate, even in public, something that Greta wouldn't allow. Grace was nothing like Greta. She was practical but sensitive - the rock Josef needed. If he occasionally lapsed into a down mood, she provided him with understanding and support. They worked together often. He designed a building and once it was completed she worked on the interior decoration. They often argued at work. Her taste was classical, while he was more adventurous in his views of design. Their clashes stayed at work and he was certain that their different approaches helped to create a comfortable and appealing atmosphere in the buildings. Their reputations soared with the many projects they handled. Though the new baby was their primary concern, they talked about starting their own company together – a dream in the future.

It was summer and they decided on a week's holiday. They rented a small house overlooking the sea and Josef insisted on towing their boat to their destination half a day's drive away. The house was clean and comfortable with a magnificent view of the sea. They relaxed, ate in nearby restaurants and took long walks at dawn and sunset. The heat of the sand during the day drew them indoors.

One morning, while Grace was reading on the beach under an umbrella, Josef set out in his boat. The sea was calm and he allowed the boat to drift. As he looked out at the endless blue, memories of sailing with his grandfather flowed back to him. Lately, he was allowing snatches of positive, precious images of his grandfather into his thoughts. When he talked of his grandfather, he called him *Farfar* once more. He recalled his sixth birthday when his parents rented a house during summer near the beach, much like the house he and Grace were renting. He woke to a choir of *happy birthday*. Shiny, wrapped presents were on his bed - a new outfit from his mother, a fire engine from his father and a gold box from *Farfar*. Inside the box was a child's military uniform and a gun. His mother's joyful face turned into a scowl. Her voice was shrill. 'No, absolutely not, no uniforms or guns. I won't allow your grandfather to turn you into a little soldier.' Josef smiled ruefully remembering crying as he tugged the gift until his mother grabbed it. He remembered too the displeasure on his grandfather's face on seeing the gift taken from him.

Towards the end of the holiday, he and Grace were strolling on the beach at sunset when they passed a woman returning from the ocean after a late swim. As she passed them he turned around. He recognised her. Carla. She was plumper now and looked happy. He watched her for a few minutes, and they walked on.

www.ingramcontent.com/pod-product-compliance
Lightning Source LLC
Chambersburg PA
CBHW070443030726
47503CB00004B/861